"Half the fun of pajama parties is being able to consume all the snacks and drinks you want before bed without worrying about the calories!"

Contents

Может, как раз сегодня я встречу его...

Alya Sometimes Hides Her Feelings in Russian

Summer Stories

4.5

Sunsunsun
Illustrated by Momoco

YEN ON
New York

Alya
Sometimes Hides Her
Feelings in
Russian

4.5 Sunsunsun

Translation by Matthew Rutsohn
Cover art by Momoco

This book is a work of fiction. Names, characters, places, and incidents are the product of the author's imagination or are used fictitiously. Any resemblance to actual events, locales, or persons, living or dead, is coincidental.

TOKIDOKI BOSOTTO ROSHIAGO DE DERERU TONARI NO ARYA SAN Vol.4.5 SUMMER STORIES
©Sunsunsun, Momoco 2022
First published in Japan in 2022 by KADOKAWA CORPORATION, Tokyo.
English translation rights arranged with KADOKAWA CORPORATION, Tokyo, through TUTTLE-MORI AGENCY, INC., Tokyo.

English translation © 2024 by Yen Press, LLC

Yen On
150 West 30th Street, 19th Floor
New York, NY 10001

Visit us at yenpress.com • facebook.com/yenpress • twitter.com/yenpress
yenpress.tumblr.com • instagram.com/yenpress

First Yen On Edition: March 2024
Edited by Yen On Editorial: Leilah Labossiere
Designed by Yen Press Design: Liz Parlett

Yen On is an imprint of Yen Press, LLC.
The Yen On name and logo are trademarks of Yen Press, LLC.

The publisher is not responsible for websites (or their content) that are not owned by the publisher.

Library of Congress Cataloging-in-Publication Data
Names: Sunsunsun, author. | Momoco, illustrator. | Rutsohn, Matthew, translator.
Title: Alya sometimes hides her feelings in Russian / Sunsunsun ; illustration by Momoco ; translation by Matthew Rutsohn.
Other titles: Tokidoki bosotto roshiago de dereru tonari no Arya san. English
Description: First Yen On edition. | New York, NY : Yen On, 2022-
Identifiers: LCCN 2022029973 | ISBN 9781975347840 (v. 1 ; trade paperback) |
    ISBN 9781975347864 (v. 2 ; trade paperback) | ISBN 9781975367572 (v. 3 ; trade paperback) |
    ISBN 9781975367596 (v. 4 ; trade paperback) | ISBN 9781975367619 (v. 4.5 ; trade paperback)
Subjects: CYAC: Language and languages—Fiction. | Friendship—Fiction. | Schools—Fiction. |
    LCGFT: Humorous fiction. | School fiction. | Light novels.
Classification: LCC PZ7.1.S8676 Ar 2022 | DDC [Fic]—dc23
LC record available at https://lccn.loc.gov/2022029973

ISBNs: 978-1-9753-6761-9 (paperback)
        978-1-9753-6762-6 (ebook)

10 9 8 7 6 5 4 3 2 1

LSC-C

Printed in the United States of America

CHAPTER 1 GL and BL

"Sibling reunions are amazing, no matter how they are done! Of course, I absolutely adore heartwarming reunions where they share their everlasting love for each other as much as the next person, but I also have a weakness for reunions where they're currently in opposing positions and are enemies!"

"I know exactly what you mean. After all, simply being blood-related siblings is already going to create exciting drama for their relationship."

After discovering that Masachika and Yuki were actually siblings, Sayaka began gushing about her love for stories with long-lost siblings to Yuki at the amusement-park food court.

They passionately shared their nerdy hobbies, unconcerned that Ayano was quietly nibbling on a churro next to them. Only after a great deal of discussion and time had gone by was Sayaka finally able to calm down and snap out of her trance.

"Oh... Sorry about rambling like that. It's just... I've never had anyone I could talk to about things like this before, so..."

Sayaka was struck with embarrassment from unloading years' worth of pent-up excitement, as she'd been hiding the fact that she was genuinely an otaku. She shyly pushed up her glasses, bit her lip, and hunched her shoulders. It was an unfamiliar sight for Yuki, seeing as Sayaka almost always maintained a serious, stiff demeanor.

Tsk! Just how adorable can one girl be?

But Yuki, smiling sweetly, didn't breathe a word of this to Sayaka.

"Don't worry about it. I understand exactly how you feel."

"...Really? I appreciate it," thanked Sayaka with a somewhat awkward smile, and yet she couldn't help but think, *What have I done? I seriously embarrassed myself.* Most closeted nerds made sure to keep their interests a secret at all costs. Even if they discovered that the person they were talking to was a like-minded enthusiast, they would still be convinced that their hobbies were unacceptable, abnormal abominations. There was always the nagging feeling that they were too interested compared with the average nerd, and this obsessive thought controlled their lives. To make matters worse, they were afraid that other geeks would figure out that they were hiding how ashamed they were, since that sense of embarrassment in itself was insulting to people with the same interests who may not be so ashamed.

This belief was shared by both Sayaka—who had worked hard to hide her interests from everyone over the years—and Yuki, which would only lead to one thing.

"......"
"......"

They had to feel each other out and see just how much of a nerd the other was. They silently exchanged glances with faint smirks on their lips...all the while Ayano quietly munched on her churro like a rabbit. Tension began to rise between them until Sayaka eventually spoke up.

"By the way, Yuki, what anime are you watching this season?"

She swiftly made the first move to ensure her victory. Although she passed it off as small talk, what she was actually doing was far more sinister. It was her way of gauging how much of a degenerate Yuki actually was. The number of anime she was watching would give an idea of how much of a nerd she was, while the content of the anime would allow Sayaka to analyze Yuki's interests. Did she like fantasy? Rom-coms? Slice-of-life? Or perhaps she liked violent, lewd shows that were barely acceptable to even air on TV?

That nonchalant question alone would give Sayaka valuable information without any risk at all. That was the kind of person Sayaka Taniyama was. This was the talent she possessed that allowed her to crush countless rivals during debates. She appeared confident, while Yuki's expression made it impossible to know how she was feeling. Ayano was folding the recently departed churro's wrapper.

"Oh… This season? Well…" Yuki started to respond to Sayaka's opening move. Of course, Sayaka wasn't expecting to win with one simple trick. In fact, she figured Yuki would just give her a few safe picks, then ask what Sayaka liked. But even that wouldn't be an issue, for Sayaka was prepared to use the ultimate counterattack by saying, "Oh, wow. Me too. It appears we're watching the exact same shows this season."

The safest position to be in is right behind your opponent, since you can simply copy their answers. The moment I made the first move was the moment I won.

Completely confident in her victory, Sayaka leisurely waited for Yuki's reply. However…

"Of course, I'm watching *Brain Hazard* and *Dream*. Those are mandatory, and that's not up for debate. There was a lot of hype for *Brain Hazard*, and people are saying it's the best anime this season, but *Dream* has been flawless ever since the first episode, so it might end up being the biggest hit. *Rental School* and *Tunnel from Another World* are both solid as well. Personally, I think *Hamezon* is the dark horse of the season. I was worried if they'd be able to do the graphic nature of the comic justice, but it turned out better than I expected. The second season of *Ganbaruon* is just as good as the first, and…"

"…?!"

Yuki went straight into battle with her guard down while completely ignoring the unwritten rule. She passionately revealed her love for fantasy, rom-coms, touching stories, mecha, and even lewd, violent dark fantasies. The information being disclosed to Sayaka came as a tidal wave, nearly making her eyes roll back in her head. She was dazed and confused; Yuki, on the other hand, was smothering her laugh with her shirtsleeve.

…Meanwhile, Ayano left to go buy her third churro.

"So? What about you, Sayaka?"

"Uh…"

It was a question Sayaka was expecting, but everything else that happened was so unexpected that she didn't know how to respond. She couldn't even use her secret weapon anymore—"Oh, wow. Me too. It appears we're watching the exact same shows this season"—since there were a few shows that Yuki mentioned that Sayaka hadn't seen yet. However, would it be okay to say that? Or would that sound like she was criticizing Yuki's interests in some roundabout way? Although taken aback, she racked her brain for an answer until Yuki, who was struggling to suppress her laughter, suddenly muttered:

"Number Zero."

At first, Sayaka had no idea what Yuki was saying. It sounded like random gibberish, and yet…there was something about the words that drew her in, and she jumped a bit in her seat. Yuki, however, didn't stop there and came in with a follow-up attack.

"White darkness…"

"…!"

"The price for power…"

"…!!"

Seeing Sayaka's body naturally react to the wonderful string of words elicited a small smile from Yuki.

"You are in the early stages of cringelord disease. I advise you get treated for it as soon as possible," joked Yuki.

"Excuse me…?!"

Sayaka reflexively began to argue that she wasn't a so-called cringelord, which was an insult fellow anime fans her age avoided, but she couldn't deny that she was somewhat excited by what Yuki said, so she helplessly fell silent…which only made Yuki's smirk broaden.

"How about we drop this silly charade already? I'm sure you've noticed, but I'm far nerdier than you are. It's not even up for discussion, so you can quit the act. You don't need to hide your true self from me anymore."

"…!"

Yuki completely revealed just how much of a nerd she was while simultaneously demanding that Sayaka rid herself of shame or reservations. The proposal was better than what Sayaka could have ever wished for, and yet...it only made her feel more competitive, not relieved.

"Heh... I wouldn't be so sure about that. Although I may have seen fewer series overall, my love for each show is not to be underestimated."

Sayaka boldly smirked and slowly pushed up her glasses. Yuki returned the look with a competitive expression of her own. That was the start of their debate, and there was no going back now.

"The voice actor's delivery during the end of last week's episode of *Brain Hazard* was god-tier, wasn't it? He was also really good in *Gun Derro* as..."

"I actually prefer the antagonist's voice acting when..."

"Oh, hey. Did you notice they changed the ending credits of last, last week's episode of *Dream*? There was a new scene halfway through that seemed very important, and..."

"Of course I saw it. Do I look like some sort of unrefined brute who skips the opening and ending credits? Anyway, I think that scene..."

The situation made a complete one-eighty, and both girls were now competing to prove who was more of an anime nerd. Their usual composed attitudes, which they were known for at school, were nowhere to be found. The only two people there in that moment were a couple of anime fanatics playing a game of verbal tug-of-war to prove who was more passionate about the medium...until Yuki suddenly stopped talking.

"Excuse me for a moment," she requested simply, sliding her smartphone out of her pocket, but when she looked at the vibrating screen, one eyebrow twitched.

"I apologize, but I need to excuse myself for a moment."

Yuki then got up from her seat, placed the phone to her ear, and walked away. It seemed to be urgent, whatever it was.

"......"

"......"

Only Sayaka and Ayano remained at the table. Sayaka silently shifted her gaze to Ayano, who immediately began devouring her fourth churro like a rabbit rapidly nibbling on a carrot; she stared right back at Sayaka.

"Hey, uh… You don't need to rush."

But Sayaka's attempt to be nice was in vain, because Ayano refused to take the churro out of her mouth, as if a curse would instantly kill her if she did, stuffing the rest of it into her mouth at once. After adding some moisture via milk tea, she swallowed the entire churro whole.

"…!…"

Ayano sat up straight and looked into Sayaka's eyes as if nothing had happened. After wincing a bit, Sayaka softly cleared her throat and sat up straight as well.

"Allow me to introduce myself again. I'm Sayaka Taniyama. I know we're classmates, but we haven't really gotten the chance to talk much before, have we?"

"Yes, this may be the first time we've ever faced each other and exchanged words."

"Yes… So… I hear that you're Yuki's attendant…?"

"'Attendant'? …Yes. Ah!"

Ayano looked up as if she had suddenly remembered something, and she slowly got out of her chair. She then covered half her face with her right hand while crossing her arms as if she was striking a pose— like someone who'd lost their mind. Sayaka blinked in mute disbelief for a few moments.

"I am the childhood friend. I am battle-maid Ayano Kimishima," she revealed with a smug (emotionless) expression. It was glorious. She pulled it off perfectly. In fact, her introduction was so incredible that Sayaka simply froze with her mouth agape, an unusual look for her. Ayano, still with a blank expression, struck yet another pose and continued in a monotonic voice:

"However, being childhood friends is only the mask we show

the world. In truth, we subheroines are actually Mr. Masachika's protectors."

After smoothly striking a pose with the summer sun shining in the background, Ayano dropped back into her seat as if she had done something phenomenal and her work there was done. She then lowered her head and bowed to Sayaka.

"...I apologize for the inconvenience. Usually, Ms. Yuki goes first and says, 'I am the childhood friend. I am the blood-related sister Yuki Suou!'"

"...What? Wait. Does she really do that? *That* Yuki Suou?!"

"...? Of course. She told me this was the proper way to reveal our true identities."

"......"

Sayaka was quietly disturbed by the fact that Ayano was neither skeptical of Yuki's claim nor ashamed. Even Sayaka, someone in the early stages of cringelord disease, could not see a future where she would be able to compete at this level.

Wh-what an aggressive first move... She starts by throwing me off my game, then she completely takes control of the conversation.

Sayaka clutched her dully aching chest, suffering from a sudden attack of the disease, and tightly clenched her teeth. She then faced Ayano, who was calmly observing Sayaka and waiting for her next move (at least, in Sayaka's mind she was), and asked in challenge:

"Since you're Yuki's attendant—maid, I was wondering if you could tell me more about Yuki and Masachika's relationship. How do they usually act around each other?"

"......"

Ayano stared hard at Sayaka as if she was trying to scrutinize the real meaning behind her question. She was probably thinking about how to answer while taking into account that Sayaka could still potentially be Yuki's rival during the election. In fact, her efforts were unnecessary because Sayaka's question had absolutely nothing to do with the election. This was simply a personal interest of hers.

Masachika and Yuki used to be the perfect rivals for Sayaka. Now there were no hard feelings among the three of them. Just a sense of trust born from their respect for one another. However, after losing the election to them, Sayaka's respect grew immensely and transformed into something purer. Put simply, she had become a fan. And in her mind, they became the ideal pair. *Hurry up and get married already. Wait. You can take as much time as you want, but please get happily married in the end, okay?* Those were the thoughts that had crossed her mind from time to time, and on behalf of their fans, she decided that she would eliminate anyone who threatened their relationship in any way, no matter the cost. So when she heard that they were actually siblings and couldn't get married, her first thought was…

Nice. If anything, that just makes it better.

Which was why…

I want to hear more about their lives as loving siblings!

As a fan, Sayaka couldn't allow this chance to slip by, but Ayano wasn't the kind of person who would thoughtlessly leak information to a potential enemy.

"…As a humble servant, I cannot allow myself to recklessly reveal such personal details."

This reaction was completely reasonable, regardless of Sayaka's intentions. Nevertheless, Sayaka expected something like this to happen.

"Oh, really? Then I suppose I will ask someone else instead."

"…'Someone else'?"

As Ayano curiously tilted her head, Sayaka took a few sips of her drink, then continued in a matter-of-fact tone:

"I have to ask someone else if you won't tell me, right? Surely, there are a few people close with Masachika and Yuki who know they're siblings. Like…Alisa Kujou, for instance. I could just ask her."

This was also a roundabout way of threatening that she was going to tell Alisa Kujou or whomever else that Masachika and Yuki were actually siblings if Ayano didn't give her what she wanted, but Ayano was far too innocent to realize.

"That…would be bad."

And that was why she replied honestly, not knowing that she was supplying Sayaka with information.

Interesting. So nobody else knows that they're siblings, not even Alisa.

Yuki and Masachika were too sharp to ever give up anything so easily and would probably have been able to avoid the question entirely—or at the very least, threaten Sayaka to stop her. Ayano's reply, on the other hand, basically revealed their Achilles' heel.

She caught me off guard at first, but she's actually pretty easy to manipulate as long as you don't lose control of the conversation.

Sayaka went for the kill after reaching this conclusion. However, she was only doing this as a fan. She was simply craving the nectar of sibling love…as a fan, of course. It would seem she was somewhat of an idol otaku in a way.

"Then can you share more about their relationship? I have no interest in telling others about their private lives. I'm just curious about how they usually act around each other," asked Sayaka calmly, despite mentally having a paper fan for cheering in each hand with Masachika's and Yuki's names on them while her eyes eagerly sparkled.

"……"

But Ayano remained silent, so she decided to soften her tone even more.

"How about you just tell me about today? What were they doing before we ran into one another?"

"……"

Ayano's gaze wandered as she considered the compromise. Her mouth opened and closed numerous times before she lowered her gaze as if she had given up. Sayaka, confident of her win, curled her lips upward; she inwardly got into position to cheer with her paper fans, and—

"Ms. Yuki was stuck under the bed…so Mr. Masachika had to pull her out."

"What?"

Her expression faded, but internally, her jaw dropped in disbelief. She reflexively asked Ayano to repeat herself, then began trying to process what was said once more amid her confusion.

Under the bed? How did she end up there? That's... That's not really what I wanted to know... Wait. Is she feeding me misinformation to confuse me?

Once Sayaka reached that conclusion, she pulled herself together and tried to rethink how she was going to go about this while taking back what she thought earlier about Ayano being easy to manipulate. She turned in her chair, facing Ayano once more—

"Ms. Yuki had basically turned into a bagworm, so it was a very difficult morning for us all."

"What are you even talking about?!"

Sayaka imagined Yuki as a bagworm, which was almost immediately overshadowed by a giant question mark.

"Ayano? You've had your fun, so can you stop teasing Sayaka? And, Sayaka, could you please not pick on Ayano anymore?"

Yuki had returned, and although she hadn't heard their conversation, she promptly reprimanded Sayaka as if she had heard it all. Nevertheless, Sayaka smiled back at her like she had no idea what Yuki was talking about.

"Oh? We were just chitchatting. That's all. I might have gotten a little too excited, but nothing more."

"Oh, really? It is not like you to get overly excited. You are usually so levelheaded. Whatever were you two talking about?"

"I was simply trying to make sure you and Masachika really were siblings. It's still a little hard for me to believe, to be honest."

"Is that so? Well, you are free not to believe it if you wish. Either way, in public, we are still going to pretend like we are nothing more than childhood friends."

Perhaps it was because Sayaka and Yuki used to be rivals during the election...or maybe they were just not compatible. Whatever the case, the two girls continued to feel each other out every time they opened their mouths. They spoke in roundabout manners to hide their real intentions while trying to draw information out of the other. However, all it took was one question from Yuki to put an end to this charade.

"By the way, Sayaka, do you like BL?"

The sudden change of topic made Sayaka swiftly arch an eyebrow. Her back straightened, and she slowly pushed up her glasses.

"Dear Yuki... There are only two types of women in this world."

"...? And they are...?"

Light glinted mysteriously off the lenses of her glasses as she declared:

"Those who like BL and those who still don't know what BL is."

"Wiser words have never been spoken."

The two girls exchanged fearless gazes. Ayano, who still didn't know what BL was, curiously blinked as she watched their odd interaction for a few moments, but she soon got up without a care in the world and left to buy her fifth churro. Ignoring her departure, Sayaka shamelessly placed a hand on her chin as if she were a scholar and continued:

"By the way, remember how Kite turned down Nakuusha during last week's episode of *Brain Hazard*?"

"Yes?"

"I bet it's because he's actually seeing Gelgar."

"Interesting..."

Most *Brain Hazard* viewers would tell Sayaka that she was out of her mind for her groundless theory, but somehow, it made sense to these two. Sayaka then gave evidence to support her case as though she was ecstatic to have someone finally agree with her.

"I became sure of it during the beginning of episode two, when Gelgar was affectionately watching over Kite."

It was nothing but wicked conjecture.

"I mean, the fact that both their weapons were made from the same dragon is more than enough to make anyone suspicious."

Groundless, despicable speculation.

"You know when they were fighting together in the desert? And he was like, 'Watch my back!'? That was totally just him proposing in an indirect way, wasn't it?!"

There was wild imaginings, and then there was this.

"…I never thought of it like that!"

Even Yuki had no choice but to agree. Although she may have enjoyed BL from time to time, Yuki never imagined scenarios like this, so she was having a really hard time keeping up. In fact, she was actually just messing with Sayaka at first and pretending to be a BL enthusiast, while in reality, she preferred GL to BL. At any rate, there was no stopping Sayaka now.

"My favorite trope is the jealous childhood friend who is unable to control his rage. The admirable best friend has been hiding his true feelings for all these years until his uncontrollable envy gets the better of him, and he aggressively takes the protagonist in his arms and— Ah, just thinking about it makes my heart race."

It was hard to believe that these were the words of the student in charge of discipline at school. Yuki began to stare off into space—far, far into space…until she suddenly spotted Masachika and Nonoa in the distance heading their way, which immediately dragged her back to reality.

Noooooo!

Sayaka had her mask off, revealing the degenerate she truly was, which was obviously not something she wanted others to know, since she had been clearly working hard to make sure nobody ever found out.

"But after impulsively making a move, he finds no reason to continue hiding his obsession, and— It's odd. Something like this would be disgusting if it was a man and a woman, but for some reason, it feels okay since they're both men."

"Y-yes, I know what you mean. If this was a comic where the male childhood friend aggressively forced himself on the female protagonist, it would be over between them…"

Yuki promptly began adjusting the course of the conversation, since Sayaka was essentially in a trance, and immediately, Sayaka's expression clouded with despair.

"Exactly… And usually, it's only after they push the protagonist down onto the bed and see the frightened look in their eyes that they come to their senses and quickly step back… Everyone is far too nice! They were in love with the protagonist for years, and yet they back off because they want the protagonist to be happy. But what about you, then? What about your happiness?!"

"…Yes, they usually end up saying something like, 'Your happiness is my happiness.'"

"And that's only because they don't have any other choice! But they're just lying to themselves! And what's wrong with the protagonist? Why would you take some good-looking yet broken pain-in-the-ass man over your childhood friend, who would cherish you for the rest of your life? Because he'd obviously make the protagonist way happier than anyone else could!" argued Sayaka fervently, her hands tightly clenching over the table.

"Why can't the people I ship ever be together? Why do these authors keep doing this to me? Do you know what I mean?!" she shouted, straining her voice.

"Y-yes, I suppose it would be like that for people who ship childhood friends…"

"Why is everyone so obsessed with some random transfer student or some classmate they just met?! Why choose some stranger you know nothing about over the childhood friend who was always there for you?! I want them to be happy, too, for a change!"

"Ha…ha-ha…"

Yuki laughed dryly, and sweat poured down her back as she looked at Masachika, who was staring at Sayaka with an indescribable expression.

Oh my god! That was a close one!

She inwardly sighed, relieved that she'd managed to maneuver the topic to something somewhat safer. Then guessing what he was thinking, she promptly joked with her brother, who was staring off into space. This let Sayaka know that Masachika and Nonoa had returned.

"How dare you say such a thing, my dear brother."

"Stop reading my mind."

The "my dear brother" part repeated in the back of Sayaka's mind like a recording.

"Brother!" yelled Yuki, a small child in a field of white clover with a flower crown in hand before her brother.

"Brotherrr," cried a young Yuki with tears in her eyes and a stuffed animal clutched to her chest as thunder shook the house.

"Brother! Seriously?" complained an older Yuki in a slightly repri- manding tone while she fixed her brother's tie.

Every possible beautiful scene between these two siblings instantly played in Sayaka's head like a movie thanks to her well-trained imagination.

"Ngh!"

She immediately grabbed her nose in a panic before any of the precious nectar of sibling love escaped.

"Sh-she called him her dear brother... How adorable..."

Witnessing the siblings' sudden intimate exchange seemed to be too much for Sayaka, and those words just slipped off her tongue.

"...You really are a nerd, aren't you?" Masachika's annoyed tone suddenly dragged Sayaka back to reality, forcing her to realize that she had screwed up yet again. Nevertheless, despite it being far too late to do anything about it now, she put on a serious expression and stood from her seat as if nothing had happened.

"My apologies for taking up so much of your time."

"Not at all. I had a lot of fun."

"Really...? Then...I'm glad. Masachika, I would like to apologize for lashing out at you earlier as well."

"Oh, no. It's cool. Besides, you helped me realize how careless we were being... Anyway, do you think...?" Masachika hesitated, and he looked indecisive. Sayaka, however, knew exactly what he wanted to say and agreed.

"Your secret is safe with us. Right, Nonoa?"

"Hmm? Yeah, sure. Whatever."

"Anyway, enjoy the rest of your outing together, you two. See you at school."

"Yeah, thanks. See you around."

"I had a lot of fun. I hope you both enjoy the rest of your summer break."

"You too."

"Later."

After saying their good-byes, Sayaka and Nonoa hastily walked away, but once they were completely out of Masachika's and Yuki's sight, Sayaka immediately covered her face with both hands and squatted until her rear was barely hovering over ground.

"I'm so embarrassed…"

"Oh…? Something happen, Sayaka? You okay?"

"I'm not okay. I was so happy that Yuki was a fellow enthusiast that I cut loose a little *too* much…"

But even though her voice was dripping with regret, she couldn't help but smile as she thought back to their exchange.

"But it was an invaluable experience…"

"Uh-huh… Okay."

"Thank you so much, Yuki… I can go another month thanks to your contribution."

"How so?" asked Nonoa, not really knowing how to react to her friend suddenly squatting with eyes wide and hands clasped together as if in prayer.

"Moe adds color to our daily lives, and the precious nectar we occasionally find gives us the energy we need to live!"

"…Word," replied Nonoa in a monotonic voice, but Sayaka expressed no concern toward her obvious indifference and stared off into the distance.

"There are some kinds of nectar that can only be obtained through seeing close, loving siblings who are blood-related."

"Yeah, totally," replied Nonoa, messing around on her smartphone... Then she realized something and looked up.

"...Wait. Is that why you always want to come over to my house?"

"Er..."

Sayaka promptly averted her gaze, and Nonoa narrowed her eyes at the back of her friend's head. Around ten seconds of silence followed before Sayaka eventually muttered awkwardly:

"...It's really heartwarming seeing just how close Lea and Leo are, isn't it?"

"...? Are they, though?"

"Just being twins makes them precious! They must be protected at all costs!" Sayaka declared firmly, making Nonoa recoil a little.

"If you say so."

She instinctively knew it would be in her best interest to agree.

"Even when they quarrel, you can tell that they still love and trust each other very much, and that's what makes them so precious..."

"Uh-huh... Anyway, maybe it's time you stand back up so we can get going. People are starting to stare."

"Huh...? Ah!"

That was when Sayaka finally realized that countless strangers' eyes were locked on her, so she immediately stood and cleared her throat.

"Hey, uh... Just in case there's a misunderstanding, I want you to know that I don't go over to your house simply because I want to see Leo and Lea."

"I know. You want to see Lea and me getting along and having fun, right?"

"N-no, that's not what I meant... You're messing with me, aren't you?"

Nonoa proudly grinned back at Sayaka's annoyed gaze.

"Dunno. Am I? Why don't you tell me?"

"This isn't a game! Stop!" demanded Sayaka, turning her head away from Nonoa before briskly striding off, leaving her friend behind. But after walking a few steps ahead of her motionless, grinning companion, she looked back and peevishly cried, "Nonoa, come on! Stop messing around already!"

"Ha-ha! My bad."

Nonoa laughed and immediately ran over to Sayaka, slipping her arms around hers, then asking in a serious voice:

"But are you sure you're cool with saying good-bye to Kuze and the others like that? We could have totally hung out with them longer if you wanted to."

After briefly glancing in Nonoa's direction, Sayaka faced forward once more and calmly replied, "I didn't want to bother them. Besides, it's not like we're good friends with them, right?"

"Yeah, but, like…this would have been the perfect chance to get to know them better and become good friends with them. Am I wrong? It's not like we're rivals any longer."

"…Still, it wouldn't be right. Even though we aren't rival candidates anymore, it's not like our relationship is any different from before."

"Yeah, I guess."

Sayaka had done a complete reversal. She was speaking with a flat tone, unlike earlier when she was passionately rambling like a rabid fangirl. In other words, she had returned to her normal self: an intellectual who didn't let her emotions get in the way… unless she was talking about her nerdy interests or she had lost her temper.

"Besides, I don't want to be friends with either of them."

"Wait. Seriously?"

"Of course. All I want to do is watch their precious exchanges from afar as a single spectator. Nothing more."

…She was an intellectual. This was a fact. Nonoa might have been narrowing her eyes at Sayaka's serious expression as if to say, "What is wrong with her?" but she really was an intellectual. Really.

"Besides, I came here today to hang out with you, Nonoa, and nobody else," Sayaka added casually with a shrug. Nonoa's eyes widened…and she grinned.

"Wow. You love me sooo much, Saya, huh?"

"Of course. You're my best friend."

"I love you, too, Saya. ♪" Nonoa grinned goofily and leaned into Sayaka. Although Sayaka continued to look annoyed, she didn't push her friend away. After that, they kept walking side by side for a while, until Sayaka suddenly exhaled deeply as if to collect herself and began looking around.

"So… What next? Do—?"

That was when she heard them.

"*Giggle.* That was so scary, wasn't it?"

"You didn't look scared to me. Hell, you looked like you were having the time of your life."

"Not at all. I don't know what I would have done if I did not have my dear brother's arm to hold on to."

Masachika glared at Yuki reproachfully as she held on to her brother's arm like a young noblewoman. Ayano was there, too. The three of them had just come out of the haunted house when they ran into Sayaka and Nonoa again, and they simultaneously froze. There was no proper word to describe the mood.

"Don't mind me. Please continue."

That was the only thing Sayaka said as she slowly pushed her glasses up by the bridge with the expression of an intellectual, precious nectar (read: blood) slowly trickling out of her nose.

CHAPTER 2

A Princess and a God

"Nonoa! Do my hair for me!"

"Hmm?"

One day during summer break, Nonoa was relaxing in her room when the door suddenly flew open. A seemingly strong-willed, adorable girl with dark-brown hair and slightly almond-shaped eyes sprang into the room. Nonoa's sister—Lea Miyamae, who was two years her junior and had just barged in without knocking—was met with Nonoa's glare.

"Lea, you should knock—"

"Who cares about knocking?! Now, come on! Please?" Lea begged and posed cutely with both hands on her cheeks.

"…Yeah, yeah."

Nonoa casually rolled out of bed, sat her sister in front of the dresser, and plugged in the hair straightener.

"…So? What do you want me to do with it today?"

"Like… I want it like you did yours last week during your photo shoot!"

"Got it."

She began brushing her sister's hair while thinking back to what style she wore the other day. All of a sudden, a mischievous-looking teenage boy poked his head into the room.

"Hey, hurry up. We're gonna be late."

"Shut up! Never rush a lady. No wonder you're not popular."

"What? Girls love me," Lea's twin brother, Leo Miyamae, replied with irritation and a raised eyebrow. Although most people would get laughed at for claiming they were popular with the opposite sex, Leo had good looks that backed up his claim. In fact, these twins, who shared similar good-looking features, modeled together from time to time, and Leo was extremely popular. All three siblings had that in common.

"You hanging out with your model friends today?"

"Yeah, we're gonna meet up with some people from the last photo shoot... Oh, hey! You wanna come?"

"Hmm? Oh, I can't. Already have plans."

"Awww. More boys for me, then, I guess," said Lea with a cheeky smile as Nonoa continued styling her hair. But after seeing her expression in the mirror on the dresser, Leo, who was leaning against the doorframe, blatantly frowned.

"You're such a ho."

"Yeah, says the guy with a new girl every week."

"Unlike you, I don't flirt with and try to seduce every girl I see, though. It's not my fault they're all attracted to me."

The twins began hurling insults while glaring at each other in the mirror. Nonoa looked at her siblings and said, as if she couldn't care less:

"Don't go too crazy, guys. Mom already told you not to—"

"Yeah, yeah. I know. Don't worry. I never go all the way. Besides, I don't like 'good-looking guys.' Like, I'm totally sick of how overconfident they all are."

"Then stop trying to seduce every last one of them."

"That's a different issue entirely. I love the attention good-looking guys give me."

"Tsk."

Leo clicked his tongue in disgust, but when he saw Nonoa looking at him in the mirror, he felt guilty and averted his gaze.

"I'll be waiting at the front door."

After pushing off from the doorframe, Leo began to turn on his heel when Nonoa suddenly asked, "Do you have a handkerchief and some tissues?"

"Tsk. Shut up. Of course I do. Stop treating me like a kid."

"...? I'm not treating you like a kid. I'm treating you like a little brother."

"Whatever," he hissed before immediately leaving the room.

"...Is he going through his rebellious phase or something?"

"Probably. He's so immature. Kids, am I right?" Lea snorted, despite being exactly the same age as Leo. Nonoa, however, didn't bother bringing it up but instead placed the hair straightener down, took a step back, and checked how Lea's hair had turned out.

"What do you think?"

"Looks good. Thanks! Anyway, see you when I get back."

"Later."

After watching her sister walk out of the room with a coquettish grin, Nonoa glanced at the clock on the wall.

"...I should probably get ready to leave, too," she muttered. She took a seat in the chair Lea had been sitting in, straightened her own hair, and braided it so that it hung over her shoulder. After that, she opened her walk-in closet, revealing countless designer outfits that cost who knows how much. Yet she didn't glance in their direction but instead pulled a bland blouse and skirt out of one of the stacked plastic wardrobe shelves on the floor. She then grabbed a plain bag and hat off another shelf, picked up her black-framed glasses, and put them all on.

"...All right, that should do it."

She looked like a celebrity wearing a disguise to go into town. She managed to conceal some of her usual glamorous features and even appeared sophisticated in a way. After double-checking herself in the mirror, Nonoa briefly practiced a few expressions, then promptly walked out the front door. She was heading to a karaoke spot at the end of an alleyway behind the train station. It honestly wasn't the cleanest place, and it reeked of cigarettes, but there were no security cameras, and the workers hardly patrolled the area. As a result, it was often used as a hangout spot for delinquents and couples who were short on cash.

"Ngh… *Sniffle…*"

"…?"

The moment Nonoa stepped into the alley, she heard someone softly sobbing and began to look around. A few moments went by, and then a little boy around five or six years old came walking around the corner. His face was scrunched up and wet with tears, as though he was lost and aimlessly wandering the streets.

"Hff… Mmm… *Sniffle…*"

"……"

A little boy was lost and crying in what you could say was not exactly the safest place in the city. Nonoa glanced at the kid…and then ignored him as if she didn't particularly care. She wasn't in a hurry, but she didn't see the point in helping the child. She understood that the societal standard was that you should be nice to small children, and she probably would have done something to help the kid if there were people she knew nearby watching. But none of Nonoa's acquaintances were anywhere in sight. Plus, although her parents told her to be nice to her younger brother and sister, they never told her to be nice to other kids. Put simply, she had no reason to help this lost child. Maybe some would claim that having a conscience would urge her to do the right thing, but she didn't have one.

She arrived at the karaoke box and told the apathetic employee that she was joining a group that was already there.

"Welcome. How many people are in your party?"

"Oh, I'm meeting someone here. Uh… They're in room number…"

Nonoa looked through her smartphone to check the room number, then went up to the third floor.

"Oh, Nonoa! About time you showed up!"

When she walked into the karaoke room, a young girl immediately ran over, and Nonoa smiled brightly.

"I'm really sorry about that. So, uh… Am I the last to arrive?" replied Nonoa in a very sweet tone for a change. She then looked around and saw three guys sitting on the sofa; they all affectionately smiled back at her.

"Don't worry about it. We're the ones who asked you to come all the way out here," replied one of the boys.

"Yeah, if anything, we should be apologizing for having you meet us here during your summer break."

"We had something we just had to tell you, though… Anyway, have a seat," requested one of the guys, pointing to the empty spot next to him. Immediately, the other two boys' eyes began to burn red.

"Wow. Real sly subtly offering the seat next to you, bro."

"You really can't let your guard down around this guy."

"Okay, guys. That's enough fighting. Nonoa, you can sit here with me."

After giving the three boys a cold, piercing glare, the girl faced Nonoa once more with a brilliant smile and gestured to the seat beside her. Now it was the three boys staring at her coldly for using the fact that she was the same gender as Nonoa to her advantage. She picked up the control tablet as if she didn't even notice and handed it to Nonoa.

"Come on. Let's sing a couple of songs first. I want to hear you sing, Nonoa."

"Oh, good idea."

"Yeah, I want to hear her sing, too."

"Sing us a song, Nonoa."

"U-uh…? …All right. But we should probably order some drinks—"

"Okay, I'll go grab us some drinks. What do you want?"

All four of them immediately began to move the moment Nonoa seemed like she needed something, and once she began to sing, each of them was having the time of their life, as if they were at a live concert. At first glance, there was nothing out of the ordinary when compared to how they always acted around Nonoa at school, but there were a few minute differences: namely, Nonoa's behavior and how everyone was reacting. If Nonoa was their queen and they were her followers at school, then Nonoa right now was their dear princess, and they were her servants who catered to her every need.

"Phew..."

The moment Nonoa finished her ballad, the small crowd erupted into applause. None of them cared that it was a mellow, sentimental song, which people usually wouldn't get this excited for at karaoke, but these four would probably react the same way even if Nonoa had sung a heavy metal or anime song. She could be tone-deaf and the worst singer in the world, and they would still probably clap and cheer from the bottom of their hearts in the same way.

"G-guys, come on. That's enough...," Nonoa said bashfully as she fanned her face, appearing embarrassed by their excessive applause. Immediately, their clapping stopped, and their expressions lit up as if they had been blessed by an actual goddess.

"Wow, I was so nervous. Singing in front of others is so scary. Know what I mean?"

Nonoa smiled self-consciously before their affectionate gazes. Her smile, perhaps also due to the fact that she was dressed more modestly than usual, evoked a strong desire in them to protect her. In fact, the four lackeys were instantly won over, their passionate gazes locking on Nonoa in unison, and she began to fidget as if she felt embarrassed by it.

"Ngh... C-come on, guys. Sing something. This is embarrassing..."

Nonoa looked away to escape their stares and gestured that the other four should choose songs.

"O-oh, uh... All right."

"Uh... Should I put in the usual rock medley?"

"Oh yeah. Good idea. Let's all take turns doing that, then."

"I'll go grab a tambourine. ♪"

They immediately began picking songs and acting like they were having fun. It was like four servants going overboard to entertain their princess while observing every little move she made in order to please her, and it was only natural they acted this way. Because these four grunts were thinking, *Nonoa only worked as a model because her parents told her to, and although she hangs out with all the cool kids at school, she's really just a shy little girl deep down inside, unsure of herself and sick of this person she has to pretend to be.* Of course, this contradicted reality. Being timid and unsure of herself was merely a story Nonoa came up with to gain sympathy from these four. In fact, it was these four who were sick of caring about appearances, how they had to act at school, and how they had to pretend to be people they were not. Nonoa knew this, which was why she had approached them and used it to her advantage, claiming she was no different.

And that was how she got together people at the bottom and in the middle of the school-caste system to form this five-person group. These depressed individuals were extremely quick to fall for Nonoa, the only person who could understand them and the first true friend they had ever had.

We're the only ones who know the real Nonoa.

The popular kids who crowd around Nonoa aren't her real friends. We're her real friends.

This secret (fantasy) gave them an ever so sweet sense of superiority, and the kindness and trust that Nonoa showed them was like a high... And that was how Nonoa became a god to them.

"Wow, that was sooo good. You guys are such great singers!"

Nonoa laughed mirthfully while giving each guy a high five after they had finished singing, making every boy grin widely. After all, special treatment like this was reserved for when they were out together, which made it even more special. Nevertheless, the group of four didn't simply ask Nonoa to come just to sing. Once the mood eventually became more relaxed, the four exchanged glances and nodded.

"So... Nonoa... We actually invited you here today because there was something we wanted to talk about," explained one of the guys on behalf of the others.

"Really?"

"Like… You remember when you introduced us to Kinjou from Class F and told us to be friends with him?"

"Oh yeah. Kinjou, right? So…? Are you all getting along? Kinjou seems to be a very lonely person, just like us…so I would really appreciate it if you could be good friends with him, too."

"Yeah, uh… About that…"

In the face of Nonoa's affectionate smile, everyone just pressed their lips together awkwardly until the girl sitting next to Nonoa bravely spoke up.

"Hey… Kinjou is…"

"Tsk! Both Suou and Kujou aren't on social media… Figures. Probably trying to act like they don't care about fame or attention, since they're running for student council president. Pathetic. Pisses me off," grumbled a teenage boy, alone in his room in a luxury apartment. This was Kinjou from Class F, a student at Seirei Academy and the student whom Nonoa had been talking about. He was…honestly what most people would classify as ugly. In addition, what he lacked in height, he unfortunately made up in width. Pimples covered his round cheeks like freckles, and his nostrils were large like a pig's. These features alone would make most harmless-looking kids targeted by bullies, but the mean glint in his eyes left a completely different impression on most people. He was far less like a harmless little piglet and more like a sly snake. By regarding others as inferior and treating them poorly, he relieved some of the pressure from his own inferiority complex. Whether online or in real life, he lived to spread rumors about and criticize those "better" than him.

"Pfft. What? Look at this asshole vacationing in Guam. Getting a little too cocky lately, huh? Let's check this punk's post history and see if he has said anything slightly offensive before… Pfft! Ha-ha! What's this? Pissed off because someone pointed out the obvious?

Yeah, sorry you had to edit your photos to make yourself look halfway decent. Freaking uggo."

Day in and day out, he wandered through various social media pages of his schoolmates and famous people to troll and roast...but today, his smartphone suddenly began to vibrate on his desk.

"Huh...? Oh!"

When Kinjou saw the name on the screen, he answered the phone, his plump cheeks soon curling into a smile.

"Heh. Karaoke, huh? Fiiine. I guess I can do that."

Contrary to his complaint, he hopped out of his seat in excitement and immediately got ready to go out. Not even five minutes had gone by, and he was already outside and heading toward the karaoke place. Obviously, he was loathed by everyone at school as well due to his awful personality, which was why he didn't have a single friend. In fact, he had never had a friend. That is, until Nonoa talked to him at school only a month ago.

"Kinjou, I heard you're always being compared with your talented brother. Is that true? 'Cause I am, too..."

Nonoa spoke to him that day while showing him a different side to her than she ever showed at school. That was when she told him "everything." She told him that she was only pretending to be a bubbly, cheerful girl because that was what her parents wanted. She told him that she was really an introvert, that she was not as good as her siblings, that she felt ashamed whenever she was home, that she couldn't be the real her at school and that it was killing her.

"I feel like you and I aren't so different, Kinjou...," admitted Nonoa uneasily, looking up at him through her eyelashes and stealing his heart. Kinjou also opened up to her after that. He told her how his father and stepmother always doted on his younger half brother. He explained how everyone was always going on about how talented his brother was, but if his parents gave him the same opportunities to learn, study, and take part in extracurricular activities, then he would be able to do everything his little brother could do and better. And yet nobody—not his parents, not his teachers, not anyone around him—realized just how talented he was. Nonoa smiled and nodded while Kinjou dumped every bit of baggage that he had, and she agreed with him. She accepted him as he was. It wasn't long after that until she eventually introduced him to her four minions, who were all in similar situations, and they almost immediately hit it off.

"*Yo, Kinjou. I heard you really dissed Kujou good at the debate the other day.*"

"*I know how ya feel, man. We're a traditional school, so we should be represented by a real Japanese.*"

"*We're really happy to have someone who finally agrees with us. The other idiots at school look at her and think she's a princess just because she's a little cute.*"

What brought them together was a mutual dislike for none other than Alisa. At times, sharing a dislike for something forged stronger bonds than sharing a like for something, and that was especially true when it came to Kinjou.

Those idiots at school are such posers. They only care about looks. Scumbags.

But these people were different, and they lauded Kinjou for his bravery for standing up all by himself against the students who were at the top of the caste system. They were eager to hear tales of his heroic exploits, and their eyes lit up with joy after each story he told. For someone like Kinjou, who raised his self-esteem solely by putting others down, being praised by others was unbelievably euphoric. He was unconsciously opening up to them, despite being a person who usually didn't trust anyone.

"Heh. I don't really do karaoke, but I guess I can grace them with my presence, since they invited me," he arrogantly muttered to himself, and yet he couldn't keep himself from gleefully grinning all the way to the karaoke box. After making his way up to the third floor, he walked over to the room number he was given and stood in front of the door.

Hmm? It's strangely quiet...

Although he briefly found it curious, he wasn't too concerned, and he promptly opened the door before strutting inside like he was the coolest kid in school.

"Yooo! What's with the random karaoke invite? Lucky for you guys I just happened to be free," he claimed, looking around the room, then suddenly realized something was off. The air was tense. The only other female member of the group aside from Nonoa had her arm wrapped around Nonoa's shoulder as Nonoa stared at the floor. Never in a million years had Kinjou been expecting to see everyone so joyless. Although taken aback, he forced himself to smile.

"Guys, come on. What's with the gloomy mood? Wait. Nonoa, are you crying? Guys, what did you—?"

"Kinjou, shut up," snapped one of the guys, cutting him off. Kinjou clicked his tongue with clear irritation and looked over...where he found everyone glaring at him, eyes burning with animosity, and he unconsciously winced.

"Kinjou...," muttered Nonoa, slowly lifting her head.

"Y-yeah? What's wrong, Nonoa?"

He took a half step back the moment he saw the look on her face— the expression of a woman who felt betrayed by someone she trusted.

"Kinjou... Six months ago, someone harassed Mimiko online until she quit modeling. Was that you?"

"Huh? O-oh, uh... Well..."

Even Kinjou understood that nothing good was going to come from admitting it, but Nonoa's four friends were glaring at him as if to say, "You told us you did it the other day," which meant there was no way he could lie his way out of this.

"Yeah, I guess...I might have done that?"

Which led him to give this noncommittal answer. Nonoa bit her lip, scrunching up her tearstained face.

"H-hey, what's wrong? Seriously, like, what are we talking—?"

"Kinjou... Mimiko was my friend. A very close friend...," cried Nonoa, fighting through her tears.

"...?!"

Kinjou was rendered speechless.

"Mimiko was a really good person who accepted me for who I really was…but she fell into a deep depression after she was harassed online, and now she won't even talk to m-me anymore…!" she wailed, her voice trembling until she couldn't take it anymore. She pushed Kinjou out of the way and ran out of the room.

"Ah…"

He reached out to her in mute disbelief as she disappeared around the corner…when a large hand suddenly grabbed his shoulder tightly from behind. Naturally, he looked back…and found that four students with wicked grins were staring down at him.

"Well, Kinjou. That's how it is. The girl you destroyed just for laughs was one of Nonoa's best friends."

"Huh? Wait. No. I didn't know she—"

Kinjou retreated a few steps while trying to pathetically make excuses, but he soon found his back up against a wall of the small room, and the other four immediately cornered him.

"You can't just say you didn't know and expect to be forgiven. Besides, that model's not the only one you hurt. You were bragging for hours the other day about how many people you destroyed."

"Oh, by the way, we recorded the entire conversation and looked into these people you mentioned that night. And wow… You've slandered a ton of celebrities and kids at school. Now…what do you think would happen if we exposed you and told everyone online who you were?"

"Wh-why would you do that? The other day, you guys were praising me for everything I did…," stammered Kinjou, not able to process what was going on as he was pierced by their disdainful glares.

"We were only pretending to be interested, dumbass. What kind of person brags about stuff like that? There's something seriously wrong with you."

"Oh, and by the way, we were totally willing to accept you if you were a good person deep down inside like Nonoa thought you were. Too bad you ended up being trash inside and out."

"That's why we had to tell Nonoa what kind of person you really were."

"Yeah, she's too pure and sweet. ♪ We have to protect her from trash like you."

Their loving gazes as they thought about Nonoa instantly sharpened into sinister grins. The contrast was mind-boggling. Hints of fanaticism could be seen in their eyes, making Kinjou sink to the floor. He understood instinctively…that these four didn't consider him to be human. They didn't care about his feelings. They didn't respect him. They weren't taking his life into account. If needed, they wouldn't hesitate to stomp on him until he drew his very last breath.

"A-ah…"

It was genuine, undiluted cruelty—something he had never been faced with once in his life. It was unmitigated rejection that went beyond bitterness or hate, and it shook him to his core as warmth slowly spread throughout his underwear.

"P-please don't…"

The words escaped his hoarse throat as he acted purely on instinct. Meanwhile, the other four's eyes brightly burned as their lips curled maliciously.

"Ha-ha-ha! What the hell, man? You make it seem like we're trying to make you 'disappear.'"

"Don't worry. We wouldn't do anything like that…as long as you make sure you don't show your face around Nonoa again. Got it?"

"Of course, you can ignore our warning, but then we're gonna expose you online, and then it's not gonna only be about you anymore. Your entire family is gonna be publicly shamed and shunned for the rest of their lives. I'll make sure of it."

"You've ruined plenty of lives up until now, so I'm sure you're prepared to face the consequences, right?"

"A-ah…"

A young teenage boy's voice trembled with fear in that karaoke box that day, but his cries went unheard.

◇

"*Sigh...* Trying to make myself cry is hard," muttered Nonoa while messing around on her phone in the restroom stall. Not even a hint of the intense grief she expressed a few moments ago remained, but that was no surprise. It was merely an act, after all. Nonoa didn't have anything against Kinjou. Truthfully, she wasn't really that close to Mimiko, and the only reason she fed him to the lions like this was to pay back Masachika and Alisa.

Dad always told me that you have to pay back the people who help you.

That reason alone was enough for Nonoa to tear down a fellow human being, and yet she felt neither guilt nor a sense of accomplishment. It wasn't anything new for her, so she felt nothing. She had been manipulating her four puppets countless times already to dispose of people who got in her way: upperclassmen who were jealous of her and harassed her, the guidance counselor who held a grudge against her, Sayaka's rival candidates during the election who spread nasty rumors about her... Nonoa never once gave direct orders to do any harm to these people. She simply provided information and triggered her minions' desire to protect her. Doing that was more than enough to motivate her four goons to dispose of anyone who got in her way, and it made sense. She chose them because she knew what kind of people they were and what they were capable of.

"Things should be wrapping up right about...now."

After Nonoa walked out of the stall, she stood in front of the mirror, worked on her expression, then left the restroom.

"Nonoa!"

Just as she expected, the four members of her group were heading her way. She greeted them with a brave yet feeble smile.

"Guys... I'm so sorry about that. I'm fine now, though..."

"Nonoa... Are you sure you're okay?"

"Yeah, I'm sorry for getting upset like that. I ran off without even hearing Kinjou's side of the story... I'm sure he had his reasons for doing what he did, right? I should probably talk to him..."

But the three male members of the group stood in Nonoa's way when she began walking back to their room, each of them wearing a somewhat cruel grin.

"Oh, Kinjou already went home."

"He seems to feel super bad about what he did... Said he was too embarrassed to even face you."

"He said he was gonna have to rethink life and stuff, so don't worry about him, okay?"

"...Really? Well, if you say so..."

They gently watched over her as if they were knights protecting their innocent princess, but to Nonoa, they looked like rabid fanatics idolizing her as their goddess.

It's so funny how people can just assume and believe things with no evidence.

There were no deep emotions connected to that thought. Only cold observation.

"Well, I guess we will just have to wait until Kinjou turns over a new leaf and comes back better than ever."

Nonoa's smile was that of an angel: infinitely pure and innocent.

CHAPTER 3 **Atmosphere and Appetite**

One day, Alisa was standing in front of a certain ramen shop. Ominously written in red on the wooden sign were the words *The Cauldron of Hell*, and it was the same ramen shop she had eaten at with Masachika and Yuki a while back. She vividly recalled that the shop lived up to its name by serving only the spiciest ramen, sending her straight to hell and back, and yet for some reason, she was about to waltz into the lion's den once more. Why? Because when she and Masachika went on a da—a...pretend practice date the other day so she could teach the clueless teenager about women, he'd told her he liked spicy food.

It's not like I'm trying to understand what kind of food he likes, though!

She was making excuses to herself. There had to be some reason why someone would love spicy food that much, and she wanted to know why. That was all. This was nothing other than her trying to expand her culinary palate. If she managed to like not only sweets but spicy food as well, then she would be able to enjoy eating twice as much. This challenge was based on that simple thought process. And maybe it would have some side benefits, too? Like maybe she was hoping that she could enjoy eating out with her friend more? Of course, she was obviously referring to Yuki and not Masachika when she came to that conclusion.

"All right."

After making every excuse she could think of and preparing

herself for what was about to come, she opened the sliding door to the restaurant—

"...!"

—and immediately, the spices in the air burned her eyes and the back of her nasal cavity. Even though she was somewhat prepared for this, she reflexively narrowed her eyes and winced.

"Welcome to The Cauldron of Hell!"

She blinked for a few moments at the chef's high-spirited voice, then shifted her gaze to the hostess...where she saw a familiar face out of the corner of her eye and did a double take.

"Uh...? Ayano?"

"...? Oh."

Ayano, who was sitting at a table for two near the entrance, lifted her head from the book she was reading, and her eyes widened slightly in surprise. After seeing them greeting each other, the hostess approached and timidly asked:

"Uh... Will you two be eating together?"

"Oh, uh... Er... Yes," Alisa responded awkwardly, thanks to her absolute lack of life experience in this regard. The embarrassment she felt was almost physically painful, but there was no way she could back down now after she claimed that they would be eating together.

"Hey, uh... Do you mind?" she asked Ayano apprehensively.

"Be my guest."

She then took a seat across from Ayano, who tucked her book away in her bag.

"......"
"......"

And then there was silence. Two beautiful women staring at each other. Saying nothing.

Uh...

The indescribable awkward silence became too much for Alisa as she closed her half-open mouth, unable to find the right words to say. She didn't have much experience initiating small talk, and her relationship with Ayano...was still extremely uncertain.

Are we even friends…? We're not, are we? After all, we've hardly ever talked to each other, especially not like this, and we've only spent time together as members of the student council. To make matters worse, we're going to be running on opposing sides during the election cycle, so while we're working together in the student council now, we're also enemies. Wait. But…Yuki and I are friends, so…

Alisa was having difficulty putting her relationship with Ayano into words, but how she was going to start the conversation depended on what kind of relationship they had. Of course, she was not against the idea of being friends with Ayano, but Ayano had never asked to be her friend, and she wasn't confident enough to claim they were friends without any confirmation, either. It was a very common conundrum for people who were socially awkward or shy. She even started hoping that Ayano would be the one to initiate conversation…but she gave up the moment she looked into Ayano's eyes. Her eyes were unclouded without a hint of embarrassment. Clearly, she wasn't feeling awkward as she sat straight up with her hands in her lap as if to say, "Go ahead. I am ready to listen to whatever it is you have to say."

"Hello, I brought you some water. Please let me know when you're ready to order."

Their bizarre staring contest paused when the waitress came back with some water. Alisa's eyes naturally shifted away from Ayano as she picked up the menu and perused the disturbing names of the food with a bitter expression on her face. She then looked back at Ayano and asked:

"What did you get?"

It took quite a bit of courage for Alisa to ask that.

"I got—"

But right as Ayano was about to reply, the waitress returned with a bowl of ramen on a tray.

"Here you go. Spike Mountain Hell ramen. Enjoy your meal."

Inside the dark-red soup…were countless spikelike fine strips of long onion stacked to make a small mountain. It was the second thing from the top on the menu, and one stage hotter than the Blood Pond Hell ramen, which Alisa ate last time.

"…This."

"Oh…"

Alisa thought carefully for a few seconds after seeing the ramen the hostess brought. She was originally planning on getting Blood Pond Hell again, but after seeing Ayano's spicier choice, she suddenly began to doubt that getting the same thing would help her progress. Plus, ordering the least spicy item on the menu would make her kind of feel like a loser. She obviously knew this wasn't a competition, but…

"Excuse me, waitress? I'll have the same thing," she ordered, stopping the waitress on her way back to the kitchen. She then faced Ayano once more.

"Oh, you don't need to wait for me. Go ahead," she urged.

"Thank you," replied Ayano before grabbing her chopsticks, submerging the mountain of long onion into the soup, and pulling the chopsticks back out with some ramen. She then began slurping her noodles in silence.

"…!

"…?

"……"

After freezing for a moment, Ayano slowly slurped until the noodles were completely in her mouth. She wiped her lips with a napkin, then began to chew…and her expression didn't change in the slightest.

I-incredible! She's eating what looks like super-spicy ramen without even raising an eyebrow… Ayano must love spicy food, too…

Alisa's fear was accompanied by admiration and a faint sense of urgency. She could still clearly remember how devastatingly hot the ramen she ordered last time was, and this was going to be spicier. Would she really be able to eat it?

I-I'll be fine! They say you just have to get used to spicy food, and I had so much trouble finishing last time because I ended up adding seasoning to make it spicier!

While trying to fire herself up, she glanced at one of the table corners and noticed the seasoning the restaurant offered: soy sauce, pepper…and a suspicious-looking small earthenware jar that stood out more than the rest. On the jar was the name *Demon Tears*—an unbelievably spicy seasoning.

I'll be okay as long as I don't put any of that in my ramen… At least, I should be okay!

She said that to herself in an attempt to summon up enough courage to eat. Meanwhile, Ayano continued to chew on the noodles of the second hottest ramen in the shop as she thought:

It's spicy… So spicy…

Ayano was mentally on the verge of tears because she couldn't actually handle spicy foods that well, either. There was a reason she went there alone that day, and it was because she wanted to train herself to be able to eat spicy food, since the two people she adored the most loved it. Unknown to anyone around her, she had been painstakingly training at restaurants that specialized in spicy cuisine whenever she had a day off or some spare time. Thanks to that, she had built quite a tolerance for spicy food compared with when she first started training two years ago…but even then, this spicy ramen was hard to handle.

It's hot and spicy… My mouth feels like it's on fire…

The spiciness only got worse after the first bite, as if little bits of the spicy elements remained in her mouth, ignited by the boiling-hot noodles before exploding like dynamite. It got to the point where Ayano could no longer tell if the ramen was burning hot or if it was just really spicy.

Ngh… Too…hot…

She honestly wanted to open her mouth wide to breathe and get some ventilation going, but she was a proud maid, and that was bad manners. If she was alone, then maybe, but Alisa was sitting right in front of her. She couldn't allow herself to show such shameful behavior in front of Yuki's beautiful rival and schoolmate.

"…! Hff."

After managing to swallow the food in her mouth while keeping a straight face, she let out a brief sigh. Of course, her instincts were telling her to guzzle as much water as she could, but she knew through experience that doing so wasn't that effective, especially since it added pressure on the stomach, so she decided to simply bear the pain. Instead, she chose to use the long onion shavings, which were relatively safe, to escape from the heat.

There was less soup on the long onions compared with the noodles…which should give her some time to breathe and relax.

That was her hypothesis when she shoveled some long onion shavings into her mouth…and then immediately regretted it. Once she started chewing, the onions' own unique flavor made it feel like her tongue was being pierced by spikes.

"…?!"

Ayano's eyes rolled back due to how surprisingly spicy these long onion shavings were. It was clear there was something different about them. The heat was nothing like hot peppers. Instead, it felt like she was being stabbed. In basic chemical terms, it wasn't like the spiciness of capsaicin. It was aniline that contributed to the onions' piercingly burning sensation. If these types of spiciness were magic types, then they would be fire and wind. They were completely different magic types, exploding in her mouth and causing so much pain that she almost wanted to cry.

I-interesting… So this is the Spike Mountain part of hell…

The conflicting types of spicy flavors didn't cancel each other out. Instead, they came after her and attacked from both sides. That was the moment she realized that this double whammy was the core of the dish. She closed her eyes, tightly squeezing her tear glands to shut off the impending waterworks while nodding a few times as if she was actually enjoying the flavor. After eventually swallowing, she slowly reached for her cup, took a big sip of water, and exhaled, feeling instant relief from having her mouth cleaned out.

"It's really good. The exquisite savory flavors of the vegetables and ground beef stand out thanks to the spiciness of the soup."

Incidentally, Ayano wasn't telling a fib. She could taste the umami that went beyond the spiciness of the dish thanks to her years of hard training, so she wasn't lying. She simply didn't disclose the fact that she had no time to enjoy these flavors because of how spicy the ramen was. Nevertheless, Alisa was oblivious to how Ayano was feeling.

"Oh… Really? I can't wait," said Alisa with an awkward smile as she felt a shiver go down her spine.

H-how can she continue eating that like it's nothing? Ayano must love spicy food…

Alisa was gradually becoming more worried as she watched Ayano quietly resume eating. She thought that maybe they could bond over a common enemy like spicy ramen, saying things like "Mmph… This is hot" and "Yeah, it is," but this glimmer of hope she once had swiftly came crumbling down like a house made of straw in the wind. Ayano was a seasoned warrior who had no need for a comrade in arms. The only rookie soldier there was Alisa.

Ngh…

She started to regret sitting with Ayano, although it was already far too late for that. Crying now about how spicy the ramen was would only make a veteran like Ayano glare at her as if to say, "Why are you even here, then?" The best-case scenario would be Alisa's order arriving at the table after Ayano had finished eating and left…but of course, life was never that easy.

"Sorry for the wait. Spike Mountain Hell ramen. Enjoy."

Ayano had finished about half her ramen when Alisa's food arrived. There was no way for Alisa to run away now, so she steeled herself for battle while grabbing her disposable chopsticks like a soldier heading into war with a rifle in hand.

"Oh, great. It's finally here."

Her first contact with the ramen was going to be crucial, and this first bite was going to let her know that—

"…?! Gfff?!"

The instant she slurped up the noodles, her throat was doused with capsaicin, and she began to violently cough. While she managed to keep the food down, albeit barely, she couldn't stop coughing.

"…! Mn! Gff!"

The coughs were relentless, and having food in her mouth made it worse. Once Alisa finally managed to stop coughing, she carefully used her chopsticks to get the rest of the noodles in her mouth…where she was in unbelievable pain. Although she kept quiet, it felt as if the inside of her mouth was on fire.

Mngh…?!

It was spicy and boiling hot, and her mouth hurt. What kind of fools made this monstrosity? And how dumb did you have to be to order it?

I guess that means…I'm dumb…too…!

It was so spicy that she could hardly even think straight as she furiously began wiping her lips with a napkin. At any rate, first contact with the ramen…went poorly.

Th-there's no way I'm going to be able to eat all this…

Overcome with utter despair, Alisa swallowed her first bite as Ayano watched.

"Are you okay? You were coughing quite a bit a second ago…," asked Ayano with worry.

"I-I'm fine." Alisa reflexively retorted to feign strength. "Some of the soup went down the wrong pipe. That's all. I guess I was a little too aggressive with my slurping."

"Oh, I know what you mean. That happens a lot to me if I'm not careful." Ayano nodded as if she could relate. Alisa responded to the admission with an awkward smile, then looked down at her bowl of ramen…and felt almost hopeless. The road to finishing the entire bowl of ramen was a long one and a task so daunting that the hand holding her chopsticks was frozen. Ayano, on the other hand, seemed to have a good appetite.

I—I guess I'll try eating the long onions in between…

Alisa's thought process led her to the same conclusion Ayano had reached. In other words, she fell for the same exact trap. *A-ack! Th-that's hot! Hot, hot, hot! Hff!*

Alisa may have had a poker face, but she was struggling due to the spiciness of the onions directly attacking her tear ducts. It was sheer willpower alone that allowed her to maintain her dignified expression, but she soon realized that the more she chewed, the spicier it got. After doing the minimum amount of chewing necessary, she forced the food down with some water. But for some reason, mixing the cold water with the piercing spiciness of the onion made her mouth feel oddly refreshed.

I don't have any other choice...!

She knew that this refreshing feeling was a sham, but even if it was all in her head, there was no way she was going to be able to finish her ramen otherwise. Once she came to this conclusion, Alisa started to blow on the hot noodles to cool them down while removing as much of the soup as she could. She ate as quickly as she could. The goal was to defeat as much of her foe as possible before her deceitful powers of invincibility wore off.

Ayano's eyes widened slightly as she watched Alisa's chopsticks move diligently.

H-how can she continue eating like that? Incredible... Alisa must really love spicy food.

It was a mutual misunderstanding born from two people who couldn't be honest with each other.

I can't let her show me up...!

Seeing the way her schoolmate ate ended up motivating Ayano, and her chopsticks began moving tirelessly, as if she was trying not to be outdone. And once Alisa saw this...

She's shoving down all that ramen like it's nothing... I have to work even harder!

It was a scene from hell. Since each of them believed the other wasn't having any trouble, the idea of giving up wasn't an option for them anymore. All they could do now was move forward through pure

stubbornness and pride until they could escape this torment. And before long…

"…! Phew… That was good."

Ayano had finally conquered the Spike Mountain Hell. The sense of accomplishment was so great that she almost wanted to raise a flag to celebrate as she gulped down her glass of ice water and basked in victory.

Ayano looks…really satisfied for some reason. D-did she like it that much? I don't get it…but I've only got a few more bites to go!

Seeing Ayano's victory encouraged Alisa to make the final push, sticking her chopsticks into the small clump of remaining noodles, when—

Crunch.

The ominous sensation made Alisa freeze in place. It was a classic beginner's mistake. While eating, she hadn't stirred her ramen even once, so all the hot peppers and minced meat had sunk and gathered at the bottom of the bowl.

…? What's this?

And since she was but an amateur, she made another grave mistake. She curiously moved the noodles out of the way and peeked into the depths of hell.

Wh-what…?! What is that?!

The lump of spiciness, which had hardened a bit after sinking to the bottom of the bowl, began to crumble, and the horde of demons who had been sealed away in the deepest pit of hell were freed. The lack of soup itself further contributed to the high concentration of spiciness, making the dish become something far more sinister than when she started. Alisa tried to pull up the noodles in a fluster, but it was already too late. The noodles were covered with flakes of red-hot pepper and black specks to the point that no amount of blowing or shaking could get enough off.

…! Am I really going to eat this?

Alisa felt as if she were standing right before the crater of a volcano in the middle of an eruption, but she couldn't keep staring at her food all day. The finish line was right in front of her, and Ayano was already waiting for her at the summit.

I won't lose. I will finish every last bite. I will finish...every last bite...

She glared at the noodles with an almost ghastly expression as she tried to drum up courage for battle. Giving up now would mean that she went through hell for nothing. And for what? Why was she even doing this in the first place? Because of some sort of rivalry with Ayano? Because she was stubborn? No...

I want to be able to enjoy eating out with Masachika!

In the deepest pit of the netherworld, Alisa admitted her true feelings, and with that determination in her heart, she brought the ramen to her lips, and—

"...! ...?"

When she opened her eyes, she was sitting on a vaguely familiar park bench. She blinked repeatedly, looking around, and noticed that Ayano was sitting right next to her, appearing worried.

"...Are you okay?"

"Huh? Uh... I..."

She began tracing her memories to uncover the mystery of how she'd gotten there, but her head was so foggy that she couldn't remember a thing. While she knitted her brow and curiously tilted her head, Ayano timidly explained:

"Ahem... The moment you finished your ramen...it was like your soul had left your body..."

"What? O-oh..."

Overcome with embarrassment, she leaned forward, head hanging under the pressure of the indescribable awkwardness in the air, then looked back up at Ayano.

"Hey, uh... Thank you. You brought me here, right...? Ah! I didn't pay! I still haven't paid for my—"

"Oh, I…I paid for you…"

"I'm so sorry! Let me pay you back! How much was it?"

They continued to chat as Alisa got her money together… Ayano hesitantly asked:

"Hey, uh… You don't really like spicy food, do you?"

"Er…"

Despite wanting to immediately deny it, Alisa had no way to pretend to be tough after essentially losing consciousness. Her eyes wandered for a while until she finally decided to admit it.

"I'm…not really a big fan of spicy food…"

"Oh…"

Alisa hung her head low and waited to be asked why she would even go to such a restaurant, but what she heard next was something she never expected to hear in a million years.

"I actually don't like spicy food, either."

"Huh…?"

"I've been trying to build a tolerance so that I can eat spicy food with Ms. Yuki and M—*ahem*—maybe enjoy myself more when we eat out…but I still can't get used to it."

Ayano revealed that they shared the exact same motive and opinion, which made Alisa instantly feel a connection between them. She felt as if she had been walking through the depths of the underworld, where only demons gleefully played, and had finally found another living, breathing human.

"I—I was actually doing it for the very same reason. I wanted to build a tolerance to spicy food so I could enjoy the same foods as Yuki…"

"Really?"

Ayano's eyes glowed with delight. They were the eyes of a lone warrior on the battlefield who had finally found an ally. After all that, it appeared that honesty really was the best policy when it came to building a relationship.

"Then if you want…maybe we could start training and eating spicy food together from now on?"

"Huh…?"

Alisa froze the instant she heard the suggestion, since she was genuinely in no condition to be thinking about what she was going to do next.

"Like… I feel like it would be a lot less intimidating if we did it together, and we could really help each other as well…"

But there was no way she could say no after seeing Ayano timidly lower her gaze and speak so hesitantly.

It looks like I might have made a new friend…

She might have had a tiny ulterior motive as well.

"Yes, sure. Let's train together. I'm really looking forward to it, Ayano."

"…! Me too!"

Alisa agreed to the proposal without really giving it much thought. It was the beginning of a long, agonizing journey that neither girl was even remotely prepared for…but that was another story.

CHAPTER 4

Brother Complex, Sister Complex

"Phew... I'm finally back..."

A man wearing a polo shirt was standing in front of a traditional Japanese-style house. He was a tall, moderately muscular man who stood with his back straight. Behind the silver-framed glasses of this middle-aged intellectual were the gentle eyes of someone who might not have been the most handsome person in the world but was someone who would make you feel safe and relaxed... His hairline, on the other hand, was clearly in danger, and he was sensitive about it, so nobody ever brought it up. This man—Kyoutarou Kuze—was Masachika and Yuki's father, who had taken some time off work for the first time in ages and just arrived in Japan.

"It feels like it has been forever...," muttered Kyoutarou emotionally as he lifted his head, which felt a bit heavy due to jet lag. He was standing in front of his parents' home after having not been back for an entire year. After opening the gate and stepping inside, a big white dog that was sleeping under the eaves of the roof sluggishly lifted his head.

"Rir, long time no see. Do you remember me?"

The dog called Rir slothfully and unenthusiastically plodded over to Kyoutarou, gave him a few sniffs, and then barked.

"Yep. That's a good doggy."

He petted the dog's head with a wry smile and added:

"Are you really gonna be able to guard the house like that?"

This dog was originally a stray that Masachika and Yuki rescued three years ago. More specifically, it was Yuki who found a puppy with an injured hind leg and said they should save it, which Masachika quickly agreed to, so they brought the dog back with them to their grandparents' house. That said, the story wasn't as heartwarming and inspiring as it may have sounded…because Yuki also exclaimed:

"It's an injured white puppy… I bet it's a juvenile Fenrir! Let's take it home and make it our familiar!"

Her intentions…were not the purest. Regardless, they ended up taking the dog home and naming it Rir at the request of Yuki…who expected far too much from an injured puppy. Three years had gone by since then, and while Rir grew quite a bit, there was nothing divine about this beast. If anything, the canine only became more sluggish by the day. The excessive pressure may have stunted its growth. Rir wouldn't survive a single day alone in the wild.

"Sigh… I wonder who he gets that from," muttered Kyoutarou in a fed-up manner as he watched Rir lazily return to his spot under the eaves. After collecting himself, he walked over to the front door, opened it, and yelled down the hallway:

"I'm home!"

Immediately, the sliding door on the left side of the hallway flew open, and Yuki poked out her head.

"Oh, Dad! You're back. Welcome home. ♪"

Her lips curled into a beaming smile as she ran down the hall and threw her arms around her father. Kyoutarou closed his eyes and tilted his head back, touched by his daughter's undying love.

I have the cutest daughter in the entire world!

There was a decent number of fathers in the world who were unfortunately despised by their daughters around this age, but there was not a hint of dislike in Yuki's heart. Although he may have been a little concerned by the fact that she'd never had a rebellious phase, it quickly became nothing more than a trivial issue when faced with such love. Kyoutarou gently smiled and hugged his beloved daughter.

"It's good to be home. You've gotten…so big, Yuki."

"Hmm? Why did you pause for a second there?"

Yuki smiled knowingly at her father's slight hesitation as he calmly checked to see how tall she had gotten.

"Because, uh… You haven't really gotten much taller, have you?"

"Because I'm already the perfect size! I fit perfectly in your arms! I mean, what's cuter than that?!" argued Yuki like a thug, making it clear she wasn't insecure about any part of her body. Kyoutarou, who was a tad worried about his daughter's development, had no choice but to agree with her clear, enthusiastic remark.

"Yeah… Of course? You *are* the cutest, Yuki."

"Right?"

Her smile became smug, and she placed a proud hand on her chest. That was when both Masachika and Tomohisa looked out into the hallway as well.

"Oh. Hey, Dad."

"You're finally home, Kyoutarou!"

"Hey. It feels good to be home."

After a brief greeting, Masachika immediately returned to the room he'd been in. It was an extremely cold welcome compared with his sister's.

Yep… My son hasn't changed a bit. Still as cold as ever.

Though he was somewhat depressed by his son's unfriendly welcome despite them not having seen each other for so long, he figured all kids were like that while going through puberty and left it at that.

On the other hand…

"How was England? Were there a lot of pretty ladies everywhere? Hmm?"

"…I see you're as restless as always, Dad."

Unamused, Kyoutarou narrowed his eyes as his father approached him with a pervy smirk. It was hard to believe this was normal behavior for a senior citizen.

"Honey. You haven't seen your son in who knows how long. Is that really the first thing you should be asking him? Welcome home, Kyoutarou."

"Thanks, Mom."

Kyoutarou's mother, Asae, emerged from a room in the back of the house with the same fed-up expression as her son. But neither of their narrowed gazes seemed to have fazed Tomohisa at all.

"Of course it is! What is wrong with you? The first thing a real man does abroad is taste their best booze and their best women!"

"Dad, you don't even drink…"

Kyoutarou's exhausted gaze narrowed further, but it was his mother's exasperated look transforming into something far more terrifying that finally shut Tomohisa up.

"Honey…?"

"…!"

"Why does it sound like you speak from experience?"

"I-it's just talk. Th-that's all. You're the only one for me, Asae…"

"But, Grandpa, you told me a while back that Westerners had great butts because their pelvises were shaped differently."

"…?! No, uh… That was because I was watching this Western movie, and…uh…"

"Oh my. Honey, you said that to Yuki? My, my, my…"

"Wait. Asae, no. Asae?"

With an ominous smirk, Asae disappeared back into the room; Tomohisa chased after her in a panic. Kyoutarou watched his parents' usual exchange with a half-relieved, half-jaded expression until Yuki suddenly spun around with the brightest of smiles.

"So? How was it, really? Were there any beautiful blond women with incredible bodies?"

"Yuki, you too? Really? …At least let me put my suitcase down."

He stepped inside with a troubled grin, then joined his son in the Japanese-style room on the left and placed his suitcase and belongings down in a corner…all while Yuki followed closely behind him, begging him to talk about beautiful British women.

"Oh, hey. Did you see any maids? England's the birthplace of maids and maid culture, right? Did you take pictures of any real maids?"

"I saw some…but none of them were young, you know? They were less maids…and more like housekeepers, I guess you could say…"

"Whaaat? There weren't any cute blond maids with huge racks and tiny waists?"

"Not that I saw…"

"Whaaat? *Boooring*," she complained before throwing herself in her brother's lap.

"Ouch! What the hell?" replied Masachika, who was sitting in a legless floor chair and playing on his phone.

"Dad's home, so it's time to stop playing on your damn phone."

Yuki rapidly punched Masachika's stomach while he glared down at her, holding his smartphone at a safe distance in the air.

They really get along so well.

Kyoutarou watched over them with warmth in his heart. There were countless siblings in the world who lived together but didn't talk, let alone even make eye contact, and yet there were no signs of these two ever not getting along. In fact, they essentially acted like best friends whenever they were together. Perhaps it helped that they lived separately, though, for the most part.

"Tsk."

Masachika scowled and grumbled, grabbed Yuki's fist to stop her, and placed his phone down. Immediately, she swiped his phone, reclined across his lap, and began scrolling.

"Oh, you're already at chapter five? Impressive for a free-to-play player."

"That's not your phone. Stop. Seriously, though… Did you already forget what you just said a few seconds ago?"

"Huh? You mean how Westerners have different-size pelvises, so they have really nice butts?"

"What the…?! The hell are you talking about?!"

"Ah…! Does that mean Alya and Masha, too…? I'm going to have to check when we go to the beach!"

"You better not. Anyway, give me back my phone already."

"Ahn. ♡"

After Masachika nabbed the phone out of Yuki's hand, she turned ninety degrees, facing his stomach while still using his lap as a pillow.

"Come on, you can't tell me you're not looking forward to seeing Alya and Masha...in their swimsuits. ♡"

"Stop drawing boobs on my thigh."

"They're eyes!"

"I don't care!"

"Yeah, yeah. That's what they all say. Don't try to pretend you're tough. I bet you're imagining them in their swimsuits right now."

"No, that's not what I meant. I—... I know it's hard for you to understand this, but I'm not looking forward to it *that* much."

"Speaking of 'hard,' there's an easy way we can check to see how excited you— Bfft?!"

Yuki's temple was suddenly met with an iron elbow, sending her to the tatami-mat floor as she writhed and groaned in agony.

Maybe they're a little...too close?

That was the first thought that came to mind as Kyoutarou watched their exchange from where he was sitting at the low table. They looked more like a stupid couple than best friends—to the point that you'd almost want to jokingly ask, "Wait. Are you two dating?"

No. No way. This isn't a comic book. There's no way they'd be...

There was no way his children would ever do anything like that. After he furiously shook his head, he casually spoke up as if to dispel any fears he had and asked:

"By the way, you two dating anyone right now?"

Masachika shot his father a questioning gaze while Yuki looked up as well, albeit still clutching her head.

"I already told you that I don't have a girlfriend."

"Me neither. I'm not really interested in dating, though."

Hmm...?

It was something he had expected, since they had told him in e-mails before that they weren't dating anyone. But what concerned him was how Yuki said she wasn't interested in dating at all.

I heard it's normal for even middle schoolers to have boyfriends and girlfriends these days, and Yuki is really cute, so surely, tons of guys have

tried to ask her out, right? Of course, I don't want her to date just any-
one, but...!

While Kyoutarou was analyzing the situation, the revived sister swiftly crawled over to her father's side, then looked up at him with a sleazy smile similar to her grandfather's.

"So? Are you going to tell me or what, Dad?"

"Tell you what?"

"About England! Did you meet any beautiful blond women or not? You had to have been invited to tons of parties as a diplomat, right? Did no politician ever introduce you to a nice, young lady?"

"Oh, that? ...Yeah, I guess there were some beautiful women, now that you mention it."

He did attend parties with a female companion from time to time due to the nature of his work, and occasionally, he would ask his single female coworker to go with him, but he usually went by himself. Sometimes, people would ask him if he was interested in dating their daughter when they found out he was single, but he never really gave it much thought, since he figured they were joking around or just try-ing to be polite. However, when he explained that to Yuki, she seemed to express some skepticism.

"Are you sure they were just trying to be polite?"

"They were obviously joking around. One man's daughter, for example, was still in her midtwenties."

Things did get a little...interesting between Kyoutarou and this man's daughter when she had a little too much to drink, though, but he figured that it was some kind of honey trap, since there was an important international conference coming up. Thankfully, the female coworker he always asked to join him at these parties happened to see him and came running over to save the day before anything serious occurred. She continued to reprimand him after that as well.

"You know you can't hold your liquor, Mr. Kuze! You need to be more careful around people like that!" she'd yelled. From that day on, she became his self-proclaimed "honey-trap lookout" and started to

attend more and more parties with him…but if anything, Kyoutarou was worried that perhaps this young, beautiful coworker of his *was* the honey trap.

She's very mature, independent, and never asks about any classified information, though…

But after giving it some thought, he realized this was nothing he should tell his daughter about, so he simply added:

"Nobody's interested in a divorced, middle-aged Japanese man with kids."

He did actually feel that way, and even if some wonderful woman ever did show interest in him, Kyoutarou had no intention of getting remarried… Nevertheless, Yuki relentlessly continued to press the issue, showing no signs of giving up.

"Then how about a sexy, middle-aged widow? Were there really no youthful older women with kids you could talk to and make a connection with?"

"Huh? Oh, uh… There is a French diplomat I met during a conference who fits that description…"

"Seriously?!"

"A beautiful French lady!"

Masachika's disbelief and Yuki's amusement clashed as they shouted over each other.

"I mean, she has a daughter who lives in France while she works abroad, so we kind of hit it off. That's all," he mentioned as if to calm Yuki's expectations, but his comment only made her further narrow her gaze.

"But, Dad, you said there *is* a French diplomat, not *was*. It sure sounds like you two are still keeping in touch, if you ask me."

"…?! No, uh…"

Kyoutarou was essentially struck speechless by her sharp observation, but it didn't end there, for his son followed up with yet another piercing attack.

"Wait. Is that who I was sending that anime merchandise to around six or so months ago?"

"…?! Y-yeah, could have been."

"Hmm? Ohhh! Now I remember! The letter!"

Their father averted his gaze for no apparent reason, but apparently, that French diplomat's daughter was a fan of Japanese subculture, so she tried to use her mother's connections to see if she could somehow get her some merchandise of a certain show she liked.

She ended up sending Kyoutarou a letter that clearly showed a lot of effort and passion, since she tried to write in Japanese, despite being far from a native speaker, so there was no way he could refuse. Therefore, he'd asked if Masachika could pick up the goods and send it to her. Everything she wanted was relatively easy to get in Japan, so Masachika took on the job to help his father out. The daughter promptly wrote a heartfelt message to express her gratitude, which Kyoutarou had forwarded to Masachika, and both Masachika and Yuki could still vividly remember it.

"*Giggle*. Oh, Dad. You should never tell a fib. It sounds like you have a close, personal relationship to me."

"No, not at all. She took me out for a light lunch to thank me, but that's it. As two people who represent different countries, deep down inside, we are always trying to read each other and are suspicious of each other to an extent, so…"

Yuki's lips only curled upward the more he tried to explain.

"A forbidden love between two diplomats from different countries… You should follow your heart, no matter what others say."

"Actually, there's nothing forbidden about it…"

"Follow your heart. Get married to that beautiful, blond woman and, while you're at it, send her beautiful daughter to Japan. Can you imagine it? One day, she suddenly rings the doorbell, introduces herself as Masachika's new stepsister, and three seconds later, they're now living together. Doesn't that sound wonderful?"

"No, it doesn't, actually! What kind of filthy smut are you reading lately?!" complained Masachika, standing behind his sister, whose brain was in full-degenerate mode.

Nevertheless, Yuki ignored her brother and continued: "By the way, how old is this daughter of hers?"

"Uh… I think she was around fourteen or fifteen years old?"

"Oh? So she would be Masachika's new younger sister! We'd probably have to fight for the position!"

"Yeah, right. You two would be best friends."

"Could this be the start of a rom-com-like war between a blond stepsister and a silver-haired schoolmate for Masachika's love?!"

"No."

"Hmm? 'Silver-haired schoolmate'? Oh, is that the girl I heard about the other day? Uh…"

Kyoutarou paused while he tried to think back… All of a sudden, the sliding door flew open with a *thud*. Everyone's eyes were naturally drawn to the doorway, where they found Tomohisa with a radiant smile.

"Alisa Kujou! Right?! Did something happen? Are you two dating?!"

He came rushing into the room noisily, knowing exactly who they were talking about.

"Sorry to disappoint you, Grandpa, but nothing happened. There's nothing going on between us." Masachika frowned as he looked away from his father's and grandfather's curious gazes. Of course, Yuki wasn't going to let him off that easily.

"She and Masachika have apparently been doing their summer homework together. Alone at home! Just the two of them! And they have been doing this a lot!"

"Ooooh?!"

"Heh. That's my boy."

"No, we've just been doing homework together. That's all…," Masachika explained desperately, clearly even more annoyed by how excited all of them were getting. Regardless, Yuki wasn't a quitter.

"The defendant claims that he's innocent, but when I was in his room the other day…"

"Who are you calling a defendant?"

Ignoring her brother, Yuki cupped the side of her mouth as if she was about to reveal a secret. After both Kyoutarou and Tomohisa leaned forward, eyes sparkling with curiosity, she grinned and continued:

"I found Alya's silver hair in Masachika's bed! Oh my gosh! I wonder what they were doing, right?! Wink, wink! Maybe they were just practicing what they learned in health class?!"

"Unbelievable. So? Did you learn anything? Did you get enough credits to finally graduate?"

"No! Now stop playing detective and making up weird scenarios, especially when it involves Alya! It's rude!" Masachika replied angrily to Tomohisa's crude remark.

With a soft smile, Yuki placed a hand on her brother's shoulder. "I know. You're a spineless virgin with no balls, so there's no way you would ever try anything with Alya. Yep. Everyone knows that."

"Excuse me? Are you looking for a fight? Because—"

"Of course not. I'm on your side. That's why I plan on helping you during our upcoming student council get-together. Alya's going to be all over you before you know it."

"I'd rather you not."

"Which do you prefer: Alya's swimsuit coming off and floating away, or being stuck on an uninhabited island together with—?"

"What is wrong with you? Are you stupid or something? I can't choose just one."

"All right, I'll make sure Alya's bikini top falls off after you and Touya are banished to an uninhabited island together."

"Wait. No. Being stuck on an island with Touya sounds like hell. You said together—"

"You interrupted me before I finished my sentence. What I was about to say was 'together with Touya.'"

"Tsk…! I can't believe I fell for such a simple trap… Who would even want to see something like that?"

"A *fujoshi* would. Plus, there are guys who like watching cute girls in bikinis but don't like it when there are other guys in the scene."

"Oh, like me, huh?"

"Exactly. So you should probably start working on turning yourself into a girl first if you want to join us."

"'First'? Great. There's more."

"Don't worry. Ordinary guys turn into beautiful women when they switch sexes. It's just one of those unwritten rules of the world."

"Even if I could do something like that, how am I supposed to explain it to the others in the student council?"

"Huh? Obviously, we'd introduce you to them as your cousin, Chika Kuzemasa."

"Wow, *great name*. That'll fool 'em."

"Don't worry! I'll call you Big Sis Chika!"

Seeing Yuki joking around and try to help Masachika with his love life erased any concern that Kyoutarou may have had.

Oh, thank goodness… It looks like I was just overthinking things. Yeah, what was I thinking?

These two siblings would never do something so taboo. Entertaining the idea at all was absurd, and Kyoutarou was embarrassed that the thought ever crossed his mind.

They're just close. Yeah… And that's a good thing.

Once he came to that conclusion, Kyoutarou warmly watched over his children with Tomohisa… Yuki suddenly wrapped her arms around Masachika from behind, then followed up by tightly wrapping her legs around him as well.

"Is something the matter?"

"Oh, no… I just gave Dad a hug earlier, so I thought I'd give you one, too."

"This isn't really a hug. It's more like a piggyback ride…and you're heavy."

"Excuse me? Did you just tell a young lady she was heavy?"

"Yeah?"

"How dare you!" shouted Yuki, baring her fangs as they drew closer to his neck, until…

"Nom, nom, nom."

"Stop biting me."

"Hmm… I'd say that's A2-grade meat right there."

"Hmph! Cut me some slack. I'm at least F1 grade."

"There is no F1 grade. We're not talking about cars."

"Yeah, I get that, but it's usually an F in these kinds of situations."

"You mean like *My Little Sister Called Me F1-Grade Meat, So I Became the Best in the School Cafeteria*?"

"Yeah, something like— Wait. Did you just say 'school cafeteria'?"

"Yeah, but that was just the subtitle. The main title is *That Time I Got Reincarnated as Beef*."

"The hell?! What kind of title is that?! I'm going to get eaten?!"

"The protagonist is reborn in another world as a Minotaur and starts working as a chef at a depraved, cuisine-ignorant school cafeteria where he cooks his own flesh, and whenever the heroines eat his cooking, they yell, 'Yummy!' while their clothes explode off their bodies."

"You can't trick people into reading this just because you stripped a few cute girls naked."

"Oh, by the way, all the heroines are literal trolls."

"Goddammit. Gross."

"How can you say that? This is a story about different creatures and races finding common ground and sharing joy through food. It's a really touching story."

"Minus the cannibalism, maybe."

"And at the very end, when the protagonist lets the school director's granddaughter eat his remaining right arm, his lips curl into a bittersweet smile, and he says, 'Well, it looks like I won't be able to cook anymore.' Heartbreaking, huh?"

"You'd have to be legally insane to want to read that."

"The story ends with the protagonist getting back at his sister, who made fun of him, by making the most incredible cuisine with his heart."

"That's the worst revenge story I've ever heard! Disgusting!"

"But, well, his sister's a Minotaur, too, and a vegetarian, so she didn't eat it."

"That ending really left a bad taste in my mouth. Ruined the whole thing."

"Other than the ending, though, what do you think?"

"I think you're sick."

As Yuki cackled, violently shaking Masachika, Kyoutarou continued to smile. He slightly averted his gaze and thought:

Yeah, maybe they are a little too *close.*

CHAPTER 5

Ideals and Reality

"Thanks for gathering here today, everyone. I know this isn't what you wanted to do during your summer break."

The people sitting in the student council room during summer break shook their heads to tell Touya not to worry about it.

"No, it's fine, but…is this about changing the school uniform?" Masachika spoke up on behalf of the others.

"Hmm? Oh, no. This has nothing to do with the uniforms. Chisaki and I are making progress regarding that issue, though."

"Are you sure you don't need our help?"

"I appreciate it, but you don't have to worry about it. There's actually something else I need help with instead."

"What's that?"

Touya's eyes slowly swept the room as he looked at every member besides Chisaki.

"…Have any of you heard the rumors about the seven school mysteries?" he asked with a grim expression on his face.

"Seven school mysteries? You mean…like Hanako of the Toilet, or anatomical models moving on their own?"

"Exactly. The mysteries at our school aren't what you'd expect, though."

Masachika shifted his gaze to Alisa, since he hadn't heard any rumors. But there was no way she would know if he didn't, owing to the fact that she had a far smaller circle of friends than he did, so all they could do was share puzzled glances.

"I have heard a few rumors before. I believe the ones I know of were the Shadowy Figure on the Roof, the Turning Statue, and the Red Schoolgirl," Yuki suddenly piped up. She was sitting across the table from them.

"Yeah, you remembered correctly. Those are three of the seven."

"Hmm… These aren't really names you hear about often, huh?"

"They aren't. You usually expect these to be like finding Hanako in the bathroom, or the school piano randomly playing at night, or a staircase that leads to a floor that's not supposed to exist."

"I know, right? I guess it'd be kind of weird for high schoolers to be spreading rumors about really cliché ghost stories like that, though… By the way, what are those three rumors about?" asked Masachika with a smirk, making Yuki's lips curl suggestively.

"Are you sure you want to hear? Some of these stories are pretty scary."

"Wait. Really? How scary?"

"As scary as finding a tiny screw near the microwave."

"That's terrifying! …But isn't that a different kind of scary?"

"*Giggle*. I'm kidding."

After laughing softly, Yuki began to explain what she had heard about the mysterious seven school wonders.

The Shadowy Figure on the Roof… Students had supposedly seen a shadowy figure from time to time standing on the rooftop of the school building, which no one was allowed access to. Although the shadowy figure appeared blurry for some reason, making it impossible to even guess the gender, every student who saw it said that they could feel an extremely strong, piercing gaze watching them.

The Turning Statue… There was apparently a plaster bust in the art room that would flip horizontally in the middle of the night. Although that was the only thing it did, there were multiple eyewitness accounts in the art club of the phenomenon, and there were supposedly pictures of it as well.

The Red Schoolgirl… Students claimed to have run into a seemingly injured female student after school somewhere on school grounds. Nobody who had seen her could remember what she looked like, but after a few days had gone by, they all had an injury in the same spot that she'd had.

"Hmm…," mumbled Masachika apathetically after hearing the rumors.

"You seem rather uninterested in the rumors," replied Yuki.

"I mean, they're just rumors, right? You can claim to have pictures as evidence, but anyone can edit pictures nowadays."

"Yes, I suppose." She nodded, seeming to agree with Masachika. They both slightly shrugged in unison. Yuki probably never believed any of the rumors from the start, and these two weren't the only ones. All the others in the room were either grinning or their faces were blank with indifference. There was one exception, though.

"Ngh… How am I supposed to walk alone after school hours now…?"

"Huh? Masha…?"

Maria lowered her head, wrapping her arms around herself. Her usual smile was nowhere to be found, and the fact that she was nervously looking around the room made it clear that she was seriously frightened. Worried by her close friend's overreaction, Chisaki, who was sitting across from Maria, immediately tried to soothe her.

"No, Masha. These are just rumors. You don't need to be scared…"

"Mmm… But you know what they say: There are dead folk where there's a vampire, right?"

"You mean, 'Where there's smoke, there's fire'?"

"Ha-ha! Wow. I guess it basically means the same thing, but the way you said it made it way more complicated."

"Huh?"

"Masha! Seriously?!" shouted Alisa in embarrassment; her sister simply blinked in a puzzled manner.

"Anyway, I'm surprised. I thought you'd be more scared of ghost stories, Chisaki," commented Masachika as he watched the sisters' exchange out of the corner of his eye.

"Huh? No way. Why would you think that?"

"I don't know. I just thought you'd be afraid of ghosts, since you can't punch them."

It was a common trope among meatheads in comics and anime, so of course it was the first thing to pop into Masachika's head, but Chisaki looked back at him, tilting her head as if she couldn't comprehend what he was trying to say.

"What are you talking about? You can punch ghosts."

"Huh?"

"Huh?"

""""Huh?""""

The other five members of the student council immediately spun in their chairs and stared at Chisaki, causing her to recoil as if she had no idea why everyone was looking at her. And because she didn't seem to be joking in the slightest…

"So, President, what are the other four mysteries about?"

"Oh, I was actually curious as well."

"Oh, right. Uh…"

…the rest of the student council simply decided to pretend like they hadn't heard anything. After all, asking her to expand on it would be like opening Pandora's box and would perhaps lead to consequences far more terrifying than the school's seven mysteries. What she'd punched was definitely not a ghost—it was something else. That was the story everyone decided to tell themselves.

"The stories I heard…"

Touya proceeded to explain the other four rumors.

The Weeping Clubhouse… There were claims that you could hear a woman crying in the school clubhouse, but nobody could figure out where the sobbing was coming from.

The Luck Staircase… You apparently had a high chance of pulling an SSR in any mobile game while on the staircase to the rooftop.

"Sorry, I need to go to the bathroom."

"You are free to go to the bathroom, but we need you to leave your phone here."

"Never mind, then."

"Hmph. Not even trying to hide it, huh, Kuze?"

The Invisible Cat… People had been hearing a cat meowing from time to time in the gymnasium's storeroom to the side of the school-yard, but not one person had ever seen the cat.

The Blooming Cherry Blossom… There was a cherry blossom tree behind the schoolhouse that would sometimes bloom out of season at night. Those who were graced with white flower petals were blessed with good luck, while those who saw crimson petals were struck by bad luck.

"And…that about does it for the seven mysteries of our school," concluded Touya.

"Uh… I know this isn't your fault…but a lot of those stories were ridiculous. I mean, the mobile game one just sounds like something that someone hastily made up so there would be seven wonders, right?" replied Masachika with a finger on his forehead as if he had a headache.

"Yeah, I…I guess so."

"The crying woman is obviously the building settling or noise being carried by the wind. I mean, the fact that she's weeping is a little concerning, but still. And that cat meowing? A cat probably just wandered into the storehouse. Nothing more, nothing less."

"Yeah, those would be the most obvious reasons."

"And that cherry blossom blooming out of season. The flowers on our school's trees are all white, and the petals' color depends on the type of cherry blossom, so there's no way anything other than white flowers are going to bloom."

"Sure…but isn't that what makes this a mystery?"

"Hmm… I feel like it just depends on who you ask. It's at night, right? Some people might think the petals look white, while others see them as pink…"

Only after being this much of a contrarian did Masachika realize that his opinions were starting to sound like complaints, and he shrugged.

"Sorry for being so negative about everything."

"Oh, no. We need critical feedback, so don't worry about it."

"Thanks. Anyway, why did you want to talk about these seven school mysteries?"

Touya frowned and crossed his arms.

"So…there have apparently been a lot of students sneaking into school after hours lately because of these seven mysteries."

"Uh…"

"It's not really a problem if they wander around a bit before going to their clubroom, but some people are trying to break into the school rooftop area, and a handful of others are even sneaking into the school in the middle of the night."

"O-oh my. Actual high schoolers are doing this?"

Yuki expressed doubt as well, as if to agree with Masachika, who was clearly puzzled that high schoolers were still up to such shenanigans.

"So these students sneaking into school at night… That sounds like trespassing to me. Is it not? I'm pretty sure our school wouldn't tolerate something like that. Where did you hear all this?"

"There's a video that was uploaded online to a private account of some students sneaking in, from what I hear. One of the students who saw the video informed us the day before yesterday."

"Wow… How stupid can you be? The world's full of idiots like that, though, huh?"

Depending on the circumstances, that video could get leaked to the public. The backlash would be brutal, and once people on the internet figured out who posted the video, everyone involved—or even somewhat related—could essentially be doxed. Not only Masachika but also Alisa and Chisaki frowned at the thought. There seemed to be some clowns at this prestigious school who were completely oblivious to how the real world worked and had little to no personal risk management.

"But, well, we did contact the student who uploaded the video, in private, and gave them a strong warning, so the video has apparently been deleted. But while the imminent crisis has been averted, this doesn't mean there won't be other students who'll do the same thing. The student in question this time got lucky because no school staff found out, but if one of the teachers heard what happened, then they would have been severely punished without question."

"Yes, we are very lucky that everything went smoothly this time," agreed Yuki.

"That's why I would like for the student council to investigate these seven school mysteries. To put a stop to these rumors and prevent people from doing anything illegal. What do you all say?" continued Touya, slightly raising the tone of his voice.

"By 'investigate,' do you mean you want us to find the cause of these rumors? In other words, to make the students lose interest, you want us to get the word out that all these mysteries have simple explanations, right?"

"Exactly, Yuki. To be honest, I don't even care if you fabricate the evidence. Like if you found a cat somewhere and took a picture with them, then you could claim this was the same cat that people had heard meowing in the gymnasium storeroom. Your goal is less about discovering the actual causes behind these rumors and more about making it seem like you discovered the actual causes. At any rate, I want to put an end to these rumors as quickly as possible."

"Honestly, I heard some members in the kendo club talking about the rumors, too. I doubt any of them would actually trespass, but it is a little concerning…," added Chisaki.

Uh… That probably has something to do with you telling them ghosts are real, thought Masachika, but he kept that to himself and replied:

"All right. I mean, this is a student issue, so it is the student council's job to do something about it."

The other members individually agreed with Masachika's point of view, and none of them seemed reluctant, bringing a smile of relief to Touya's face.

"Thanks, everyone. I want to get started right away…but Chisaki and I have a meeting about the school uniform that we must attend, so we probably won't be able to help. I know I'm the one who suggested investigating these rumors, so I'm sorry…"

"Yeah, we're really sorry. The meeting's probably going to last the rest of the day, so I doubt we'll be able to help at all."

Both Touya and Chisaki looked apologetic, but the other five members didn't seem to care.

"No, don't worry about it. If anything, you're doing us a favor handling the most difficult task. Plus, you're letting us stay at your family's house when we go to the beach, so this is the least we can do."

"Exactly. Five people is more than enough. Let us handle this."

"Yes, there is nothing you two need to worry about."

"I agree with the others. Good luck."

"Yeah… Good luck… I—I can't say I'm not scared, but I won't let you down!"

Touya and Chisaki gently smiled, relieved.

The group continued to discuss the plan in detail for a while after that until they came up with enough concrete ideas.

"All right, so let's split up and start investigating. We're gonna need to wait until night to look into about half of these, though."

"Yes… But unfortunately, Ayano and I have a curfew, so…"

"It's not your fault, so don't worry about it. Alya, Masha, and I can take care of all the night ones. Sound good, you two?"

"I'm fine with that."

"Y-yeah, sure."

"Again, thanks, everyone. And sorry to leave you three with the night shift. I'll make sure to tell the teachers what we're up to just in case. Of course, I won't tell them about the trespassing. I'll tell them that there are many students who've been feeling uncomfortable lately because of these seven mysteries."

"Sounds good. Thanks."

They decided to take a short break after the meeting before starting the actual investigation.

"Oh, Kuze. Hold on."

"Yeah?"

Each member went off on their own during the break, with some going to buy a drink and others going to the bathroom. Masachika did the latter, but on his way to the bathroom, Chisaki suddenly called out to him from behind. When he turned around, she took something out of her bag and tried to hand it to him.

"Here, you can borrow this."

"Is this…?"

What Chisaki was handing him…was a Buddhist rosary, and one with beautifully polished obsidian prayer beads at that. It was strangely authentic-looking.

What is she trying to give me this for?!

Masachika froze, unable to process why an upperclassman was trying to lend him prayer beads.

"You know, just in case you run into a real one, you can use this," added Chisaki as if she'd picked up on how bewildered he was.

"Oh… Uh… A real one? You don't mean a ghost, right? And how am I supposed to even use this…?"

Was he supposed to sandwich it between his hands and roll the beads while reciting some sort of Buddhist prayer? He began to daydream about comic books where priests did that to exorcise ghosts.

"'How'…?"

On the other hand, Chisaki seemed somewhat puzzled by his question, but she soon began weaving the prayer beads under and over her fingers…as if she was wearing brass knuckles.

"First, you do this."

"…Uh-huh."

She squeezed the beads wrapped around her fingers tightly and formed a fist before throwing a fierce straight right.

"And then this!"

"Got it."

Put simply, punch them. Don't waste your time chanting some Buddhist prayer. Punch them. It appeared violence really did solve all problems.

"Oh, but if you're having trouble getting close enough to strike,

I recommend taking the beads off and flicking them at your opponent."

"You make it sound like everyone can do that. I mean, I'm a professional nerd, so of course I can do it."

"Oh, perfect. Then here. Take the Renyouhou Renheki Gaiju and protect the girls for me, okay?"

"That's clearly an item you're supposed to get in the last dungeon. Are we sure that I can even equip it at my level?"

"Don't worry. You can still equip it even if you don't have enough strength. It'll just absorb some of your life force instead."

"Oh, that's it? Well, gee! I'm relieved to hear that!" he exclaimed sarcastically, then carefully accepted the prayer beads.

…How in the world does she have such a nice smile?

Masachika still had no idea how much of what she said was a joke, but he made a promise to himself that he would never wear these beads, no matter what happened.

"All right, then. Let's start the investigation."

"What are you talking about? We already finished investigating the first case."

As Alisa's fed-up voice echoed down the staircase leading to the rooftop, Masachika's pupils widened, and he smiled shakily as he turned around.

"Ha-ha-ha. What are you talking about? We're just getting started…right?"

"No. Just now, we've been standing on these stairs—"

"And nothing happened. Nothing at all. The five thousand gems I've been diligently saving after watching ad after ad every single day did not disappear, right? That was just my imagination."

"Sigh…"

Yuki was wearing an eerie grin next to her brother, who still couldn't accept reality.

"Ha…ha-ha…! We still need to try a few more times before we can be sure the rumors were false. Wouldn't you agree?"

"You mustn't, Ms. Yuki. You would only be digging yourself into a deeper hole."

Yuki, who had the same bothered expression as Masachika, was about to move out of free-to-play territory until she was stopped by Ayano, her very rational maid. The siblings were crushed. Not only did they not get any SSR draws, but they also didn't even pull a single SR. A complete failure. If anything, it seemed like they were getting worse draws than usual. The investigation had just started, and they were already losing their sanity, but not because of any ghost. Meanwhile, Maria, who never played mobile games, smiled nervously as she observed their despair.

"Um… Are you two okay? Do you need me to pat you on the head?"

"He doesn't need any consoling."

"Yes, please."

"Unbelievable!"

A few minutes went by before Masachika finally recovered mentally and was able to ignore Alisa's disgusted "I hope I never end up like him" gaze as he swiftly pointed up the staircase.

"To the rooftop! Come on!"

"Why are you suddenly so excited to go to the rooftop…?"

"Why wouldn't I be? Aren't school rooftops magical?"

"How are they magical?"

Although Alisa furrowed her brow skeptically, Maria was firmly nodding.

"I know what you mean. ♪ It always feels like something wonderful is going to happen on school rooftops."

"*Giggle.* Yes, the protagonists in young adult novels always gather on the school rooftop, and something wonderful usually happens to them." Yuki added to Maria's excitement by smiling elegantly and agreeing. Ayano was air.

"You hear that, Alya? Plus, the fact that the door to the rooftop is normally locked makes this even more exciting. We're about to have our own secret base," Masachika said enthusiastically.

"Uh-huh." Alisa sighed as if she couldn't keep up with Masachika as he weirdly and passionately looked up at the door to the rooftop.

"You're free to feel however you want, but don't forget we have a job to do."

"Yeah, yeah…"

After giving Alisa a half-hearted reply, Masachika climbed the stairs, then began scrutinizing the door to the rooftop area.

"Hmm… The door seems to be installed correctly. The doorknob and keyhole don't seem to be broken, either, which means there's no way anyone forced their way through…right?"

"Yeah, it doesn't look like any students broke into the rooftop area."

After thoroughly examining the door, they concluded that there was no way anyone got onto the rooftop without a key.

"All right, then! Let's do this!"

"Okay. ♪ Allow me to unlock it."

The door to the rooftop area was finally opened with the key Maria had borrowed from the faculty room.

"Whoa…," muttered Masachika, his voice brimming with excitement as the door to a new world opened before his eyes. He squinted in the bright light of the sun but then—

"It's filthy! What the hell?!"

He frowned at how *not* magical the dirty sight was. Of course, he wasn't expecting it to be spotless, since nobody ever cleaned it, but this was on another level. The entire rooftop area was covered in something black, bird droppings were scattered about, and green moss was sluggishly growing under the fence.

"Wow…"

"…This is something else."

"This is… This is awful…"

The three who were expecting the rooftop to be a magical place of fantasy were met with crushing disappointment and brutally shattered dreams. Alisa rolled her eyes at her particularly depressed sister and decided to remind everyone what they had come to do.

"So what do you want to do? I believe the easiest option would be to explain to everyone that the mysterious shadowy figure appearing here was just an ordinary person, but what do you all think?"

"I agree... Perhaps we could leave some footprints near the fence facing the schoolyard and then take a picture of them? After that, we could simply spread a rumor that a maintenance worker or someone had been fixing something on the rooftop. After all, nobody can disprove it, since we now know that there have not been any students sneaking onto the rooftop," suggested Yuki.

"Yeah, that sounds reasonable... In fact, that might be our only option," agreed Masachika, then he suddenly realized that all of them were staring right at him.

"...Wait. Me?"

"Your shoe size would be the most believable, yes?"

"And your weight should make it easier for you to leave footprints. Congratulations. You always wanted to hang out on the school rooftop, right?"

The two candidates for the next student council president were perfectly in sync while clinching the argument. Although what they were saying was perfectly reasonable, it was painfully obvious that they just didn't want to step foot onto the filthy rooftop.

"Whaaat? Seriously? In my shoes?"

But Masachika was no different. In fact, nobody wanted to step onto the filth. He shifted his gaze to Maria in hopes that there had to be some other way, but...

"*Sniffle*... Playing with sparklers on the rooftop... Having lunch on a picnic blanket... Secretly smoking between classes..."

She appeared to still be chasing a dream...which smoking definitely shouldn't have ever been part of. Therefore, Masachika had no choice but to turn to Ayano for help.

"Uh... I could do it if you would like me to?" she replied, giving him no choice.

"No, I'll do it…"

After returning to the first floor and grabbing his shoes, he stepped onto the rooftop area and began making footsteps while sweating under the burning summer sun.

I have to wonder if there has ever been a student council job this miserable before…

When he looked down at the schoolyard, countless students in sports clubs were working up a sweat with their friends, living their teenage years to the fullest. When he looked up, birds were freely soaring in the sky. *Ah, how wonderful it must be,* Masachika thought. *I'll never forgive those damn birds for covering the entire rooftop in crap, though. Never.*

"Masachika? You stopped moving. Is everything okay?"

(Caw! And I'll never forgive you, either, you asshat. Caw! Whose idea do you think this was?)

Tsk… Whatever.

The frustration only continued to build. First, his dreams were crushed by the filthy reality of this rooftop, then he was made to do this miserable job… It was all too much for him. Unable to control his urges any longer, he impulsively executed his eleventh-most "thing he wanted to do on the school building's rooftop." After taking in a deep breath, he ran over to the fence and yelled at the schoolyard:

"Where is my youth, dammit?! Where is my adventure?! You're all a bunch of idiots!"

"You're the only idiot here."

And he was immediately shot down by Alisa's sharp tongue.

CHAPTER 6

A Storeroom and a Locked Room

"*Sigh*. That was so embarrassing."

"The voices in my head got the best of me…"

After finishing their work on the rooftop, Alisa and Masachika began heading toward the schoolyard to check out the gymnasium storeroom. Out of the remaining rumors, the two that they could investigate during the day were the Invisible Cat and the Weeping Clubhouse, so they decided to split up into two groups. The running partners for the upcoming election were grouped together, save for Maria, who was sent to the clubhouse with Yuki and Ayano due to its size.

"Who impulsively screams like that? You looked insane."

"But…I made sure to keep my voice down so that nobody in the schoolyard could hear me…"

Alisa and Masachika's exchange continued like this until they reached the storeroom. Once they opened the heavy metal door, they were hit with a blast of hot, dusty air, and they reflexively grimaced. Countless particles of dust illuminated by the sunlight danced in the air, making it seem as if stepping even one foot inside was a health risk.

"Wow… Are we really gonna go in there?"

"…Complaining isn't going to help anything. Let's just get this over with."

Soon after coming to terms with reality, they stepped inside and began to listen carefully to see if they could hear any cats meowing.

"……"

"……"

"———ow."

"…! I heard something!"

"Seriously? Where was it coming from?"

"Shhh!"

Masachika walked over to Alisa's side, strained his ears, and heard…

"Nice! Let's go for another!"

"We've got this!"

""""Yeah!"""""

"Ugh! Masachika, go shut the door! I can't hear anything with all that noise!"

"Yes, ma'am."

He closed the heavy door just as his irritated running mate commanded, immediately preventing the wind from passing through any longer, which made the already blistering storeroom feel hotter. Nevertheless, they decided to continue listening for a cat while they told themselves it wouldn't be for long.

"……"

"……"

But even after twenty seconds of complete silence and concentration, all they could hear were the voices of the students playing sports outside. It wasn't long before Alisa muttered in annoyance:

"I can't hear it anymore. *Sigh*… I could hear something up until a few seconds ago, but…"

"Hey, it's not a big deal. Here, let me open the door. It's getting hot, and it's really dark in here," suggested Masachika, trying to calm her. He reached for the door, and—*thud!*

"Hmm?"

The door wouldn't open. He could almost crack it slightly open but not all the way, as if it was getting stuck on something.

"…? What's wrong?"

"Oh, it's just this door. It's…"

Fearing the worst, he grabbed the handle with both hands and began to pull as hard as he could, but it still wouldn't budge.

"What? C-can you really not get it open?"

"…It's stuck."

Alisa's expression was a mix of panic and skepticism as she approached him, so he stepped aside and let her have a go, but the door still couldn't be opened. That was when Masachika's phone began to softly vibrate. When he slipped it out of his pocket, he noticed he'd received a message from Yuki:

> Hey, it's your understanding, genius sister, Yuki.

He already wanted to throw his phone at the wall, but he decided to painfully wait for her next message instead. Thankfully, not even a minute went by before he received it:

> I decided to create a wonderful situation for my good-for-nothing brother, who brought Alya back to his place multiple times and still didn't have the courage to do anything.

…They actually went on what was essentially a date the other day, but since Yuki didn't know that, he couldn't say anything. It didn't help that he couldn't remember what happened during the second half of the date, either.

> Just so you know, I basically combined a good old rom-com cliché with something that's been popular lately among a few communities. It's called The Only Way Out of the Storeroom Is by Having Sex and—

"The hell?!"

Unable to take it any longer, Masachika immediately threw his phone into the giant blue high-jump mat, where it sank as if it were being absorbed into the abyss. Meanwhile, Alisa jumped, startled by his sudden screaming, and turned around.

"Wh-what's wrong?"

"…No, it's nothing. I was just a little irritated since I couldn't get in touch with Yuki."

It was actually the opposite, but contacting the person behind this and asking her to save them surely wasn't going to work. Furthermore, Masachika found himself now skeptical of the meowing Alisa had heard earlier as well. It probably wouldn't be that much of a stretch to assume that Yuki was playing videos of cats meowing on her phone to trick them, and it was all so she could lock Masachika and Alisa in this storeroom from the outside.

Yukiiiiiiiii!!

He clenched his teeth so that he wouldn't yell; meanwhile, he inwardly screamed her name… Then another message appeared on his phone screen:

> Don't worry. I'll make sure to unlock the door a little later so you two don't get heatstroke.

Oh, gee! Thanks!

> So you better squeeze a boob or two before then. In fact, if you do decide to go all the way, I'm fine with that, too.

She can't honestly believe we'd really do anything like that, right?!

As he retrieved his phone, he was so angry, he could practically feel the fumes of rage escaping between his clenched teeth.

"…I can't get in touch with Masha, either," Alisa suddenly said, shaking her head.

"…Oh. All right."

That was something Masachika was already expecting, since Yuki was obviously going to consider that before even doing all this. It wouldn't surprise him if she had told the people playing sports outside not to worry if they heard any noise coming from the storeroom.

…Which was why Masachika came to a single conclusion.

"Well, I sent a message to the student council group chat, and I'm sure one of them will come to check on us after they finish their side of the investigation, so the only thing we can do is wait."

He didn't have much of a choice.

"All we can do is wait? Why not yell for help? Surely, someone out there will hear us."

"Don't even try. They wouldn't be able to hear you. Trust me. All that would do is make you hot and thirsty."

"Hmph…"

Alisa didn't argue, since they didn't have any water. Instead, she thought for around ten seconds of other ways they could escape, but absolutely nothing came to mind.

"…How about we search for the cat until someone comes to help?" She shrugged.

"Wow, look at you. You're really serious about this, huh?"

"What's wrong with that? That's the whole reason we came here in the first place, and I actually heard a cat meowing, too."

"Mm… Yeah, that's… Yep." Masachika nodded and hummed noncommittally. In his mind, it was highly likely that sound was also Yuki's doing, but he couldn't tell Alisa that, since he didn't have any evidence, and there was no way he could tell her why he believed Yuki was behind this. Alisa, perhaps seeing his response as agreement, decided to turn on the lights first, and flipped the switch by the door.

"Uh…?"

"Oh, right. That reminds me… The lights don't work in here."

There were two fluorescent lights on the ceiling, with one being completely burned out and the other only emitting a faint orange light that was hardly useful at all. Furthermore, now that the door was closed, the only half-decent source of light was a tiny window high on one wall and close to the ceiling. Unfortunately, most of it was blocked by various pieces of equipment and supplies, so while Alisa and Masachika could see each other, most of whatever was by the walls was shrouded in darkness.

"...Well, we're not going to find anything when it's this dark, so let's just wait for someone to come help us."

"We can use the flashlights on our phones. Come on. Let's keep looking."

"Seriously...?"

Masachika failed to persuade Alisa, who was determined to track down the cat, as one might expect from a straight A student like her, so he decided to help, albeit reluctantly. They split up to search for clues, each taking one side of the storeroom, until around five minutes went by.

"It's too freakin' hot!"

They still hadn't found any cat, let alone heard one, and the humid heat of the storeroom was getting so bad that Masachika had to take off his uniform jacket. After undoing his tie as well, he hung them on the side of a basket for balls nearby, then began flapping his shirt collar to cool his sweaty chest.

"*Sigh...* I hope Touya gets the summer uniform changed fast. I can't take this anymore..."

"...Yeah, it really is hot."

He hadn't been expecting an answer, so when he heard Alisa agree, his eyes were naturally drawn in her direction...where he saw her also taking off her school jacket. She undid the ribbon around her neck as well, then proceeded to pull her jumper's straps off her shoulders, leaving it on only to cover her lower body. Alisa softly exhaled while she fanned herself with both hands.

Mmm...

Seeing her like this inevitably reminded him of what had happened over a month ago in the student council room when she was hypnotized, immediately making him feel uncomfortable in a way no word could describe. That was when Alisa suddenly looked over in his direction as if she could feel him staring at her, and the moment their eyes met, she knit her brow and swiftly turned her back to him, covering herself.

"What do you think you're looking at?"

"O-oh, sorry…"

It wasn't like she was scantily dressed. If anything, it looked like a school uniform worn by students at any other school during the summer. All she did was lightly undress a little, so why did it look so strangely suggestive?

Ugh… The only way I can stop thinking about it is if I focus on finding that cat.

After coming to that conclusion, Masachika began his search for the cat once more, but…

"…Nothing. Not a single clue."

He tried opening and moving boxes and equipment, but there was no sign of a cat ever being there. Then again, the name of the mystery was the *Invisible* Cat, so not seeing the cat made sense.

"If the cat's not down here, then maybe they're up there?"

Masachika shifted his gaze toward a shelf around head-high and frowned. Sitting on the shelf were small cones, a line marker with bent wheels, a cardboard box with who knows what inside—countless items usually not used were scattered about, and even trying to take one thing off the shelf seemed like it would be a real pain in the ass.

…I mean, if we're going to be investigating tonight as well, then maybe we should wait to do this until we have Masha's help?

There's no reason for us to aimlessly search in this heat when we can do this at night, thought Masachika, so he looked over at Alisa to ask her what she thought.

"Hey, Al—"

His breath caught in his throat…because Alisa was on all fours under the hurdles stacked by the wall as if she was looking for something in the very back. Her rear shook side to side while the hurdles rattled, bumping into one another. *Sst! Sst!* The hem of her skirt danced to the beat, entering dangerous territory, perhaps due to her keeping her upper body low so that she wouldn't hit her back on the bars. Since Masachika was standing, he couldn't see anything, but he would probably have a clear view of her underwear if he squatted.

…Seriously?

One corner of his lips curled at the unexpected chance to see up Alisa's skirt. It was as if her gently rocking butt was inviting him. There was something undeniably seductive about seeing her perfectly plump, milky-white thighs, only barely visible in the darkness, with sweat dripping down them. *Ah, where is that sweat coming from? How I wish I could check with my own two eyes—*

"Mmph!" grunted Masachika as if he was violently coughing, and he drove his fist into his temple to rid his mind of these lewd thoughts. He then exhaled deeply to cool his overheated brain, since it seemed the humidity was doing something to him.

Relax, Masachika... Randomly catching a glimpse of panties is what makes it so incredible. It's something you have to be lucky to see. Purposely looking up someone's skirt is peeping! It's not even close to being the same thing!

Masachika scolded himself, although perhaps not for the reason most people would, and he continued to twist his fist into his temple while glaring at Alisa's skirt.

It doesn't matter how wide-open she's making herself right now. Using that to my advantage to take a peek is something only a monster would do! It would betray her trust...and that's why I'm not going to peek, no matter what! No matter what... She has really nice legs, though.

Her legs were mysteriously alluring—tightly wrapped in knee-high socks with only the top of her thighs spilling out as they squished against each other. Masachika's eyes were naturally drawn to every move they made.

Yeah... This isn't peeping. So...I'm okay, right?

Grinding his fist into his temple, Masachika gazed intently at Alisa's legs in a daze as if he was delirious with a fever... All of a sudden, the phone in his hand started to vibrate. He jumped in a panic, as if he had fallen asleep in class and someone had poked him to wake him up. His eyes pointlessly wandered to each side before he looked at the screen and noticed it was another message from Yuki:

> **It must be so hard seeing Alya on all fours with her beautiful hips facing you. It must be sooo hard—**

Although he was midsentence, Masachika promptly turned off the display in silence and was immediately overcome with unbelievable embarrassment and discomfort. His eyes darted around the storeroom in search of the eyes watching them, when—

"E-eek!"

He reflexively turned in the direction of the shriek, only to find Alisa recklessly trying to crawl backward out from under the hurdles as they banged and clanked together. And seeing her desperately try to escape with no regard to appearances or modesty—

"…?!"

—Masachika promptly looked up and away before he actually did see her panties. Alisa, on the other hand, immediately ran over to his side as if that was the last thing on her mind, and she threw both her arms around him with a tense, twitching expression.

"Wh-what's wrong?!"

"Th-th-there's a rat…!"

"Huh? A rat…?"

Knitting his brow, he lowered his gaze as Alisa looked up, and their eyes met. That was the moment that she apparently realized she was wrapping her arms around him, and she promptly looked down at her arms in disbelief and let go in a panic. Immediately, she wrapped her arms around herself as if to suppress goose bumps, then set her eyes on the darkness beyond the hurdles, her expression twisting in fear and disgust.

"I…I found a dead rat…behind those hurdles…"

"…Gross. Seriously?"

Masachika grimaced as well at the sound of those unfortunate yet disgusting words… He noticed Alisa was now staring at him again as if to say, "Go see for yourself just in case," so he reluctantly held up his phone and walked over to the hurdles.

"All right, then…"

After getting on all fours, he slipped under the bars, then timidly held his smartphone's flashlight up and illuminated the area around the wall.

"Guh…!" He grunted with disgust the instant he found the rat to his right, hidden in the shadow of a giant rope used for tug-of-war. He scooted back out from under the hurdles in a fluster and returned to Alisa's side.

"…Did you see it?"

"Yep. Blech. That was disgusting!"

He had actually never seen a rat up close before, which was why he only had a vague image of them being unsanitary creatures…but all he felt from seeing its decomposed body was disgust.

"Hmm… But isn't this kind of proof that there was a cat? I think I saw teeth marks in it…"

"Y-yeah… But it's not like we can take a picture of that and use it as proof, right?"

"Yeah, of course not. Even if we blurred the picture, people would be crying and vomiting and whatnot. It'd be hell. Everyone would probably start avoiding this area like the plague if we did that."

Both Masachika and Alisa rubbed their arms while trembling. They had experienced fear unlike anything these seven school wonders could have ever given them. An eerie chill ran down Masachika's spine as a clammy sweat began to drench his body, so he promptly walked briskly over to where he had hung his jacket and began undoing the buttons on his collared shirt.

"Ugh… Man, that was gross! I feel disgusting!"

With only an undershirt covering his upper body, he pulled a handkerchief out of his pocket and began wiping the sweat off his neck and chest.

"H-hey?! What do you think you're doing, getting undressed in front of me?!" muttered Alisa with panic in her voice.

"Huh?" Masachika turned around as he wiped the sweat off his body. He noticed that Alisa's eyes were restlessly wandering in the darkness.

"I'm not getting any more undressed than this, you know. Besides, you can hardly see me, right?"

"True…but that's not the issue here."

"Really? But you're going to see me in a swimsuit at the beach, which means I'm not going to be wearing a shirt, so…"

"L-listen. Any girl would be worried if she was locked in a small room with a guy and he started stripping, okay?!"

Masachika was at a loss for words. After all, it was obvious that some girls might feel threatened in a situation like this, even if it was someone they knew.

"…You're right. That was insensitive of me."

"O-oh, uh… I mean, it's not that big of a deal…," Alisa replied awkwardly as Masachika sincerely bowed.

"<You're making my heart race… That's all…,>" she added softly in Russian.

Because you're wary of what I might do…right?

Masachika immediately came up with that self-serving interpretation and ignored what she was saying. Awkward silence followed for the next few seconds until Masachika suddenly smirked to clear the mood and joked:

"But, well, I guess I'd feel worse if I was talking to some weak little girl, but you? I don't know."

"Wh-what's that supposed to mean?!"

"I vaguely remember you smacking the crap out of a guy when you two were alone in a small room together not too long ago."

"Th-that was… That's because…"

Alisa stammered as she thought back to what happened in Masachika's room a few days ago. Her eyes began to wander even more restlessly than a few minutes ago until she suddenly shot Masachika with a piercing glare.

"That's because you completely ruined the mood!"

"Huh...? Did I...?"

"Yes!" she snapped before looking the other way as if to say that this conversation was over.

"If you say so." He wryly smirked back.

"<If you actually tried, then I would have...>"

His smirk froze the moment he heard her whispers in Russian.

Uh... What could she mean by that?

She would have...what? What would have happened if the mood wasn't ruined...? Alisa's expression was hardly visible in the darkness, but she was fidgeting with the ends of her hair like she usually did. Alisa must feel—

"Meow."

""?!""

Their hearts skipped a beat, and they immediately looked up to see where the sudden meow came from...and on top of a cardboard box on the shelf was a black cat.

"".......""

".......".

Masachika and Alisa silently observed the cat after their unexpected encounter...while the cat, just as surprised, stared hard back down at them as if to say, "What are these two creatures doing here?!" Their quiet staring contest went on for a few more seconds after that until Masachika came to his senses. But the moment he pulled out his phone to get a picture, the cat slouched, ready for battle. Masachika froze for not even half a second, but that was still more than enough time for the cat to turn around and disappear into the shadows of the cardboard boxes.

"Ah...!" he grunted, overcome with surprise, and immediately began to chase after the cat in a panic. But when he quickly moved the cardboard box that the cat was hiding behind, his eyes were met with by the blinding rays of the sun, and he squinted.

"...? What the...?"

Facing him in the wall was a square hole...and beyond that hole was what appeared to be some sort of rain cover with its opening facing down. Masachika lightly jumped and looked down the hole, discovering that he could see the ground outside.

"Hmm…? Did there used to be an exhaust fan here or something?"

That was the feeling he got, and after examining the edges of the hole, he noticed that there were marks from something having been installed there.

"Is this how the cat is getting inside?" wondered Alisa after coming over to see what he was looking at.

"Yeah, sure seems that way."

He casually glanced in her direction…and froze for a few seconds before quietly facing forward once more.

It's basically see-through. Ha-ha.

Put simply, the light peeking inside from the hole was illuminating Alisa's upper body. Clearly visible under her collared shirt, which was soaked from sweat due to the heat and fear, was a lacy yellow bra, and to make matters worse, it was tightly sticking to her skin. The curves…were incredible, and far too stimulating for a boy in the middle of puberty.

That Time I Avoided Seeing Panties and Ended Up Seeing a Bra Through Her See-Through Shirt.

The unexpected twist caused Masachika's brain to short-circuit and inwardly perform terrible monologues, but Alisa didn't even seem to notice as she faced the wind coming in through the hole and exhaled with relief.

"Finally, some cool air," she muttered. But Masachika, if anything, was feeling hotter than before, and his brain felt like it was going to explode thanks to this unexpected gift from the gods. Nevertheless, he quietly moved the cardboard box back to where it had been in order to keep himself from staring into the gates to heaven any longer. He then began moving things back into place while pretending not to notice Alisa's annoyed gaze. It was as if her eyes were saying, "Why did you move the box back after I just told you how good the air felt?"

"…Well, we found the cat, and if we cover that hole, then we won't have to worry about them sneaking in here any longer."

"…? Yeah…"

Although confused by Masachika's sudden gloomy tone, Alisa began to clean up as well. It took only a few minutes until everything was back to where it was… Just then, they could hear Yuki's voice coming from outside the storeroom.

"Masachika? Alya? Oh my. Whyever is the door locked?"

After what Masachika considered a shameless remark, the door handle began to rattle and click as if it was being unlocked.

"About time." He shrugged…when it suddenly hit him.

Hold up… I can't let Alya go outside looking like that!

Although there was most likely nobody around, it would be a complete disaster if a guy saw her like this. Even Yuki wasn't going to let something like this slip by without saying something, which was already bad enough. There was a 100 percent chance she would call Masachika later to mess with him, saying something like, "So? How was it? It looks like you made Alya sweat until you could see her underwear. It must have been fun."

Wh-wh-what should I do?! I have to do something to cover Alya, but what? Just pointing it out might not be a good idea, but if I don't say something, then there's no way I can get her to do anything about it, so— Ahhh! There's no time!

He desperately racked his brain for a solution for those two seconds, then Masachika grabbed his jacket, which was hanging on the basket nearby, and gently draped it over her shoulders from behind.

"…? What are you doing?"

Alisa turned around with a skeptical glare and was greeted with a gentle, confident grin. His eyes brimming with compassion made her jump in surprise. They gazed into each other's eyes as they stood so close that they could almost feel the other breathe. It was like a romantic scene from a movie where a guy put his jacket over the girl's shoulders under the eaves of a building after her clothes got soaked in the rain. Alisa almost felt as if she was being held tightly in his arms from behind. It wouldn't be odd if she felt like she was in danger, and yet she didn't move. She simply squeezed his jacket tightly in her hands with her eyes still opened wide. Masachika's gaze affectionately narrowed even more as he softly added:

"Madam, I can see your bra right through your— Bfft?!"

His speech was interrupted by a powerful slap, knocking him flying back.

"Y-y-you should have said something sooner, you jerk!" yelled Alisa in almost a shriek as the door to the storeroom opened, revealing Yuki. But when she stepped inside, all she saw was Masachika buried in the mat used for the high jump, and she blinked in a daze.

"Um… What is going—?"

"Hmph!" snorted Alisa, cutting off Yuki as if to clear up any doubt, and she immediately stomped her way over to the door. Yuki moved out of the way in a fluster, and just like that, Alisa stormed off into the distance.

"Oh, you must have been able to see her bra through her shirt," she muttered with evident satisfaction a few seconds later.

"How the hell did you figure that out just from that?"

"Hmph! I have rom-com radar, so I can easily detect the waves."

"Wow… I bet that's really useful…," muttered Masachika wearily as he slowly sat up on the mat.

"We found the cat and found out how it was sneaking into the storeroom."

He decided to make the first move after seeing his sister's gleeful expression.

"…Seriously? Show me."

Masachika escorted his seemingly curious sister outside and around to the back of the detached storeroom.

"See that? At first glance, it looks like nothing more than a hole for ventilation, but there isn't actually an exhaust fan installed anymore, so it's basically a tiny door to the storeroom," he revealed, pointing at the rain cover hanging over the wall.

"Oh…? Hmm…"

Yuki thoughtfully surveyed the area…until she suddenly came to some sort of realization and stopped.

"…? What's wrong?"

"…Hey, did you actually see the cat using this hole to go inside?"

"Hmm? I mean, I didn't actually see the cat walk through it, but I followed it to the hole in the wall when it disappeared, so it's safe to assume this is how it's getting inside, especially since there didn't seem to be any other way in."

Yuki slowly lifted her head and argued with a serious expression:

"How would the cat get inside from here?"

"Huh?"

"How could the cat use this hole to get inside?"

Only after she mentioned it did he finally realize it. The area behind the storeroom was almost completely flat, and there was nothing the cat could use to climb their way up. Although cats in general could jump high, this cat would have had to jump around a meter and a half to reach the ventilation hole.

"Good…point…"

A chill instantly ran down Masachika's spine. *This is one of those stories that gets scarier the more you think about it*, he thought. Then a faint sound could be heard coming from the slope to their left, getting their immediate attention.

"…!"

Standing in the grassy slope was the black cat from the storeroom, looking at them as if to say, "What's your problem?" They stared at each other for a few seconds until Masachika finally came to his senses and swiftly pulled out his phone to take a video. But the instant he hit the record button, the cat glanced over at the storeroom, then took off like a cheetah chasing a jackal before leaping high into the air and *effortlessly climbing up the concrete-block storeroom's wall like a ninja*.

""That was…insane…!!""

The video Masachika took was posted online later and went viral.

CHAPTER 7 | ## Stargazing and a Scolding

"So, uh… Ready to do this?"

It was seven at night, and all club activities had finished for the day. After eating an early dinner of convenience-store meals in the student council room, Masachika hesitantly looked side to side at the two girls with him.

"L-let's do this…," cheered Maria, her voice trembling as she raised a fist in the air, clearly terrified.

"Let's get this over with."

Meanwhile, Alisa was wearing a straight face as if this wasn't a big deal, but she was restlessly tapping her finger with her arms crossed… Masachika was genuinely worried already, and they hadn't even started.

"Uh… Masha? Are you okay? Because you don't look okay at all."

"Wh-what? Of course I'm okay. I… I'll do my best!"

Though her eyes were twitching, she set her lips in a straight line and held up her clenched fists, showing that she was more than determined to do this. Her display of strong will was something that would naturally bring a smile to anyone's face, but…

"Saying you'll 'do your best' means you're obviously not okay."

Because that meant she was scared. Her anxiety forewarned of the difficulties that lay ahead, and yet Masachika simply added:

"Just don't force yourself to do anything you don't want to do, okay?"

He then shifted his gaze to his other side.

"What about you, Alya? Are you okay?"

"…? Yes? Why wouldn't I be? I'm not a scaredy-cat like Masha."

Alisa lifted an eyebrow skeptically at Maria as if she wanted to roll her eyes, so maybe it was only Masachika's imagination that she was pretending to be okay. Regardless, bringing that doubt up wouldn't lead to anything good, so Masachika simply sighed and opened the door to the student council room. Immediately, the motion-sensor lights illuminated the hallway.

"See, Masha? The lights still turn on. Besides, it's not even dark outside yet, so there's nothing to be afraid of." Masachika shrugged, looking back.

"Yeah…," Maria agreed with a nod as she timidly stepped out into the hallway, followed by Alisa, who looked kind of annoyed as she closed the door.

"So… How about we start with the art room, then check out the area behind the school building? …After that, we look for the Red Schoolgirl while making our way back around the building."

"O-okay."

"Sure, that works."

After receiving their consent, he took a step forward—

"Wait!"

—when all of a sudden, Maria grabbed his right hand from behind. He promptly turned around to find her on the verge of tears and glancing at the window.

"Don't go too far ahead! I'm scaaared."

"…You can stay in the student council room and wait for us, you know."

"I'll be attacked the moment I'm alone!"

"By what?! None of the school's ghost stories were about monsters or killers, you know!"

He couldn't help pointing out the obvious, since Maria was uncharacteristically jabbering with terror as if she were being chased by a stalker like in a horror movie. Nevertheless, she continued to anxiously glance at the window, and her delicate hands, holding Masachika's right, were trembling with fear.

"It always happens like this… You think everything's okay one second, and then the next, bam—something comes flying in through the window, right?"

"None of the ghost stories we talked about had anything flying through the window or attacking anyone. Is this better?"

Masachika sighed and moved to Maria's side to shield her from anything that might break in through the window. Meanwhile, Alisa sighed as well and took Maria's other side just in case.

"…There. Now you should be okay if anyone suddenly comes out of one of the classrooms, too, right? That's not going to happen, but you get my point."

"Y-yeah… Thanks, Alya." She nodded awkwardly, wrapping her hand around Alisa's left hand. Immediately, Alisa's eyebrows rose sharply, but she noticed Masachika's gaze on the other side of Maria, stopped herself, and shrugged. Masachika and Alisa were now indirectly connected through his right hand and her left via Maria, and because Maria was a head shorter than them, she looked like a child going on a walk with her parents…despite the fact that she was the oldest among them.

"This in itself is a trope in horror movies, though. One second, you're holding hands like this, and the next thing you know, the person you were holding hands with is now *something* else, and—… Sorry."

Masachika immediately apologized when he saw the look in Maria's eyes. They were the eyes of someone who couldn't believe what they were seeing. However, she almost immediately gasped, turned to Alisa, and timidly asked:

"Alya…? You're the real Alya, right?"

"Yes, so stop taking Masachika's jokes so seriously."

She was mentally slamming her head against a wall.

"<Then where is my biggest mole?>" Maria asked suddenly in Russian.

"<…What kind of question is that?>"

"<Don't worry about it. It's not like Kuze understands us.>"

He understood. Painfully so. But after Alisa glanced in his direction, she almost immediately looked away and muttered:

"<...On the inner side of your right thigh.>"

Oof...

It was not like he could do anything with that information, though. Maybe he could wonder if Alisa had a mole, too? Regardless, he couldn't help but glance at her thighs hidden under her skirt while he simultaneously thought back to what happened today at the gymnasium's detached storeroom. *Now, then... Did she have a mole on her thigh?* wondered Masachika as his mind explored the possibility.

"Yep! You are the real Alya!"

However, Maria immediately glanced back in Masachika's direction, causing him to look away in a fluster. He wasn't confident that he managed to avert his gaze in time...but Maria didn't seem to be concerned in the slightest, curiously tilting her head and grumbling in thought.

"Now, then... Kuze... You..."

After racking her brain for another few seconds, she placed a hand over her mouth as if she was in complete shock.

"Wh-what are we going to do?! I can't think of a question I could ask him to prove he's the real Kuze!"

"Oh... Yeah."

"Alya? Can you think of any good questions?!"

"Huh...?"

Alisa frowned in annoyance, but after seeing how desperate Maria was, she began to think, allowing her eyes to wander. A few moments went by before her lips unexpectedly curled into a malicious grin, as if she was struck by the most sinister of ideas.

"All right... Tell me exactly what you said to me when you offered to run with me for student council president."

"Wh-what kind of question is that?"

"What's wrong? The real Masachika would know the answer to that."

His lips pulled back in a grimace, and his expression tensed at her obvious bait.

Yeah, I remember... I remember the extremely embarrassing thing I said! And you want me to relive that moment right here, right now?!

It was as if she was using this for some sort of humiliation fetish, but right when Masachika was about to demand that she change the question, Maria gently stepped away from him with tears welling in her eyes. It was as if her pleading gaze was saying, "What? No! This can't be happening. Tell me this isn't happening," which was something he couldn't ignore.

Sigh... Tsk! Looks like I've got no choice.

Acting embarrassed meant losing. In fact, if he was bold about it and reenacted the dialogue with pride, then it would end up embarrassing Alisa instead.

It's your fault for making me do this, Alya. You've got no one to blame but yourself. Take this!

After mustering up the courage, Masachika cleared his throat and put on the most serious expression he could, then faced Alisa, gazed into her eyes, and recited:

"'You're not alone. From now on, I'll be there for you and support you.' That sound about right?"

"...It was, 'You won't be alone anymore. From now on, I will be by your side to support you,' but you were close," corrected Alisa in a strangely discontented tone, wiping the smug grin right off Masachika's face.

"Huh? Oh, right."

Not even another second went by before he was overwhelmed with unbearable embarrassment, and his face gradually turned red.

Huh...? Seriously? Wait. The hell is she doing memorizing what I said word for word? This goes way beyond just being embarrassing!

The fact that she accurately memorized a quote from an embarrassing moment for Masachika—the fact that Alisa etched those words forever in her mind as if this was a cherished memory for her—made Masachika mentally writhe in agony.

"Wh-what are you blushing for?" sassed Alisa with a piercing glare…right as her cheeks began to flush as though she was suddenly overcome with embarrassment as well. She immediately averted her gaze, perhaps realizing this herself, and faced Maria as if to play it off while hoping Masachika didn't notice.

"See? He's the real Masachika…so come on. Let's go," she dryly demanded with a straight face. However, Maria seemed like a completely different person from a few minutes ago. She was smiling warmly with her head tilted.

"You're so cute, Alya."

"Wh-what? Where did that come from?"

"Ah, to be young… Oh, hey. I know. How about we do this?" said Maria. She pulled Masachika's and Alisa's hands together and essentially made them hold hands.

"There. I figured you two should be holding hands, since you're so close."

"What?! Why?!"

"I feel like we're talking about something completely different now."

Alisa and Masachika immediately let go of each other's hands, which made Maria raise an eyebrow as she lovingly smiled.

"Oh, come on, you two. You're both so shy."

"I have no idea what you're even talking about."

"Weren't we holding hands because you were scared, Masha?"

"Yep. ♪ That's why I want you two to hold hands, okay?"

"I'm sorry, but I'm not sure how that'd help you."

"Masha, at least make sense."

They sharply pointed out the obvious to Maria, who somehow perfectly left out any reason why that would make any sense…which, for some reason, made her pout with displeasure, slide over to the opposite side of Masachika, and hold his left hand.

"Fine. I'll just hold hands with Kuze if you're going to be like that."

"I still have no idea what's going on?!"

"M-my poor sister has lost her mind…"

Masachika shrieked hysterically while Alisa placed a hand on her forehead as if she had a headache, but when they saw how strangely smug Maria was holding his hand, they promptly gave up trying to understand her. After exchanging tired glances, Masachika and Alisa joined hands once more, and the sight instantly made Maria smile in satisfaction.

"Good. Now let's move out. ♪"

She mirthfully pointed forward...still holding Masachika's hand with her right hand.

"......"

Alisa glared at her sister like some low-level thug, with one eye wide open and the other one closed as if to say, "The hell?! I thought you'd let go of him if I held his hand! Tsk!" Nevertheless, she almost immediately realized that she would be wasting her time arguing, so she let out a brief sigh and faced forward.

"Shall we get going? Let's just get this over with."

"...Yeah, let's do this."

Masachika, who was also in a state of resignation, stared into the distance as he began to walk. In his right hand was Alisa's slightly cold, slender hand, and in his left was Maria's warm, soft hand.

Hmm? Is this a harem? Hooray... A beautiful woman on each side... I'm peaking in high school...

Despite the stupid things he was thinking, he was actually very nervous. Although he had held hands with Alisa a few times before, he was far from used to it, and this was the first time he was holding hands with Maria. The fact that these two things were happening at the same time fried his brain to the point that he didn't know what to do. Should he swing his arms? Were his hands getting sweaty? Was he walking too fast? Too slow? More important, was he even holding their hands the right way? Countless questions crossed his mind; there were so many that he was having trouble containing himself any longer.

Th-this is... Yeah... I need to solve these mysteries as soon as I can and end this.

Sandwiched between a strangely mirthful older sister and a some-what annoyed little sister, Masachika decided that he needed to put an end to this investigation as soon as possible. Therefore—

"Nothing unusual about the art room! Next!"

"Nothing unusual about the cherry blossoms behind the school! Not blooming yet! Next!"

"We barely looked around?!" complained Alisa, since Masachika was spending only around ten seconds on each mystery. And yet he shrugged with an air of nonchalance, as if he wasn't concerned in the slightest.

"The whole point of our investigation was to prove that these mysteries were baseless rumors, right? So what's the big deal? I made sure to take photographic evidence, too."

"Sure, but…"

Being a serious person by nature, Alisa seemed bothered by their process, but when she glanced over Masachika's shoulder and saw her sister, her discontent was replaced with a sigh.

"Masha… Stop being scared already," she requested unreasonably.

"…?! I-it isn't a switch I can just flip on and off," Maria replied pathetically as she slouched over. The night had finally begun to swallow their surroundings in darkness. Her eyes darted around fearfully while she gently leaned into Masachika.

…Alisa frowned and huffed.

"Plus, the next mystery we're about to investigate—… It sounds so scary. I mean, there's no way I *cannot* be scared."

Maria appeared to be avoiding talking about the next mystery at all, and she leaned into Masachika more…until she was essentially clinging to him. With her right hand still latched on to his left, she wrapped her left arm around his forearm. Their arms were wrapped around each other's. It wasn't long before his elbow disappeared into the mounds of her chest, his expression disappeared, and Alisa's patience…disappeared.

"…Let's hurry up and get this over with," she hissed with irritation as she strode off, jerking Masachika along by the hand. But even then, Maria continued to cling tightly to his right arm, and Alisa's knit brow only continued to furrow when she saw that. After stomping her way back to the school, Alisa began to rush down the hallway.

"H-hey, maybe we could slow down a little...?"

"Why? We still need to circle the entire school building, right? So the faster we finish, the better."

"Yeah, I guess..."

And yet he felt like something was off with her being in such a hurry, so he timidly asked:

"...You okay? You're not pushing yourself too hard, right?"

"......"

Alisa's hand, which was wrapped around his, twitched, but even then, she still didn't look back at him.

"Alya doesn't like to show weakness," whispered Maria.

"Wait. What? Alya, are you scared?"

"...No," she replied like this was no big deal, but she still didn't look back. Luckily, she started to gradually slow down, which allowed Masachika to catch up with her, but she promptly looked away as if to hide her face.

"...Are you afraid of ghosts or something? You seemed completely fine last year when everyone was telling ghost stories and playing scary games while preparing for the school festival."

"I told you already. I'm not scared," claimed Alisa stubbornly, still facing the other direction.

"Yelling 'boo!' and trying to scare Alya doesn't really work, but she doesn't like scary stories," explained Maria.

"Oh, I can see that. She lets her imagination run wild and ends up scaring herself, huh?"

There was a sense of understanding in his voice, but Alisa still shot Maria a piercing glare before immediately looking away once more. She couldn't have made how she felt more obvious.

"Well, I guess there's nothing you can do about that," he said with an awkward smile. After all, the Red Schoolgirl was much closer to a real ghost story than the others, and there were about as many detailed witness accounts of this mystery as there were of more famous ghost stories like the Slit-Mouthed Woman and Teke Teke.

They said that a schoolgirl would appear somewhere inside the main building after school, wearing Seirei Academy's school uniform with a green ribbon. Her long black hair extended to her waist, and she would always be bleeding whenever she appeared, which was how she got the name *the Red Schoolgirl*. Seeing someone hurt would make most people worry for them, but you must never talk to her or help her, no matter what. In addition, even if you did happen to check on her, she would simply say, "Thanks. I'm fine now, though," before walking away. However, within a few days, those who spoke to her would find themselves wounded in the exact same spot she had been. It was as if the Red Schoolgirl were transferring her injury—her pain—to others...

But it's not like a little cut's gonna kill you or anything. There's something strangely realistic about this story... The fact that it happens within a few days increases the amount of uncertainty, too.

Whether this story was true was unclear, but there was a way to deal with this schoolgirl if they ever ran into her. First, they couldn't approach her. Instead, they were to leave the school building as quickly as possible. They should be able to tell her apart from the other students, since they knew what she looked and dressed like. Plus, the motion-sensor lights shouldn't turn on if she were a ghost, so if they saw a girl standing all alone in a dark hallway...then they needed to proceed with caution.

Honestly, a lot of that feels like it was made up after the rumors started coming out...but there have been victims, apparently.

According to Touya, there were two incidents of students getting hurt. The first incident happened last year in November. A male student in the track-and-field club ran into the Red Schoolgirl, who had hurt her right leg. Three days later, he tore his Achilles tendon. The second incident happened this year in June. The vice manager of the brass band club happened to run into the Red Schoolgirl, whose shirt was soaked in blood around the stomach area. Five days later, that same vice manager was in the hospital for appendicitis. The rumors after that spread like wildfire due to the popularity and personal magnetism of this brass band student, and it was unintentionally what would spark this entire "seven wonders of Seirei Academy" craze.

In other words, this Red Schoolgirl was the alpha and the omega of these seven mysteries. Huh, it sounds kind of cool when you put it that way.

Masachika smiled softly as his wild, nerdy imagination took off. He was very confident going into this compared with the Kujou sisters, but that was simply because he didn't believe anything about this ghost story. It wasn't that unusual for someone in track and field to tear their Achilles tendon, and the whole appendicitis thing was a bit of a stretch. The student didn't bleed from their stomach, so it was kind of hard to believe that this was some sort of injury transferred from the Red Schoolgirl.

It'd be far more believable if that kid got stabbed in the stomach or something.

After giving them a brief summary of his observations, he shrugged and looked over at Maria.

"Besides, the other mysteries up until now have been completely bogus. I mean, you never heard any woman weeping in the clubhouse, right?"

"Y-yeah... I guess you're right."

After all, Maria, Yuki, and Ayano patrolled the Weeping Clubhouse earlier that day for almost an hour, and they didn't hear even a single sniffle. When they eventually cracked open a window, they concluded that the howling wind was the culprit...or at least, that was the story they went with. Out of the six mysteries so far, they only actually solved the one about the cat in the storeroom. The rest were all fakes, according to their investigation. Therefore, it was highly likely that this last ghost story was some student's work of fiction as well.

"This is how all ghost stories are. Whenever something kind of weird happens to a student, they embellish the story when they tell it to their friends, and then the rumors start, and the story gradually transforms into something completely different," stated Masachika, showing no signs of fear. If anything, he was kind of making fun of the entire situation, which seemed to help ease the other two girls' fear. Maria was finally able to slightly loosen her grip around him, and she slowly nodded.

"Yeah… It makes sense when you put it that way…"

"Right? Plus, making it a schoolgirl is way too cliché. Wouldn't you agree? So many of these ghost stories and urban legends use young women for some reason. You have Hanako, the Slit-Mouthed Woman, Teke Teke, Lady Hasshaku… I mean, these stories would be way more believable if you told me some greasy, fat, balding middle-aged man was randomly appearing in the school building at night. At least, that'd be original," argued Masachika with a completely straight face.

"That'd also be something you'd call the police for," joked Alisa.

"True that."

The three laughed. Even Maria's expression relaxed, and she seemed to ponder for a moment.

"Wait. Isn't there an evil spirit that looks like an old man, though? The, uh… The sly baby geezer?"

"Is he supposed to be a baby or a geezer? Or a newborn old man? Anyway, it's *crybaby* geezer."

"I'd rather run into a greasy middle-aged man than whatever that is…"

The tension in the air almost completely disappeared thanks to Maria's ridiculous comment. Before they realized it, the investigation they started on the first floor had already made its way to the hallway on the third floor. They continued to casually peek into each classroom. Eventually…

"…Hmm?"

Once Masachika approached the last classroom at the end of the hall, he experienced a faint warmth in his pants pocket. It felt like having a hand warmer in there, despite it being the middle of summer.

"What's wrong?"

"Not sure…," he replied vaguely to Alisa's skeptical gaze. He promptly shoved his hand in his pocket until his fingers were touching the source of the heat.

"Oh my. What's that?"

"Chisaki lent it to me…and it's getting hot for some reason…"

In his hand were the black prayer beads. It was the rosary with the strong-sounding name that he had been given just in case, and for some reason, it was burning warmly in his hand…as if it were trying to tell him something.

"Tsk. Quit trying to scare us. Get a hobby."

"Huh? No, I'm not trying to scare anyone… But if this were a horror movie, the most common trope would be that these had been possessed by an evil spirit…," joked Masachika, trying to explain things to his frowning election partner… Suddenly, a hand appeared from around the corner of the hallway a few meters ahead.

"…?!"

It was an eerily white hand clutching the wall while slithering around the corner.

"""……"""

Each of their eyes were drawn to the hand. They watched in absolute silence as the fingers gripped into the wall. It was at this moment that Masachika's gut was telling him that something horrifying was about to emerge from the darkness, and his survival instincts were violently ringing an alarm, telling him to get out of there as soon as possible. And yet, despite that, his legs wouldn't move. Both Alisa and Maria seemed no different. They, consciously or unconsciously, clung tightly to his arms without taking a single step away. Before long, the hand grabbing the wall pulled a body around the corner, revealing *it*: a Seirei Academy uniform and a green ribbon, long black hair, and, peeking out from under those bangs, the bloody face of a woman.

"Eek!"

"N-no…!"

Maria and Alisa each tensely shrieked. Even Masachika genuinely wanted to scream, but their trembling warmth pressing against his arms temporarily diluted his fear. He was surprised by how calm he felt as he rapidly racked his brain for ways to get them out of there.

Maybe we should run...but Alya might not be able to, and Masha definitely won't be able to. If she did, she'd probably collapse in fear. I mean, this entire situation must be very traumatic for her... Then that leaves me with...!!

After making the split-second decision, he threw their arms off him, put on a half smirk, and began to run...forward...heading right for the blood-covered female student.

"Come on, seriously?! This is way too creepy! I didn't tell you to take it *this* far!" Masachika scolded, his voice trembling. His bright tone was flat, unfitting for such a tense moment, but he felt as if it helped free the two behind him from fear, even if only temporarily.

His decision was to make them think that the Red Schoolgirl was a prank that he was in on, so he was sprinting toward the girl while making it humorously seem like he felt she had gone too far. However, he was tightly squeezing the prayer beads that Chisaki lent him, and though he was acting like he was joking around, he planned on taking this very seriously. What Masachika needed to prepare himself for was the potential of getting injured, and he couldn't hesitate to resort to violence if necessary. He purposely rid himself of every other emotion and thought:

Wow... I'm probably gonna die tonight.

The thought popped into the back of his mind as if it had nothing to do with him. At the very least, he knew he wasn't going to get out of this unscathed because he instinctively knew this was *real*, and all he had were some beads that he didn't know would work on it. The odds were against him, but there was no other way out of this. To make matters worse, this mysterious girl's face was bloodied and injured, so if the ghost story was true, then that would mean Alisa's and Maria's faces were in danger. And as their friend—as a man—he wasn't going to allow that.

First, I'll push her back around the corner, then punch her with these prayer beads… Even if that doesn't work, the Red Schoolgirl's curse only hurts whoever she first talks to. Plus, the effects should appear within a few days, so I should be fine, since it's still summer break.

He probably wouldn't be able to go to the beach with the others, but at the very least, he would be able to protect Maria and Alisa both mentally and physically.

So bring it on!

Once he got into range, he quickly eyeballed the girl in search of the best place to strike… Then he realized something rather peculiar.

Huh? She's bleeding from her side, too… Wait. Her legs and right arm are bloodied up…

She has way too many injuries, right? That was the first seed of doubt that was planted in his mind, when suddenly, another hand reached out from around the corner and grabbed the schoolgirl's neck from behind.

"I've got you now… Oh? Kuze?" uttered the owner of said hand as she emerged from around the corner, looking pained.

"What the…?"

It was their student council vice president, who wasn't supposed to be there, making Masachika unconsciously freeze.

"Oh! Masha, Alya, hey."

"Huh? Oh. Hey?"

"Good evening?"

The Kujou sisters replied awkwardly, taken aback by the unexpected twist. Chisaki, on the other hand, was acting no different than usual and continued: "The meeting ended early, and I was a little worried, so I came… Anyway, is it okay if I handle this?" Then to the mysterious female student, she said: "I'm not going to let you get away this time," Chisaki barked, glaring hard and making her jump. She immediately turned to Masachika with her blood-filled eyes and reached out to him.

"H-help…," she cried in a hoarse voice before being helplessly dragged away by Chisaki, disappearing around the corner, never to be seen again.

"D-don't come down too hard on her, okay?" Masachika requested (for some reason) as he tilted his head curiously.

Uh... What? What was that? That wasn't a real ghost...right? Which means that was just someone trespassing who Chisaki beat up? I guess that is a lot more plausible...setting aside the fact that it's strange she'd beat up a weak, little girl.

Or perhaps it was some sort of prank that Masachika had no knowledge of and nothing to do with. The girl could have been an ass who liked scaring people, and if that was the case, then the so-called blood smeared all over her face might have been something she did partially to conceal her identity.

Yeah, that sounds about right. Wow, I guess I shouldn't jump to conclusions, huh? I can't believe how serious I got... How embarrassing! Ha-ha-ha!

Masachika desperately did everything in his power to forget the fact that Chisaki had sacred paper talismans wrapped around her left hand like a makeshift boxing glove. He continued to scratch his head to hide his embarrassment... Two hands tightly clenched his shoulders from behind.

"Masachika... What's the meaning of this?"

"Kuze? Do you think you could explain yourself?"

After hearing those two bone-chilling voices coming from behind, he turned his head stiffly like a rusty gear and checked over his shoulder. Alisa looked like she was smiling, but her eyes definitely weren't, and Maria's lips were blissfully curling so much that it seemed unnatural. They were genuinely even more terrifying than the bloody girl from a few moments ago...to Masachika, at least.

"No, uh... W-we, uh... It was a prank. She just went a little overboard, so Chisaki had to...go have a talk with her...or something?"

Words once spoken could not be taken back...which meant Masachika had to try to make his story consistent, but it was all in vain. Alisa's eyes immediately creased, while Maria's smile deepened. Both of their fingers slowly tightened, burying themselves into his shoulders.

"No, I… I was the one trying to tell Chisaki that she had gone too far, so…"

But their grips didn't loosen. Instead, they ended up lecturing him for a while after that, despite the fact that he was completely innocent.

Heh. Whatever. I'm a man… I don't do the things I do in hope for something in return…

Sitting on his knees in front of the two girls, he let his eyes idly drift in a daze toward the heavens outside the window. The stars forming the constellations in the Summer Triangle sparkled brightly in the night sky. Being a knight that night was such a wonderful feeling, and to be able to see these beautiful stars with two beautiful sisters was like a dream come true. Today was—

"Masachika! Are you listening?!"

"Kuze, you need to reflect on what you've done!"

"…Yes, ma'am."

—his unlucky day, apparently. One shouldn't run from their problems.

A few days later, the student council used its connections to inform the masses of what they found during their investigation of the seven school mysteries, and thus, it put out the fire before the week even ended. Although the students half joked about Vice President Chisaki defeating the Red Schoolgirl, the members of the student council accepted it without question.

"Is it just me, or is this way more mysterious?"

"You can say that again."

A certain pair of siblings were still discussing the seven school mysteries after all was said and done.

CHAPTER 8 | **Beauty and the Bonehead**

"I-I-I-I'm in love with you! P-p-p-please go out with me!"

Is this guy okay? That was the first thought that came to Chisaki's mind when she heard this boy's unrestrained, stuttered confession.

"......"

It all started in Seirei Academy's disciplinary committee room. Chisaki was sitting in a chair, leaning back with her arms crossed, staring hard at the boy in front of her. At a glance, he seemed to be your run-of-the-mill otaku. He was big both in height and width and would probably move like a sloth. His hair was wild and unkempt, and he had the face of a middle-aged man, save for the plethora of pimples. His eyes behind black-framed glasses were restlessly darting in every direction. That, in addition to his hunched shoulders, made him look extremely sheepish.

I feel like I've seen him somewhere before...but we've never talked.

The color of his tie made it clear they were in the same grade, and she could vaguely remember seeing him in middle school as well, but they had never had class together, let alone a conversation. So why would he randomly stop by the disciplinary committee room today to confess his feelings like this?

Did he lose a bet or something? Is this some form of bullying?

The school year had just started a month ago, so students were being grouped together, and the classroom hierarchy was beginning to take form. Therefore...although it may be rude to admit it, it would be no surprise if obviously low-caste students were being bullied and made to confess their feelings to the most coldhearted member of the student disciplinary committee.

Bullying... When will it ever end? I thought I put a stop to it in middle school.

But there were new students who transferred to Seirei Academy from different schools, so maybe that had something to do with it. Chisaki considered the possibility and asked directly, "Are you being forced to do this? If you're being bullied, I can help you."

"Huh...?"

The student stared in bewilderment for a moment, his mouth agape, then promptly shook his head wildly.

"N-n-no, I'm not being bullied! Th-that's not it... I'm seriously..."

"...What?"

Chisaki squinted, having absolutely no idea what he was trying to say. Of course, she knew what most guys at school thought about her. She heard the rumors. Some said she was like a coldhearted drill sergeant, while others called her Donna, as if she were some sort of mafia leader. At any rate, Chisaki struck fear in the hearts of most boys at school, and she liked it that way. After all, it was far better to be feared than underestimated and looked down upon, and that was why she couldn't comprehend the fact that this boy liked her. It would make more sense to her if he had transferred from a different school, since even she knew that she was extremely attractive. It would be no surprise if a guy or two asked her out just because she was pretty. However, the student in front of her had known of her since at least middle school.

"So... What's your name?"

"Huh? Oh, uh. Kenzaki. Touya Kenzaki."

"Okay then, *Kenzaki*. What is it about me that you like?" she asked with a cold stare.

"Oh, uh..."

He ducked his head and rounded his shoulders, seeming to shrink in on himself further.

"You're strong and brave and so cool…but you still have very feminine qualities as well. I fell in love with how honest and true to yourself you are."

"…! O-oh. Uh…!"

Chisaki was caught off guard by how direct and honest he was with his feelings. After all, this was the first time someone of the opposite sex had ever been so straightforward about their love for her before. It wasn't that nobody had ever confessed their feelings to her, but most of them were cocky, like *"Oh, you don't have a boyfriend? Well, today's your lucky day. I'll be your boyfriend"* or *"I like strong-willed girls. Be mine."* They were all just trying to control her. Of course, she put each of these pieces of trash in their place before separating them by burnable and nonburnable and throwing them out, but that was a different story altogether. At any rate, Chisaki was shaken by the unexpected, genuine display of affection.

"Ahem!!"

She cleared her throat as if to persuade herself she wasn't bothered, then put on a confident, indifferent grin.

"Okay, I appreciate it and all…but I have no idea who you even are."

"Oh! O-of course. That's why…maybe we could be friends first…?"

His voice gradually trailed off until it was almost inaudible, and Touya continued to hunch forward as if he wished he were invisible. There was something about his pathetic, timid behavior that reminded Chisaki of her old self—which annoyed her—and she callously replied, "I hate guys who don't say what they want."

"…! Oh…"

"And I hate indecisive guys, too. Wishy-washy, weak guys are a no go as well. On second thought, I basically hate all men, so there's no way I'm ever going to date one."

"D-do you think you could make an exception…?"

He persisted (meekly) despite her purposely being extra harsh to get him to leave. Chisaki was genuinely taken aback, finding herself once again shaken by his unclouded eyes, so she promptly looked away to make sure he wouldn't notice, then dismissively waved him off.

"Then do you think you could become at least a little bit cooler? Hmm... Like becoming the student council president? Yeah, how about this: I will consider dating you if you become the student council president."

"Th-the student council president?!"

"What? You can't even do that?" taunted Chisaki, though she was well aware that it was a completely unreasonable demand. Student council president was a surprisingly valuable position at this school, which was why student council students were always after it. There was absolutely no way for your average, inexperienced student to become the student council president, let alone make it to the election. They would be squished like a bug long before that.

Nevertheless, that was far from a problem. Chisaki simply said the first thing that came to mind, and it would make this easier for him to give up and leave her alone. However...

"...All right."

"...What?"

"I'll be back when I become president."

It was the first clear, confident thing he had said to her. He then swiftly bowed and exited the room, leaving Chisaki to stare in a daze with her mouth agape in mute amazement...

"...Wait. Is he being serious?" she muttered almost unconsciously, before shaking her head and adding:

"No, there's no way."

He probably realized I wasn't planning on giving in, so he just said that so he could leave with some dignity.

She continuously told herself that while trying to erase that intruder from her memory. Little did she know that having to consciously force herself to forget about him meant that she was at least somewhat interested in him.

Around a month had gone by since that day.

I haven't heard from him since... Hmph. And he said he was in love with me... Not like I care or anything!

Although she wouldn't admit it, Chisaki was slightly disappointed while she patrolled the school... She suddenly heard the suppressed giggling of a boy and girl coming from the art room. She softly sighed. There were tons of kids like this, even at a school with a relatively high number of wealthy students. Once school was out, couples would secretly meet in clubrooms—or any empty room, for that matter—for some fun. But unfortunately for them, illicit sexual relations were prohibited on school grounds. Even a kiss was a major issue if a teacher caught them.

Tsk! School is not a place for flirting and fooling around!

When she swung her bamboo sword, a piercing whiplike sound echoed down the hall, causing the giggling students in the art room to instantly cease.

"The gate's about to be closed and locked!" she yelled before promptly walking away. Normally, the disciplinary committee would handle indecent acts like this, but Chisaki wasn't the kind of person who would walk inside and reprimand them. As long as they went home, she was happy, and if they stayed, then whatever happened to them was their own fault. If a teacher caught these students in the act, it was none of her concern.

"Tsk. Ridiculous."

There were countless graduates from this school and parents of students who were politicians and businessmen—important representatives of Japan, and they took notice of what happened at the school, so if someone were suspended, then there was no hope for them after they graduated. All that awaited was darkness. Their paths to any of the top companies in Japan would be permanently blocked, and that was not hyperbole.

Was a temporary feeling of intense passion worth the risk? It didn't make any sense to Chisaki. Perhaps love fried the brain to the point that it made people stupid. With that thought in mind, she casually shifted her gaze to the world outside the window...

"Hmm...? Is that...?"

She narrowed her eyes at two students wearing their gym clothes, standing near the school gate. She leaned closer to the window and observed them for another few seconds until she was sure that it was the student council president and vice president.

"...? What in the world are they doing?"

They were standing side by side right outside the school gate, facing Chisaki's left, and looked to be waving and talking to someone. There was nothing unusual about student council members staying after school, but there was something odd about them wearing gym clothes in front of the school gate. Chisaki watched, puzzled, until the person talking to them suddenly came into view.

"...?!"

Running over to greet the two student council members was the guy she had just been thinking about a few moments ago, and even from a distance, she could tell how utterly exhausted he was. Although his silhouette seemed to be a bit slimmer, his massive body and rounded shoulders left no doubt as to who he was. With both hands on his knees, he breathed heavily, trying to catch his breath, as the student council president and vice president warmly patted him on the back.

"......"

Why was he with two student council members? The answer was obvious. Because he was also a member of the student council... which meant...

"Is he really serious about doing this...?"

Those were the words that slipped off her tongue before she

immediately shook her head. *Even if he is serious, so what?* she thought. Surely, there had to be something wrong with him for taking her suggestion seriously, since it was merely something she came up with on the spot to turn him down.

I said that to break it to him gently, so there's something really wrong with him for taking me seriously... I didn't do anything wrong.

I didn't do anything wrong, and none of this is my fault...but I guess I could throw him a bone, thought Chisaki with a faint sense of guilt. After descending the stairs to the first floor, she bought a sports drink at the vending machine and waited for Touya in front of the school building's entrance, but...

"You've really improved your endurance, Kenzaki."

"Yeah, for real. I'm guessing you don't really feel that sore after your workouts anymore, huh?"

"Yeah, I guess I have improved...compared with a month ago, at least."

When Chisaki heard their voices getting closer, she quickly hid behind one of the shoe lockers. After giving it some thought, she immediately realized that there was no need for her to hide...but after declaring that she hated men, she was too embarrassed to actually be seen talking to one. Plus, simply explaining what she was doing there was a daunting task.

I don't have any other choice now.

After going back and forth between ideas, Chisaki placed her bamboo sword and sports drink down, waited for the student council president and vice president to change into their indoor shoes, then attacked them the instant they stepped into the hallway.

"Huh—?"

"Wha—?"

Once the surprise attack knocked them both unconscious, she gently leaned them against the shoe lockers.

"Hmm? Guys? Is—?"

Chisaki instantly turned around when she heard Touya's voice, and their eyes met.

"Hmm? Chisaki? What are you—? What the…?! What happened to them?!"

His eyes opened wide in astonishment the instant he saw their limp bodies lying against the shoe lockers, but Chisaki couldn't focus on that right now. She stood up with a calm expression and grabbed the sports drink.

"Long time no see," she commented as she tried to act normal.

"Huh? Oh yeah. Long time no see. So about the student council president and vice president…"

"You decided to join the student council? Just assuming since you were with these two."

"Y-yeah, but, uh… They—"

"Wow. You're a member of the student council now."

"Wh-what unwavering resolution and strength… I'm so in love with you."

"Wh-what?!" she goofily shrieked.

"Oh, sorry. It just came out."

Flustered, Touya began to dart his gaze around, so there was no way for Chisaki to pretend to be mad and yell at him for teasing her. Instead, she narrowed her eyes, smugly lifted her chin, and roared:

"Don't tell me you took what I said that day seriously? I'm going to be honest with you. I only said that to get rid of you, so if you're foolishly thinking about becoming the student council president or something, then stop."

She was trying to be as clear and arrogant as possible to make sure he understood…but what she got in return completely took her by surprise.

"O-oh yeah… I mean, I figured as much…," replied Touya uncomfortably as he scratched his cheek.

"…?!"

While she stood in mute amazement, Touya stared off into space and calmly continued, "I mean, I'd be lying if I said I wasn't doing this to get your attention at least a little…but even without that, I figured this would be a good opportunity to change…to change myself."

"…To change yourself?"

"Y-yeah, I realize I'm not that attractive…and I wanted to change that."

"…And yet you still confessed your feelings to me? Wow."

"Er…! That's, uh… I heard that you should tell women how you feel as soon as possible, so…I did."

"…Wouldn't that usually be after you have some sort of relationship?"

"Y-yeah, I had a feeling that was the case…," he admitted, meekly rounding his shoulders…before immediately straightening his back and standing tall. His eyes faintly trembling, he gazed right into hers, and he clearly stated with a somewhat quavering voice: "But I don't regret a thing. I got the chance to improve as a person thanks to you! So there's nothing you need to worry about…"

His voice suddenly lowered into almost a whisper as he trailed off, and he averted his gaze. However, Chisaki's eyes opened wide as if he had read her mind.

"E-excuse me?! I'm not worried about a thing! I just thought I'd make sure you didn't take what I said seriously!"

"Hmm? Doesn't that mean you were worried—?"

"What?! Don't get cocky! I would never concern myself over a man! Anyway, here! We had extra, and I don't want it, so you can have it! Bye!" she sputtered in almost one rambling breath before pushing the sports drink into Touya's hand, grabbing her bamboo sword, and running away.

"Oh, uh… What about these two? Did—? …She's fast."

Before he could finish his sentence, she was gone, harboring a heart confused like never before.

Me? Worried? Pfft! Not in the slightest! If you're going to be like that, then I'm going to intentionally make sure I don't care, even if it's the last thing I do! From now on, I'm not going to care what you do or where you do it, no matter what!

Like a stubborn child, Chisaki made this vow to herself. Regardless, she stuck to it and worked hard to make sure she didn't have any contact with Touya after that.

"Chisaki! We'll patrol the school building this week, so—"

"I'll handle things inside the school building."

"Why…?"

Touya was always jogging after school around the schoolyard, so she needed to make sure there was no way she would accidentally run into him.

"Chisaki, you have a minute?"

"What?"

"I wanted to talk to you about putting up flyers for the exercise—"

"Please ask someone else to do it."

"…! Oh… Okay…?"

The leader of the disciplinary committee seemed taken aback by Chisaki's harsh, point-blank refusal, but Chisaki didn't have a choice… because the school newspaper had plastered the bulletin board with a special article about Touya. She did everything she could to keep him out of her sight, but some things simply weren't avoidable.

"Now, a word from the student body treasurer, Touya Kenzaki."

Each student council member spoke at the closing ceremony for the first semester. Chisaki tried to look away from the stage when she heard the familiar name, but when she accidentally caught sight of the man in the wings, her eyes naturally opened wide.

"Good morning, everyone. I am the student body treasurer, Touya Kenzaki."

So this was what it felt like to hardly recognize someone. His body had clearly changed over the past month and a half, and while he was still somewhat chubby, he didn't look like a lazy sloth anymore. He even looked dignified, with his back straight as he stood tall and proud. Chisaki forgot to look away as she gazed intently at him onstage, and Touya immediately looked back at her, straight in the eyes. It wasn't merely her imagination, and it was Touya's words that would prove it.

"I plan on running for student council president next year, but I still do not have a running mate. There is someone I have in mind, though. In fact, I don't plan on running for president with anyone but her!"

Chisaki's heart began to race violently when she heard the declaration. Meanwhile, the surrounding students, mainly the boys, began to show excitement.

"And I will do whatever it takes to make her my partner!"

What is he doing? wondered Chisaki in somewhat of a daze; all the students around her erupted into applause. It even made her clap two—three times as well…before she lowered her hands in a fluster, feeling her cheeks getting warm. Was it because she'd reflexively started clapping? Or was there another reason why she was blushing? It was still far too early for Chisaki to know why.

The day after the new semester began post-summer break, Touya stopped by the disciplinary committee's room just like he had some time before, taking Chisaki completely by surprise.

"Chisaki! Please run alongside me for student council president as my vice president!"

The man bowing his head right now was a completely different person from the boy who had stood there over four months ago. The fat he had all over his body had vanished and was replaced with ripped muscles. His hair was trimmed nicely and combed, and his eyes were brimming with confidence as he gazed straight into hers.

"…!"

His transformation struck Chisaki silent for a moment, but after she cleared her throat, she looked him back in the eyes.

"…Why? I told you to become the student council president before

I would even consider anything else, but if I run with you, that would mean I'd be helping you."

"I understand that, but I cannot imagine having a running partner other than you!"

"Er…"

She looked away because he was being so direct, but he continued, "Of course, if I am elected with your help, I'm not going to use that to pressure you into dating me. But…I'm no longer that indecisive, weak boy anymore, and I plan on continuing to grow into a man you can respect! I want you to be there by my side to see for yourself, so will you do me the honor? I beg you!"

"U-uh…"

Despite it being a very selfish request, Chisaki couldn't immediately turn him down when he was being so straightforward and genuine, and before she realized it, her mouth was moving on its own.

"You claim you're not weak anymore, but maybe you only *look* strong? I'd have to see it for myself to believe it. Hmm… How about this: You beat me in a kendo match, and I'll consider your proposal."

What am I saying? thought Chisaki the moment the words came out of her mouth. If she didn't want to do it, then she could have just told him so without setting any conditions.

"…All right, I'll meet you in the second kendo training hall after school." Unsurprisingly, Touya made this declaration after only a two-second pause. Chisaki agonized over why she couldn't just turn him down as she watched him bow and leave the room.

"You are the scoundrel who has been trying to woo my lady, aren't you?!"

"…! Uh…"

Touya was taken by surprise the instant he stepped inside the kendo training hall after school. And who could blame him? Some random girl wearing a kendo *gi*, her hair in two spiral-curled pigtails like an aristocrat in the 1800s, suddenly started to verbally attack him. Moreover, she was accompanied by three girls who somehow looked very natural standing there (positioned asymmetrically for some reason), as if they had been lying in wait for him.

"Wh-who is 'my lady'?"

"Why must you waste my time asking questions you already know the answer to? Who else could it be other than the noblest lady of them all: Chisaki!"

"O-oh…" Touya nodded, overwhelmed by the noblewoman's presence.

"I know why you came. You irreverently wish to challenge my lady to a duel, yes?" the noblewoman claimed, flipping her hair (one large curl) back.

"Know your place!"

"It's troubling, isn't it? How arrogant can one man be?"

"You are in for a rude awakening if you think you can beat her that easily just because you are a man."

"I don't think that at all… Anyway, why are you all standing kind of sideways like that?"

"That is none of your concern! If you wish to challenge my lady…"

The noblewoman paused, then snapped her fingers.

"Ayame Shinbashi!" On the right, an energetic girl with simpler pigtails announced her name with her head held high.

"Kikyou Oomori," stated the tomboy to her right with a hand over one eye.

"Kurasawa Hiiragi," stated the girl standing on the opposite side, pushing her glasses up the bridge of her nose. Only after the three footmen introduced themselves did the noblewoman in the middle with spiral curls speak up.

"I am Sumire Kiryuuin, and if you wish to fight my lady, you will have to get past us first!" she proclaimed loudly, flipping her hair back again. It was a declaration of war so explosive that nobody would be surprised if something actually exploded in the background. It was as if Touya had just met the four generals of the demon lord's army.

He took a step back…and shifted his gaze toward Chisaki, who was holding her head behind them as if she had a headache.

"Hey, uh… Chisaki? Who are these…pleasant individuals?"

"…They were my kendo team's *senpou, jihou, chuuken*, and *fuku-shou* in middle school."

"…And you have them call you 'my lady'?"

"No, never. I'm not their boss or a noblewoman or anything like that. If anything, I should be calling Sumire 'my lady,' since she's older than me. And you know she only calls herself Sumire to fit in. Her real name is Viol—"

"How dare you speak to my lady and ignore me!" shouted Viol—Sumire as she leaned toward Touya and blocked Chisaki from his sight. She then snapped her fingers once more, and the smallest girl of the bunch, Ayame, took a step forward.

"If you wish to fight her, then you have to get past me first!"

"U-uh…?" said Touya hesitantly as he looked straight down at the little girl in front of him. There was a thirty-centimeter height difference at the very least, so it was hard to believe she would even stand a chance, regardless of Touya's sex.

"Uh… I mean, if I have to…"

Touya decided to accept her challenge, seeing as there didn't seem to be any other way around this…

"Hmph! Absolutely pathetic!"

"Heh! He lost the very first match…"

"What a letdown."

"Oh my. How embarrassing."

The match was over in the blink of an eye. The moment they were given the signal to fight, she vanished right before his eyes, only to reappear with her bamboo sword already thrusting into his throat.

"Cough! Hack! Hack!"

"A-are you o—?"

"My lady! He does not deserve your concern!"

"But he's seriously—"

Chisaki tried to run over and check on Touya, who was crouching and coughing violently, but Sumire promptly stood in her way, looked Chisaki right in the eye, and whispered, "Your sympathy would only hurt a man with such resolve. He would feel like you aren't taking him seriously."

"...!"

Chisaki froze, and after a few more seconds went by, Touya managed to stand up on his own and got back into stance with his bamboo sword.

"*Cough...!* I would like to request a rematch!"

"Oh? Still haven't had enough, huh? All right, I'll beat you up as many times as you'd like!"

And just as Ayame claimed, she made Touya kiss the floor multiple times over the next two hours, but even then, he didn't give up. He started practicing kendo at the dojo after that day and continued to challenge the four demon generals—the four kendo "sisters"—to matches until he eventually managed to beat every single one of them once.

"Chisaki, I've finally made it."

It was October by the time Touya was finally able to challenge Chisaki to a match...but that obviously still wasn't enough reason to go easy on him.

"...I will train hard, and I will be back."

Though he had somewhat improved through his matches against the four kendo (unrelated) sisters, Chisaki was a whole different beast. Match after match, he went home battered and bruised, hardly exchanging a word with her as she quietly continued to accept each of his challenges. She kept her heart buried deep inside her because if she didn't, she wouldn't be able to keep her inconvenient emotions from bursting out.

But one day, out of the blue...

Wait. Aiming for his hand before exams would be... He said he was studying hard, too...

Touya was putting all his muscle into his next swing as he aimed for the face, so Chisaki was just about to capitalize on this opening and strike his hand…when that thought suddenly crossed her mind. That second of hesitation alone led her aim astray, and she missed. So by the time she realized what was happening, Touya's bamboo sword was right before her eyes.

Whack.

The soft impact shook her head, but it was soft—far too soft for a bamboo sword.

"…Huh?"

He'd gone easy on her. The moment Chisaki's brain recognized this, countless pent-up emotions were suddenly freed.

"Seriously?!" she yelled, her voice a mix of humiliation and rage. She then grabbed the bamboo sword touching her head, ripped it out of his hands, and threw it at him.

"What do you think you're doing?!"

She glared at Touya through her mask, making her anger no secret.

"Oh, uh…! I'm sorry! I know it's rude to hold back, but when I realized I was about to hit the girl I'm in love with, my body just tensed," he exclaimed in a fluster, cradling the bamboo sword he'd caught in his arms.

"What…?!"

She was speechless for a few moments after that, angrily grinding her teeth, until she eventually shouted furiously, "Ugh! Whatever! Fine! You win by default! The upcoming election?! Sure, fine! I'll be your running mate!"

"…?! Y-yesss!!"

Although it took him a split second to process it all, Touya was now raising his arms into the air and cheering like a child. Chisaki huffed and puffed while she glared at him.

"Are you sure, my lady?" Sumire, who had been acting as the referee, asked suddenly.

"…Yeah, why not?" replied Chisaki, looking away with a pout, despite her face not being visible behind the mask.

"Besides, all we're doing is running for student council president and vice president together. It's not like this means we're going to be dating," she quickly added, but she realized that it sounded like an excuse.

"Yessssssssss!!"

Still dressed in his kendo gear, Touya was aggressively posing with his hands in the air as if he had just won gold at the Olympics. While she watched him out of the corner of her eye, Chisaki started to get the feeling that one day soon, she was going to start genuinely wanting him to win the election…

"And after that, Touya got even cooler…"

"U-uh… That's nice…"

Chisaki was sitting in one of the spectator seats at her family-owned dojo's arena as she bragged about her boyfriend to her cousin whom she had not seen in ages. However, this younger, female cousin couldn't help but grimace…

"Hey, uh… Chisaki? That cool boyfriend of yours is about to get himself killed, like…right now."

"Oh, come on. Touya beat me. There's no way he's gonna lose to anyone here."

"He won by default, though, right? Plus, this isn't kendo. It's hand-to-hand combat."

Her cousin's worried gaze shifted toward Touya, who was grimacing in the center of the arena. Looking down at him with bloodthirsty eyes was a man even larger and more muscular.

"His opponent's the disciple you relentlessly turned down when he asked you out, right? I mean, he looks pissed. Like he wants to kill Touya."

"What? I honestly don't remember that," commented Chisaki flippantly, which made it crueler.

"Touya, you can do it!" she then cheered innocently. Touya raised his right arm and smiled, which only made his opponent more enraged.

"I—I get this is an amateur match, but maybe letting an actual amateur participate in the martial arts festival wasn't a good idea... H-hey, we can still throw in the towel, you know? It's still not too late to give up."

"What? But Touya looks really pumped for this."

"Only because he has to act tough when his girlfriend is yelling and cheering for him like this!"

"Right? He's so manly and cool."

"You are being overly optimistic! Open your eyes!"

But the worried cousin's cries were in vain as the referee swung his arm, starting the match. It was only a matter of seconds before the match ended...with Touya face-first on the mat. So being a good sport, Chisaki personally made sure to run down and greet the opponent...with her fist...before burying him in the corner of the arena.

CHAPTER 9

Adoration and Arrogance

One day during summer break...

"I wonder if my dear brother can be hypnotized, too?" Yuki muttered, sitting on the bed in her room with a book on hypnosis in hand. The book was titled *Hypnosis for Idiots: Welcome to the Hypnotist Club*, and it had an interesting history. Namely, it had been used that fateful day in the student council room, which had ended in tragedy. Despite promising her brother that they would seal this book away so that nobody would ever get hurt again, Yuki couldn't give up something so fascinating simply because they had failed once. She had purchased this book with her own money, and ever since then, she had been testing various types of hypnosis on her guinea pig, Ayano. Nevertheless, the samples proved to be far from adequate, since Ayano's "Loyalty" was already at max level, and she would submit to and serve Yuki, regardless of what she was ordered to do. *I really want to try this out on someone, but if I tried it on a friend, and it didn't work, then...*, she thought. Suddenly, it hit her: Masachika.

"What do you think?"

"Meow?"

Ayano, who was snuggled up with her head in Yuki's lap, looked up at her with eyes full of wonder, then sat up and began brushing her bangs to the side with her right hand curled into a ball.

"Oh...," Yuki muttered. She then raised both hands to clap...but froze. Her eyes were locked on Ayano, who was sitting femininely on her knees with her legs somewhat spread open, and she suddenly got the urge to reach out and massage the maid's chest.

"Hmm...? Have you gotten a little bigger since I last checked?"

She tilted her head to the side, ignoring Ayano's curious gaze, and rubbed her maid's chest with a serious expression.

"O-oh? Oooh! They're so big, you can lift them...," murmured Yuki with admiration as she lifted Ayano's chest. She continued to enjoy her maid's bosom for a few more minutes after that before finally clapping with clear satisfaction. Immediately, Ayano froze in place, slowly blinked a few times, then curiously tilted her head.

"...Did it work?"

"Yep. Mission Kitty-Cat was a success... Do you think it will work on Masachika, though?"

"Sir Masachika? ...I believe it would be difficult."

Ayano tilted her head to the other side, seemingly unconcerned with the fact that she had been hypnotized to act like a cat.

"Yeah, they say the hypnotists are resistant to hypnosis, too." Yuki shrugged. "Oh, look at the time. I have to get ready for violin practice."

After Yuki stood up from her bed and began getting ready, Ayano immediately went to her aid, pressing her lips tightly together as if she had formed some sort of resolution.

A few days later, when Yuki was getting ready to go to the Kuze residence to hang out, Ayano suddenly approached her.

"Lady Yuki."

"Hmm?"

"It's about the hypnosis... I prepared a few things that may help you."

"Huh? Hypnosis...? Ohhh, right! I was going to hypnotize my brother! You went out of your way to prepare something for me?"

"It was my pleasure. I figured that you would need some sort of tool to aid you if you wished to hypnotize Sir Masachika."

"Oh? An enhancement item? I could definitely use one of those."

"I did a lot of research…and came up with this," revealed Ayano, pulling a dark-pink candle out of her maid uniform's pocket. "It's a scented candle that apparently helps relax the body and thus makes it easier to hypnotize people."

"It's just like those erotic fan comics."

"In addition…I prepared this."

Ayano went through her cell phone for a few seconds, then handed it to Yuki. Displayed on the screen was a questionable picture of two giant eyes with squiggly waves radiating from them.

"…What's this?"

"It's apparently a hypnosis app."

"It's just like those erotic fan comics!" Yuki repeated jokingly, but the next thing Ayano took out of her pocket…was a massive, rugged collar.

"…What's that?"

"A collar that apparently forces the wearer to obey every command."

"It's just like the ones you see in those another-world fantasy shows! …Wait! Don't tell me you plan on having Masachika wear that?!"

"No. I thought you could make me wear it…"

"That'd be pointless."

"Oh…"

"Why do you look depressed?!"

Yuki turned toward the strangely well-built collar with a hand on her forehead as if she had a headache. What appeared to be numerous power stones of all colors decorated the collar, giving it an unusually strong presence, which made it hard to believe this was a gag gift.

"Where did you even get that sketchy collar?"

"So…when I went shopping the other day, a street vendor wearing a hood called out to me… And despite not telling them what I was looking for, they gave me this and told me I didn't need to pay anything for it…"

"Whoa. Sounds less like an another-world fantasy and more like a this-world secret occult society. You better not even think about using that, okay? I've seen this before. Whoever uses that will become a shell of their former self, and then that street vendor's going to be like, 'Humans are so foolish,' and laugh."

"Oh…?"

"Wait. Hold up. Don't tell me you got the scented candle from this person, too?"

"I got this at the hundred-yen store."

"Seriously? You really can get anything there."

"It was two hundred yen, though…"

"The hell? That's way too expensive. Lying dirtbag store," joked Yuki. Then she suddenly noticed that Ayano seemed somewhat depressed.

Oops… Maybe I went a little too far. She went through all that trouble to find this stuff for me…

After reflecting on her behavior, Yuki softly cleared her throat, shifted her focus back to the candle, and suggested:

"But, well…why don't we give it a try? The candle and app could work…"

"…! Yes, I completely agree!"

"Thanks for finding this for me, by the way."

"It was nothing."

We'd probably have a better chance of hypnotizing him with a five-yen coin tied to a string, thought Yuki cynically as she grinned at her attendant's instantly improved mood.

"There was a time when I used to truly believe that, too," muttered Yuki with her eyes on her brother, who was sitting on the side of the bed with a vacant stare. Last night, she handed Masachika the scented candle and claimed that it improved sleep; she had him bask in the smoke for the entire night, then used the hypnosis app when he had just woken up and was still half asleep…and it actually worked.

"Seriously?"

"Congratulations. It worked."

"Yeah, uh… So… How about we get some fresh air in here and crack open the window?"

"As you wish."

After maid-mode Ayano did that, she opened the door that led to the living room to air out the bedroom, allowing the hot air from outside to pass through while simultaneously diluting the strangely sweet fragrance lingering in the air. And yet Masachika still showed no signs of returning to normal—he stared idly at the floor with a vacant expression.

"…What should I do now?"

Never in a million years did Yuki think her brother would actually get hypnotized, so she hadn't considered what she would do if it worked. On top of that, she didn't have the heart to say, "Well, at least we know it works, so let's call it a day," after all the effort Ayano put into this, either.

"Hmm…"

Yuki racked her brain for a few moments until she was struck with an epiphany, and she began looking through her phone. Once she opened the hypnosis app, she pointed the screen at Masachika and suggested:

"You will become a cool, doting guy who cannot hold back his love any longer."

When she tapped the screen, her phone began to ring eerily, causing Masachika's body to twitch. His pupils gradually began to focus… until out of nowhere, he looked at Yuki and smiled sweetly.

"Hey, Yuki… Cute as always, I see."

"Ew! Blech! Gross!" bitterly hissed Yuki, not even pausing between each word, but Masachika simply shifted his gaze to Ayano without a care in the world.

"You're really cute, too, Ayano."

"Th-thank you?"

"Heh! What's wrong? You look puzzled… Oh?"

He stood from the bed as if he noticed something and gently reached out to touch Ayano's black hair.

"You have some lint in your hair."

"Ah! P-please accept my sincerest apologies! I'm so embarrassed…"

While the corners of her eyes began to burn and she lowered her head in shame, Masachika gently placed his right hand on her cheek, kindly lifted her chin, and smiled the most loving of smiles.

"There's nothing for you to apologize about. This is just proof of how hard you work. You should relax more, if anything."

"N-no, I couldn't…"

"Really? You're such a hard worker. Thank you for always helping out… I love you," he declared as he affectionately caressed her cheek, causing Ayano's eyes to immediately open wide in shock…

"Fshhh…"

"A-Ayano…!!"

"Uh-oh. ♪"

Ayano's eyes spun, and her knees gave out, but before she hit the ground, Masachika swiftly grabbed her in his arms, picked her up like a princess, and gently laid her on the bed before tenderly rubbing her head.

"Ha-ha. You're so cute, Ayano."

He looked back at Yuki as if he was seeking approval, but she immediately got into a defensive stance and lowered her posture, causing his lips to curl sweetly as he approached her.

"Wh-what? You want some of this? I hope you don't think you can scare me just by telling me you love me, because it's not happening. It takes a lot more than that to scare me. Unlike Ayano, I— Ah! Hey?!"

——Five minutes later.

"I love you. I love you more than anyone else, Yuki."

"Oh-hyo, oh-hyo, oh-hyooo! What is this?! It's...! I'm going to squeal!"

Yuki was sitting in Masachika's lap while he embraced her from behind, whispering sweet nothings into her ear. Sitting cross-legged, he gently rubbed her head and cheeks, causing her to shriek and squirm, unable to take it anymore.

At first, something felt wrong about Masachika acting so loving and cool, but seeing him so confident and unashamed strangely made her more than just okay with it. *Once you start feeling embarrassed, you've already lost the game*—there seemed to be some truth to that saying.

"What's wrong? What are you thrashing about like that for? Aren't you the shy one this morning?"

"Hff! H-hey, uh... Do you think you could stop whispering into my ear? You're giving me goose bumps..."

"Really? All right... Then look at me. I want to see that cute face of yours when we talk."

"No, no, no! No way! I probably look so weird right now!"

Yuki stretched her arms and legs and began flailing them about, but that wasn't going to help her escape Masachika's grasp. Although his touch was gentle, his grip around her was surprisingly strong, making apparent his unwavering will to never let her go.

"Heh... Ha-ha...! I'm impressed. It takes a lot to make me blush..."

"Heh! It does, huh? You're so cute when you blush, you know? I'll honestly tell you how much I love you as much as it takes if it means I get to see you like this some more...because I love you more than anything in the world."

Her lips audaciously curled broadly into a smirk as she crossed her arms over her chest within her brother's embrace.

"All right, bro! You've asked for it! An eye for an eye! A tooth for a tooth! Hypnosis for hypnosis! I hope you're ready for this brand-new, new move I learned the other day!"

The redundancy of that sentence was only further proof of how uneasy Yuki felt, but that didn't stop her from curling into a ball as if she were increasing her chi, until all of a sudden, she swiftly thrust her right fist straight into the air and shouted, "Let's do this! Angel mode activ—"

"You don't have to do that, Yuki. You're already an angel in my eyes."

"Blarghffaaa."

Against all odds, Masachika promptly put a stop to her secret transformation. The doting brother did not even consider waiting for her to finish, and all the chi she had built up dispersed in vain as she froze. Masachika lovingly tightened his arms around her and placed his chin on her shoulder.

"My sweet angel who loves her family more than anything else and is always doing whatever she can for her family... I'm so happy to have a sister like you."

"U-uh-huh..."

Yuki was feeling genuinely bashful—far too embarrassed to joke anymore after such a relentlessly sweet compliment. But as her face slowly got redder, a faint voice suddenly started to groan behind her.

"M-mmm..."

"A-Ayano! You're awake?! Help!" cried Yuki. She looked over her brother's shoulder and realized Ayano was sitting up in the bed. However, the moment Masachika laid eyes on Ayano, she averted her gaze.

"O-oh, right. I just remembered that I was in the middle of preparing breakfast...," she sputtered before promptly leaving the room and leaving her master behind as well.

"A-Ayano! You traitor!!"

"Hey, now. Don't say that. We're family, right?"

"Stop whispering into my ear!"

She thrashed about like an unruly kitten until she looked like she was struck with an epiphany.

"Oh! B-bathroom! I need to go to the bathroom!" she claimed out of desperation.

"Hmm? Really? All right. Off you go."

And Masachika simply let her go. After immediately hopping to her feet, she rushed to the bathroom, slammed the door, and began doing everything she could to catch her breath.

"Oh god... That was intense... *Huff... Huff...*"

Even Yuki couldn't hide how flustered she was after experiencing her brother's shameless, sweet love. It wasn't like those videos that talent agencies put out to introduce their models, where the handsome guy just whispers something sweet into the camera. Because what Masachika did was...real. Furthermore, Yuki knew that he spoke from the heart because she herself had hypnotized him so that he wouldn't be able to control the boundless love inside him any longer.

"W-wow... Seriously? My brother loves me waaay too much," she joked, covering both her cheeks and twisting her body back and forth...because if she didn't do that, the embarrassment was going to light her on fire as the butterflies burst out of her stomach.

"Dammit... Damn it all... My brother is too damn cute."

After squirming in the bathroom for a good bit until somewhat calming down, Yuki returned to the living room... She returned...to the living room...and...

"I love watching you cook, Ayano. Your skills are captivating."

"Ahn..."

"What is this?! Some kind of newlywed role-play?!" jeered Yuki the moment she saw that her brother was holding Ayano from behind in the kitchen as he whispered sweet nothings into her ear. Nevertheless, the moment she realized that her brother might target her again, she lost the courage to take another step forward into the kitchen, grinding her teeth where she stood in the doorway. Meanwhile, Ayano, who was in the middle of being showered in Masachika's love, was completely frozen in place with an uncracked egg in hand. Hints of crimson began to illuminate her cheeks, and her eyes spun on her blank face.

"A-ahhhhhh..."

Her voice trembled like never before, and the egg shook in her violently trembling hand.

"S-S-Sir Masachika! You mustn't! The egg…! The egg…!!" she suddenly shrieked off-key, her voice unbelievably shaky, as if she was worried the egg was about to fall straight onto the floor.

"Hmm? Oh, we can't have that. Here, you need to be careful when you hold eggs."

With his left hand still wrapped around Ayano's stomach from behind, he gently cupped his right hand around the hand Ayano was using to hold the egg, immediately causing her to jump, and her body began to tremble even more intensely.

"We mustn't! The egg…! My eggs—!!"

"Stop trying to get my brother to fertilize them!"

Unable to take it anymore, Yuki rushed into the kitchen and ripped Ayano out of Masachika's arms.

"Masachika, go watch TV or something and stop bothering Ayano! She needs to cook!"

After forcing her brother out of the kitchen, she turned around and faced Ayano, who was crouched in place with only her egg-holding hand on the kitchen table.

"…So? Do you have the energy to cook still?"

"Y-yes, of course…"

"Stop rubbing your stomach like there's a baby in there," snapped Yuki, glaring reproachfully at Ayano, who was rubbing her abdomen and blushing.

"Hmm…"

Yuki glanced at her brother, who was casually watching TV after eating breakfast, and cocked her head in puzzlement.

"What's up? Something wrong, Yuki?"

"All right, I'm sick of this," she replied with a wry grimace to her sweetly smiling brother, who had his head curiously tilted.

"…?"

At least an hour and a half had gone by since she hypnotized

Masachika into being a cool, doting brother, and she had finally gotten used to it. In fact, she was genuinely getting annoyed. Even when they were eating, he kept trying to feed her and wipe her mouth, which was more than enough sweetness for a lifetime.

The hypnosis isn't wearing off at all... Maybe I should have done a better job airing out his room?

Since today was a hot day, Yuki closed all the windows and turned on the air conditioner after airing out Masachika's room, but it appeared she wasn't able to completely get rid of the scented candle's hypnotic smell. There was absolutely no sign of him ever snapping out of it.

"Hmm... It looks like I need to hypnotize him again," she muttered to herself, pulling out her smartphone. She then walked around to the other side of the table and wrapped her arms around him.

"What are you doing? Is this some sort of new game?"

"Yeeeah, exactly. It's a cool new game. Here, check it out."

"Hmm? Check...what...out...?"

While Yuki showed him her phone over his shoulder, Masachika's voice gradually began to fade as his unblinking eyes locked on the screen. Once he was ready to be hypnotized again, Yuki commanded:

"You are a cool guy with an attitude. You're always super confident and as rude as could be, but it's okay because everyone around you loves you," she almost randomly demanded, without giving it much thought, then tapped her phone's screen, causing it to ring eerily. Masachika's arms began to twitch as his wavering eyes gradually focused... All of a sudden, he lifted his chin with an audacious smirk and looked at Yuki.

"Yo, seriously? You've got your arms wrapped around *me*, but you still can't take your eyes off that phone? Bold move..."

"Ew! No," uttered Yuki sincerely with a straight face. She glared back at her smug brother. She was fine with the doting brother from earlier, but this was too much. She couldn't even force a smile. In fact, just looking at him kind of irritated her.

"What's wrong? Are you jealous that I spend so much time with Ayano?"

"Oh god."

As she held out her phone and began taking a video of her arrogant sibling, he stood from his chair, turned around, and combed his bangs back while confidently leaning back.

"Hey, yooo. What's going on? I get that you want to save every moment you spend with me, but could you at least wait until I get dressed?"

And yet he undid the top button of his shirt, casually plopped back down in his seat, and faced the smartphone camera with a saucy, sideways glance.

"Oh god... Is it just me, or is the cocky bro inside my bro having trouble finding who he wants to be? I wonder how Masachika's going to feel when he snaps out of it and sees this."

Yuki smirked maliciously because the only thing on her mind was getting revenge for what her "doting" brother did to her earlier, despite Yuki herself being 100 percent responsible for it. It was unjustified resentment simply because he made her hot and bothered, but she was able to effortlessly look away from that inconvenient truth. For the next ten minutes, she continued to record her brother doing various narcissistic poses that only someone really good-looking could get away with... Just then, the intercom rang softly. Yuki looked up and immediately felt as if something was off, since Ayano wasn't moving, despite always being quick to act.

"...? Ayano?"

When she glanced to her side, Ayano was sitting at the table in a daze. Yuki figured the silence was due to Ayano turning into air like she always did, but it appeared that she still hadn't recovered from Masachika's assertiveness in the kitchen earlier. Therefore, Yuki had no choice but to place her phone down and answer the intercom herself.

"Yes? Who could it...be...?"

Assuming it was a delivery, she peeked at the intercom camera…
and discovered there was a silver-haired maiden standing outside.

"…What?"

She froze. Masachika never told her that Alisa was coming over.
Did he forget to? That wasn't like him. Plus, Alisa already came over
the day before to study, and they purposely waited until she went
home so that Yuki could come over unnoticed and stay the night.
Therefore, there was no way Masachika would forget something as
important as Alisa visiting two days in a row…which meant that Alisa
came over unannounced—a surprise visit. But that said, it was still
ten thirty in the morning, which was a little too early to be going to
a friend's house.

…?! Alya? Wh-what is she doing here?

Yuki froze in front of the intercom camera, completely overcome
with surprise… Masachika suddenly popped up behind her, reached
out over her shoulder, and pressed the answer button before Yuki
could even process what was going on.

"Alya? What's up?"

"Oh, Masachika? Sorry for coming over out of the blue like this.
I think I forgot my phone at your place yesterday…"

It all finally made sense to Yuki… It made sense, but at the very
same time…

*She's really dressed-up for someone who just stopped by to grab
her phone.*

Being a woman herself, she could tell that Alisa clearly came
dressed to kill. Now, if Alisa claimed that she normally dolled up
whenever she went out, then that would be the end of the conversation, but Yuki had a gut feeling that wasn't the case.

"No prob. Come on up."

"…? Okay."

"…?!"

While Yuki was busy staring with suspicion at Alisa on the mon-
itor, Masachika suddenly unlocked the entrance and invited her in.

Although puzzled by the way he was speaking, Alisa didn't say another word as she stepped inside.

"Oh god. This is bad," muttered Yuki with a blank face as she began rapidly racking her brain for a solution. There were multiple things bad about this. First off, Masachika was still hypnotized. Next, there was the fact that Yuki and Ayano were hanging out at the Kuze residence this early in the morning. And last but not least, Ayano was dressed as a maid, while Yuki was wearing straight-up loungewear.

Yeah! I can't let her see me dressed like this!

After almost instantaneously coming to that decision, she took a step toward the bedroom... But she noticed Masachika was already heading toward the front door, and she froze.

"...! I need to dehypnotize him first!"

Once she came to that split-second decision, Yuki leaped toward her phone.

"Ayano! Slow Masachika down! Wait, no! Hide our shoes!"

"...As you wish."

Yuki unlocked her phone as Ayano headed toward the front door.

First, I need to make sure our shoes are hidden, and I need to make sure Masachika is himself when he answers the door, too...

Rapidly mapping out a plan in her head, Yuki opened the hypnosis app... She opened the hypnosis app... She...

"...Where's the dehypnotize function?!" she shouted shrilly, unable to find the one thing she needed. She was left with no other choice. She had to rely on the only way she knew how to dehypnotize someone...but before she could even take another step, the doorbell rang, and she froze.

"Yo, you're here."

And it was almost immediately followed by the sound of a door opening and Masachika greeting Alisa. Yuki clenched her teeth tightly, for she was now facing the worst possible scenario.

I've got to change!!

She dashed to her room while undoing her ponytail, then fast-forwarded into something more formal and appropriate for visitors. After making sure she was wearing a ladylike smile, she headed to the entrance to greet Alisa...and completely froze yet again. Because Masachika had one hand against the closed front door with his other hand lifting Alisa's chin. Ayano was staring in awe, putting no effort toward hiding.

"Wait, wait, wait..."

After Yuki passed by Ayano, who was standing upright and stock-still for some reason, she immediately tried to cut in between Masachika and Alisa... At that moment, Masachika grinned at Alisa like a savage beast and exclaimed, "I want you to bear my child."

"Seriously? You're just repeating a line you saw in a lewd video game ad online!"

"...Okay."

"Bffft?! Am I hearing things?!"

Hearing Alisa agree almost made Yuki lose consciousness. But when she turned her wide eyes to her schoolmate and noticed the vacant look on her face, it all made sense.

"Ack! I completely forgot how easily susceptible she is to hypnosis!"

The lingering fragrance of the hypnosis candle must have gotten her the moment she walked through the door. Yuki found it hard to believe that any of the candle's scent made it all the way over there... so Alisa must be more vulnerable to hypnosis than she thought. Either that, or Alisa had become addicted to being hypnotized by Masachika.

While Yuki was considering all the possibilities, Masachika wrapped his arm around Alisa's waist and began walking toward the living room. Alisa simply wore a vacant stare and surrendered herself to him.

"Huh? No, hold up."

But right as he was passing Yuki, she grabbed his shoulder and stopped him with a serious expression.

"Yuki, read the room," he warned with a somewhat bitter smirk, glancing back at her.

"What the hell do you think you're doing?!" she shouted in almost a shriek, then promptly swung her fist in an attempt to knock him unconscious. However, right as her punch was about to connect, he suddenly grabbed her wrist and stopped her.

"Whoa. Nobody likes a disobedient brat, ya know?"

"Shut up and get a hold of yourself, ya filthy cheater! Ayano, grab my br—grab Masachika for me! ...Ayano?"

She saw Ayano take a step in front of her brother, so she asked for help... But she suddenly noticed the look in her maid's eyes, and it gave her a terrible sense of foreboding.

"Sir Masachika... Very well. I will bear...your child..."

"You too?!"

Yuki finally understood why Ayano had been idly standing there for so long. The lingering aroma of the scented candle must have hypnotized her as well, and there was only one person to blame.

This is all my fault!

Ayano had been used as a guinea pig to practice hypnosis until she became unbelievably susceptible...by none other than Yuki. Although she was distressed, she saw Ayano trying to throw herself on Masachika and immediately gave a flustered command.

"Ayano! Sit!"

"……"

"Dammit! It didn't work! Is the difference in power between us just that great?!" she desperately shouted, pulling her wrist free. She then stood before her brother, blocking his path with her arms spread wide as she bravely looked up at him; his arms were wrapped around Alisa and Ayano.

"When I touch your shoulders, you will wake up from your trance! Got it? Three, two, one... Wake up!" she clearly stated, desperately placing both hands on his shoulders and shaking him. However...

"Yuki, what's wrong with you today? Are you jealous? Don't worry. I'll always be your bro."

"It's not working! Ugh! What should I...?"

Before she could get another word out, Yuki felt her right wrist being grabbed, and her body suddenly felt like it was floating in the air. But by the time she finally realized what was happening, she was already staring at the hallway ceiling.

"...Huh?"

Because she unconsciously broke her own fall and Masachika's sweep was gentle, she didn't really feel any pain, but the fact that she was caught off guard and didn't even see it coming horrified her. Nevertheless, the instant she caught a glimpse of her brother taking two girls into his room, she immediately got up and desperately went after him in full-panic mode.

"M-Masachika, let's calm down and think this through! Having your way with two hypnotized women is something that's only supposed to happen in fanfics! Wait... I guess this is kind of unique, since the man's also hypnotized... Ack! What am I thinking? Your first time isn't supposed to be a threesome! That's only something you're supposed to see as a bonus harem ending after clearing all the routes! So could you at least start with beating the individual routes?!"

She clung to his shoulders from behind, desperately trying to stop him, but Yuki's petite body was fruitlessly being dragged across the floor as he walked.

"...! Ugh! That's it!" she desperately screamed after realizing that they were now inside the living room, only steps away from his bedroom...

"Hmm? Huh?! Ow! Ouch! What the...?! Did I sleep wrong? My neck is killing me," Masachika grunted painfully as he woke up with an aching neck.

"Damn, that hurts... Hmm?"

He sat up with a hand on his neck, then realized that he had been sleeping not in his pajamas but in plain, everyday clothes. Masachika curiously began surveying his room when...

"Why am I—? Whoa?!"

...he spotted Ayano on all fours bowing to him, and he jumped.

"Wh-what's wrong?"

"I am truly sorry..."

"For what? I have no idea what's going on."

"The scented candle I gave you last night...was actually a hypnosis candle...and thanks to its effects, Lady Yuki had you hypnotized all morning."

"What? Hypnotized?"

An image of Alisa, half naked in the student council room, suddenly came to mind...which he quickly tried to erase from his head while simultaneously remembering that Alisa had no recollection of what had happened that time.

"O-oh, so that's what happened? I was hypnotized...which is why I don't remember anything?"

"Yes... That is most likely what happened."

"Uh-huh...," he replied without emotion, genuinely still unable to process what was going on. There wasn't much he could do, though, since even if he had been hypnotized, there was no way he would be able to remember.

"...So why does my neck hurt?"

"That's... Well... I only remember bits and pieces of what happened as well, so I am not exactly sure...but I believe Lady Yuki had to choke you out from behind to stop you."

"What?"

Her explanation only made him more confused.

"...Eh. Whatever. Where's Yuki? And stand up. It's not your fault. You don't need to apologize."

"I do. I was the one who brought the scented candle and found the hypnosis app..."

"...The what app?"

"This..."

Displayed on the smartphone in Ayano's hand was a giant closed eye accompanied by a faint, fishy vibrating sound.

"...What's this? And what's that noise?"

"Oh, this is apparently a sound wave that is supposed to wake you up from hypnosis. I was playing it for you while you were asleep... Oh! Right, you wanted to know where Lady Yuki was. Lady Yuki has... already returned to the Suou residence..."

"Huh? Why?"

"Um... She wanted me to give this to you..."

With extreme reluctance, Ayano slipped a folded piece of loose-leaf paper out of her pocket, but when he unfolded it, all that was written was *"I'm sorry"* in absurdly large letters in Yuki's handwriting.

"...What's this all about? ...Wait. You said she had to 'stop' me? Like, was I doing something so bad that I needed to be choked out?"

"It's probably better for you to see for yourself..."

Ayano glanced at Masachika's smartphone by his bedside. In spite of the bad feeling in his gut, he turned it on and immediately saw notifications from the second-year students in the student council.

> Kuze, what's wrong? If something's bothering you, let me know.
> Are you okay, Kuze? Were you possessed when investigating the school's seven mysteries?
> Well, I think you're cool. Yep.

While Touya and Maria seemed concerned about him, Chisaki appeared to be trying to make him feel better about something. However, all these messages could be traced to a single source: a video file that Yuki had uploaded. Masachika tapped the screen, opening the file...

"Hey, yooo. What's going on? I get that you want to save every moment you spend with me, but could you at least wait until I get dressed?"

"Huh?!"

Masachika was rendered speechless the moment he witnessed the man in the video—he was having a hard time believing it was him. The guy in the video was posing like a narcissist. He promptly locked the screen, unable to take it any longer, but that didn't change the fact that the upperclassmen in the student council had all seen the video. His entire body felt like it was on fire.

"Y-Yukiiiiii! What… What have you done?!"

He clenched his jaw, furiously grinding his teeth as he sat on the bed, and desperately fought against the overwhelming embarrassment…until it suddenly hit him. He still hadn't receive a text from Alisa.

Which means Alya probably hasn't—… Oh, wait! She left her phone at my house yesterday, so there's no way she could have seen it! So if I delete it before she spots it, then…!

The person he was worried about watching the video most still hadn't seen it yet. That sudden glimmer of hope was enough to make him forget that Yuki had already gone home, and he dashed out of his room.

"Hey! Yuki—"

Right as he rushed into the living room…he discovered Alisa slumped over the table and faintly trembling, and he froze.

"…! Pfft! Hfff…!"

Alisa had her face buried into her left arm, her back softly bouncing as she inhaled with each faint laugh, and in her right hand…was her phone, which was supposed to be on the table in Masachika's room.

"Hey, when did I tell you to stop shooting? Oh, I get it. You're tired of looking at me from the other side of the lens. You want to see me up close with your own two eyes. Heh! Fine…"

"…!!"

Masachika heard what was clearly his own voice coming from the phone and collapsed to his knees.

"Y-Yuki... Yukiiiiiiiii!" he growled from the depths of his heart while on all fours. "What did I doooooo?!"

"Pfft!! Hff!!"

Alisa's almost silent cackling as she inhaled with each laugh meshed with the cries of Masachika's soul. That was when the phone in his hand began to vibrate, so he looked down at the screen and saw it was a message from Yuki:

> It's your fault for being so popular.

CHAPTER 10

A Ditz and a Pro

"Sigh…"

An unbefitting, sorrowful sigh echoed in the cute room decorated with countless stuffed animals of all sizes. The one sighing was Maria, who was lying in bed while clutching a cat plushie in one arm and gazing at a picture in a golden locket she held in her other hand, uncharacteristically listless.

"Sah…"

The name of the man she loved fell from her lips. Her voice, which was usually brimming with mirth when she uttered his name, was now filled with pain and sadness.

"Will we never meet again…?" she muttered pessimistically before almost immediately shaking her head, burying her face in her pillow, and curling into a ball.

"…Just a little longer. Just until summer break is over…," Maria repeated to herself, holding the locket close to her heart, perhaps in hopes that they would be reunited one day—or perhaps fearing their reunion.

Knock-knock.

After a few minutes went by, Maria heard a knock, so she lifted her face off the pillow just enough to see the door with one eye, and replied, "Yes?"

"…Masha? Can we talk?"

"…! Alya?!"

Maria jumped up in her bed with so much energy and excitement that the gloomy mood from earlier seemed like a distant dream. She got over things quickly, to say the least.

"Wh-what's wrong?!"

It was rare for Maria's distant sister to stop by her room—so rare that it would only occur once every two weeks at most, which is why she immediately ran to the door. Although Alisa was somewhat taken aback by how quickly her sister answered, Maria's face instantly lit up with a bubbly smile as if to say, "Alisa's here! Nothing else matters!"

"...Were you sleeping?"

Alisa seemed a bit worried that she was bothering her sister, after seeing her disheveled hair, but Maria proudly puffed out her chest and smiled even wider, dispelling any worries Alisa once had.

"Nope! I was just rolling around in my bed! Anyway, what did you need?"

"Oh..."

Alisa rolled her eyes, since her sister seemed to be overly proud about being a lazy bum.

"Uh..."

She then paused for a few moments and looked away. She fidgeted with her hair before hesitantly continuing:

"You know how we're going to the beach next week...and we need a bathing suit? Well, I was wondering if you already got yours."

The last time the Kujou sisters went to the beach was more than four years ago, and because they hadn't gone swimming for fun since then, they had far outgrown their old bathing suits. Of course, they had their school swimsuits, but even Alisa understood that wearing those outside school was social suicide. Therefore, she wanted to talk to someone who was in the same predicament as her. In other words...

"Not yet. I was considering going bathing-suit shopping today or tomorrow, though," replied Maria with a brilliant smile, since she had a good idea what Alisa was going to say next. Lo and behold, Alisa glanced in her sister's direction but immediately averted her gaze once

more and suggested, "Then…how about we go together? I'm free right now, so we might as well…"

Alisa invited Maria on a date! Maria's IQ decreased by 5!

"Yeah, sure! Let's go! *Giggle!* Alya and I are going on a date!"

"It's not a date."

"When do you want to go? I'm free all day."

"Oh, uh… How about in thirty minutes?"

"Okay! I'll start getting ready right now!"

As excited as a dog with its tail wagging furiously—she looked as if she was about to start humming gleefully at any moment—Maria closed the door and started to get changed. It was hard to believe this was the same young woman who'd been moping in bed only a few minutes before, but once again, Maria could get over things quickly. After she finished getting ready, the Kujou sisters departed from their home and started their adventure.

"*Vroom, vroom!* Let's go!"

The instant Maria reached out to grab Alisa's hand, Alisa coldly brushed her away.

"I'm not going to hold your hand."

"Aww. ♪" Maria pouted and rushed after her sister, who had begun walking ahead dismissively.

"Come on, Alyaaa! Wait for meee! You're walking way too fast!"

"No, you're walking too slow."

"You're just going to feel even hotter in this sun if you walk that quickly. Come on, let's take our time and talk."

"I don't have anything I want to talk about."

"Alya! How can you be so cold?!"

They continued this exchange until they reached the closest train station and headed to the platform, attracting attention all along the way.

"Masha, over here."

"Whaaat? But we'd be closer to the stairs if we got on over here."

"I don't care. We're getting on the women-only car."

"Hmm… Fine. ♪"

Maria reluctantly followed Alisa over to the next train car. Obviously, she knew what women-only cars were, and she also understood that some criminals partook in molesting innocent people, but she had never been touched by a creep before, so the reality still hadn't sunk in. In other words, she lacked any sense for danger.

…Technically, she had almost encountered a few train perverts in the past, but either her menacing little sister would kick the stuffing out of them or the menacing vice president of the student council would snap their wrists before they could get their hands on her. So she was never a victim thanks to them, but conversely, she lacked any awareness.

"You need to take the women-only cars, especially when you get on the train alone. Got it? And if there aren't any, you need to be alert at all times. Don't be playing on your phone."

"Yes, ma'am. ♪"

And yet, still following the advice of her concerned sister and friend was perhaps one of Maria's virtues. But after she agreed to be careful, a wrinkle suddenly creased Maria's brow.

"Alya… Did somebody touch you?"

"Huh? No way. I never let my guard down, unlike you."

"Hmm… I usually have my guard up, too. Sah's the only man I'd ever let touch me!" Maria pouted, puffing out her cheeks and placing both hands on her hips in an offended manner.

"Yeah… Right…," Alisa muttered, frustrated, while checking out Maria from head to toe. It was no surprise she felt skeptical, either, since Maria's outfit that day had her shoulders and midriff exposed, which didn't really come across as "guarded." Her smooth, healthy, milky-white skin was attracting an incredible amount of attention, and yet Maria mirthfully placed a hand on her hat and casually posed, either unconcerned by or unaware of their gazes.

"Oh, my outfit? It's cute, right?"

"…I'll admit that it's cute, but I wouldn't wear it."

"What? But it's breathable, so it'll keep you cool on hot days like this."

"You're going to catch a cold," Alisa replied curtly and glared at the rudely gawking men around them. After she promptly grabbed Maria and dragged her onto the train, they rode for around fifteen minutes and got off at a large station where they usually went to shop for clothes. Then they headed over to the sizable shopping mall across the street. But once they took the elevator up to the women's clothing floor, Maria's eyes instantly began to sparkle as she took in the various articles of clothing.

"That outfit is so cute!"

And she immediately stepped into a shop that obviously didn't sell swimsuits... Alisa promptly grabbed her by the wrist and stopped her, as if she had predicted her sister would do this.

"We're here to buy bathing suits, right? Come on."

"Whaaat? Wait. I'll be quick. I just want to look a little. ♪"

But Alisa continued to drag her away as if her sister's pitiful cries were no concern of hers. She didn't hesitate at all, since she was painfully aware of how her free-spirited sister went wherever there was something that caught her eye if left to wander of her own accord.

"Ah! That's the skirt I saw on TV!"

"......"

"Oh, they're having a going-out-of-business sale! Alya, everything is half price!"

Even Alisa was genuinely tempted when she heard that, but she had no intention of joining one of her sister's never-ending shopping sprees, so she made sure to keep facing forward and press on. Only when they finally reached the entrance to the bathing-suit shop did Maria finally begin to calm down.

"Wow! Look at all the cute bathing suits!"

...Calm as a kid in a candy store for the first time. After a brief sigh, Alisa took a quick look around, then frowned.

"...? Alya? What's wrong?"

Alisa took a sweeping glance of the shop once more...then curiously tilted her head.

"Is it just me, or are all these really revealing?"

"Hmm... I don't know. They all look like ordinary bathing suits to me."

Maria pointed at a one-piece swimsuit hanging on a wall.

"If you're that worried, then you could wear something like that. It—"

"You could see my legs if I wore that."

"...Your legs?"

Taken aback by her sister's unexpected remark, Maria turned around and faced Alisa with a completely serious expression, only to discover Alisa looked beyond serious as well. She blinked for a few moments.

"Uh... Alya? You can usually see people's legs when they wear bathing suits. Like—"

"No. This isn't the school pool. There will be boys with us at the beach, right? Your thighs should be covered just like they usually are."

"Um... So...?"

Maria was officially confused.

"We need a bathing suit that covers our stomach and thighs," Alisa stated with a straight face as if this was obvious.

This isn't good, immediately thought Maria. While she knew her sister never let her guard down around the opposite sex, Alisa was going to be the proud new owner of a wet suit as this rate. From Maria's point of view as a fellow woman, that was out of the question, and as someone who loved her little sister, she wanted Alisa to wear something cute. Nevertheless, recommending a bathing suit to her sister would only have the opposite effect. It was glaringly obvious Alisa would simply criticize her taste in clothes and ignore anything she suggested, which Alisa made clear earlier today when she said she would never wear a shirt that exposed her midriff. Therefore...

"Alya, I think it's a good thing that you're modest, but there's a time and a place for everything."

Saying there was a time and a place for something would get the attention of any decent person—or at least, anyone who was trying to be a decent person, and Alisa was no exception. Her eyebrows twitched, and she gazed down at Maria, who was looking straight into her sister's eyes.

"Although we're officially going to the beach house for student council business, it's really just a social trip to get to know one another better. In other words, we're supposed to relax and have fun, so shouldn't we dress appropriately for the occasion?" argued Maria sincerely.

"...I get that, but how does showing more skin help anything?"

"Because if you completely cover yourself like you think everyone's a creep, then it's going to look like you're not even interested in socializing or becoming friends with anyone. It would kill the mood, at the very least. Besides, you know how Japan has a culture of 'naked bonding' as they call it, right? Like going to bathhouses and hot springs together, right?"

"Hmm..."

Alisa was at a loss for words, since Maria did have a point, and obviously, Maria wasn't going to let this rare opportunity slip by.

"Besides, we're going to a private beach, so it's not like a bunch of random strangers are going to see you in your swimsuit."

"...Masachika and Touya will be there."

"Don't worry about that. Touya only has eyes for Chisaki. And Kuze? I'm sure he'll be busy staring at me."

"Huh?"

Maria boastfully puffed her chest out before her sister, who was raising her eyebrows in bafflement.

"Kuze is a boy, after all, and you know how they are. They're obsessed with girls' chests. They can't stop staring. So...when he sees me in my cute bathing suit, he's probably not going to be able to look away."

She bashfully covered her chest with both hands and squirmed a bit, but her uncharacteristically vain remark made Alisa smile stiffly and lit the flames of competition in her blue eyes.

"Heh... Aren't you confident? Are you suggesting that this plump chest of yours along with that plump stomach makes you better than *me*?"

Alisa made sure to emphasize the word *me* as she crossed her arms, leaning her upper body back as if to show off her figure. She then glanced at Maria's exposed midriff with a meaningful gaze and sniffed haughtily, but Maria wasn't fazed by such low-level taunting.

"You still have so much to learn, Alya. Boys like girls with a little meat on them. I think your well-toned body is wonderful, though," she replied as if to console her little sister while proudly emphasizing her chest as well. One of Alisa's eyes immediately began to twitch in annoyance at her sister's unusually bold attitude, since she took a lot of pride in her appearance. She worked far harder than Maria to maintain her figure, so it was unforgivable to be told that the fruit of her labor was inferior to what she considered excessive softness due to a carefree lifestyle; there was no way she would ever acknowledge such as fact.

"Hmph. Aren't we full of confidence today? Don't blame me if you start feeling embarrassed next to my perfect figure, though."

"Go ahead. I guess that means you're going to be getting a bikini?"

"...Hmm?"

"It'd be pointless if you didn't show off your stomach. ♪ Don't worry. I'll wear a bikini, too. ♪ Oh, hey. This one would look great on you."

Maria was already picking out swimsuits before Alisa could even process what had just happened. That was when a sales associate with glasses and hair tightly pulled back approached them and chimed in.

"Sorry for interrupting, but I believe that swimsuit might be a little too small for you. I recommend going one size larger," she suggested, pushing up her glasses.

"Huh?"

Maria promptly turned around, looked hard at Alisa's chest, and commented:

"Alya, have they gotten bigger *again*?"

"L-like you're one to talk."

"Yeah, I guess you're right... Do you think it's Mom's cooking? They just won't stop growing."

She shifted her gaze away from Alisa, who was twisting her body in odd positions and looking straight down at her chest in a troubled manner.

"Brace yourself, Alya. Your back isn't going to be happy."

"Brace myself for what? ...Is this really the appropriate time to be having this conversation?!"

But right as she was about to snatch the swimsuit out of Maria's hand, the sales associate swiftly grabbed one that was a size larger and slid in front of Alisa.

"How about trying this on?"

"Huh? But..."

"You'll never know unless you try. First, put this on and see what you think. It should give you an idea of what kind of swimsuit is best for you. Please follow me."

Before Alisa knew what was happening, she was being politely pushed into a changing room.

"I'm impressed. Thank you," said Maria, giving the sales associate a thumbs-up.

"I'm only doing my job."

"A real professional... By the way, I didn't catch your name."

"My apologies. I'm Watanabe, the shop manager."

She pointed at the name tag on her chest while pushing up her glasses, causing light to reflect off the professional's lenses.

"By the way, are you two sisters?"

"Oh, yes. Yes, we are. ♪ I'm the older sister, by the way ♪," added Maria, since people always thought she was the younger one due to her being shorter and having a youthful-looking face. But Watanabe conveyed not even a hint of surprise, nodding as if she understood completely.

"Yes, I can tell. And you are searching for the perfect bathing suit for your little sister, yes?"

"Exactly! She'd choose a wet suit if I wasn't here to stop her... Hold on."

That was when Maria suddenly realized she didn't hear a single sound coming from the changing room, so she cracked the curtain open slightly and poked her head inside.

"Alya, is everything okay?"

"What the...?! What is wrong with you?!"

Alisa suddenly turned around in utter astonishment, grimacing, with the bathing suit still in her hand...just as Maria expected.

"Hurry up and get changed. ♪ The shop manager is waiting for you."

"But... But this..."

It was only natural Alisa would be hesitant, since the bathing suit in her hand was, in a way, the most bikini of all bikinis in existence. It was solid black with no ribbon or frills. In fact, there was hardly any bikini. It was thin string with a little bit of fabric attached to it. That was all. It was like something you'd see a Western supermodel wear on the runway or in a magazine.

"I can't do it! I can't wear this!" she cried, thrusting the bikini forward...

The hero of this tale, Watanabe, suddenly appeared.

"How about this one?"

In the shop manager's hand was a pink bikini that would clearly cover far more than the other one. The edges were frilly and cute in a girly way.

"Oh, I guess I could wear this..."

Were these really the words of a girl who claimed she wasn't going to expose her thighs and stomach? Alisa was completely oblivious to the obvious door-in-the-face technique being used against her as she accepted the bikini being handed to her. A few minutes went by, and then she emerged from the changing room in the bikini.

"You look sooo cute. ♪"

"That looks very good on you. That bikini style is extremely popular this year, but you're the first person I've seen who has managed to look this good in it."

"R-really?"

She probably would have just brushed it off if it was Maria saying that, but even Alisa seemed to fall for the professional's smooth compliment.

"But I feel like pink's a little too cute for me…"

"I see. Then how about this?"

As Watanabe swiftly extended her arm to her side, another sales associate suddenly appeared with a new swimsuit. Perhaps all the employees there did special training for this sort of situation.

"This one is the same style, but as you can see, it has a more elegant look to it with its flower pattern over blue—"

Alisa continued to try on six bikinis in the end thanks to Watanabe not exaggerating or overselling any single item.

"Hmm… This one could work."

At long last, it was when she tried on a sky-blue striped bikini with big frills did Alisa's lips finally curl into a pleased smile, and Maria immediately capitalized on this moment, knowing this would be her only chance.

"Yeah, that bikini is so cute."

"Y-yeah, but…"

Alisa checked herself in the mirror once more as if the excitement had started to wear off.

"Maybe it is a little too revealing," she worried, frowning.

"Whaaat? That's nothing compared with what I'm going to be wearing," Maria interjected with a mystified expression and held up a white bikini with only a few pieces of string holding the thing together in the middle. In other words, her cleavage would be in full view for anyone to see. Being presented with an even bolder choice started to make Alisa doubt herself.

"But my legs…"

Even then, she couldn't help but feel concerned as she looked down at her exposed thighs. And once again, Watanabe appeared out of nowhere with a piece of fabric in her hand.

"Then how about wearing this pareu cover-up if you're worried about showing too much leg? If you purchase this with your bikini, I could give you a special discount of…"

It was as if a calculator magically appeared in Watanabe's hand as she rapidly punched in a number at the speed of light, then showed it to Alisa.

The words *special discount* alone had Alisa inclined to accept the offer, and a few minutes later, she was standing in front of the mirror while wearing the pareu. She nodded slowly.

"All right, I'll take it…"

"Thank you very much. I'll have someone grab you a new bikini and pareu from the back."

Once the shop manager, Watanabe, clapped her hands, an employee immediately disappeared into the back of the store. Although the expeditious procedure somewhat weirded out Alisa, she and her sister went to the register together and purchased their swimsuits.

"Thank you very much. Please come again."

The Kujou sisters left the store together as Watanabe and her extremely well-trained employees saw them off. Now that Alisa had accomplished her goal, her mind was already set on going home… but Maria, on the other hand, acted like she was just getting started; she looked over at her sister with sparkles in her eyes.

"So what's next?"

"'What's next?' I figured we'd go home…"

"Whaaat? Come on, let's look around some more. ♪"

"No way. You take forever."

"You're such a meanie." Maria pouted, but her complaints didn't slow down Alisa, who was walking straight toward the elevator. Nevertheless, there was something about her little sister's curtness that was making Maria wonder if there was a specific reason why she wanted to go home.

Hmm... Oh! Maybe she wants to put on a bikini fashion show? I get that! Buying new clothes is so exciting, after all!

...Maria could be kind of an airhead from time to time, according to her friends and family, but she was painfully unaware of this trait of hers, and she would never admit it, either.

She was probably just too shy to really enjoy herself because that shop manager and I were there. I bet she plans on having her own little fashion show once we get home. Wow, just thinking about it makes me want to have a fashion show, too. ♪

Because it all made sense in her head. Everything she said was based on logic from her point of view. The only problem was that...

"All right, Alya. We can go home, but I want to join you, so can you wait for me before you start the fashion show?"

"...What are you talking about?"

...Maria always went straight to her conclusion without any buildup, so her so-called airheaded remarks simply sounded extremely sudden and random to the listener. Obviously, this was no exception, since Alisa had no idea what she was talking about and shook her head, giving up trying to understand what Maria meant. This randomness was nothing new to her.

"Anyway, here. I'll take your swimsuit back home with me."

"Really? Thank you so much. ♪"

Alisa took the plastic bag out of Maria's hand before briskly heading over to the elevator. After Maria saw her off, she checked her watch, pondered silently for a few moments, then got on the next elevator and took it to the first floor, where she left the mall without even checking out another store.

"Hmm... I wonder if I can walk there from here?" Maria muttered to herself while taking a path with her phone's map app open. Her destination was a certain place she would go whenever she had free time, and she had been doing this ever since she returned to Japan. Although she usually went there by bicycle, she was going to walk there today. She was going to walk there, and yet...

"Oh? What's that shop?"

Maria's eyes were still drawn to every cute store in sight, and her legs naturally took her into a little knickknack store on the street to the right as if she were being slowly sucked inside. After ten minutes of window-shopping, she departed from the store and took a left without even thinking about it, despite the fact that she needed to take a right to reach her destination. She continued walking for a few more minutes when...

"Hmm?"

She suddenly realized that she had strayed extremely far from the path she was supposed to be taking, so she stopped and checked the map app on her phone again.

"Hmm... Oh, I think I just need to go this way."

And once again, she began walking in the complete opposite direction without a moment of hesitation. If it wasn't clear...Maria was extremely bad with directions and got lost easily. She would usually tell her friends and family that she liked going for walks around town, but in reality, she was merely lost half the time. Of course, she would never admit that, though, because...

"Oh my. That's strange... I'm here."

...no matter how bad she was with directions, she would somehow always miraculously arrive at her destination. Out of nowhere, she caught a glimpse of a familiar sight out of the corner of her eye, so she started heading in its direction in a somewhat bewildered manner. Her destination was the corner of a large park with tons of equipment for children to play on. Maria resolutely walked straight down the path until she reached a large dome-shaped piece of playground equipment with holes of all different sizes. After briefly stopping in front of it, she climbed up to the top, unfolded a small plastic sheet, and sat on it before briefly scanning the area as if she was looking for something.

"...Just as I thought. He didn't come," she muttered downheartedly with a pout, looking up at the sky as if to hide the loneliness in her heart.

"It's okay, though. I'll wait. Destiny is something you create for yourself, after all," she added as if she was trying to convince even herself of that. She puffed out her cheeks and began quietly watching the clouds go by. She waited like this for another twenty minutes in the hot summer sun when…

"Oh, there you are! Hey!"

She jumped, taken aback by the sudden voice, but she almost immediately realized that it wasn't *his* voice, and she lowered her gaze with a hint of disappointment. Standing at the foot of the dome were seven elementary-school kids whom she knew.

"Maria!"

"Big Sister Maria's here!"

"Let's play!"

As seven smiling boys and girls merrily looked up at her, she cheerfully grinned back and climbed down the dome.

"Sounds good to me. ♪ What do you want to do today? I'm not going to lose this time ♪," she replied brightly, and just like that, she joined the elementary-school children and began to play her heart out. They played a game of hide-and-seek where the entire park was fair game, they played games together on their phone in the shade when they got tired, and Maria even enjoyed girl talk with the girls in the group. The entertainment continued until the sun began to set, and the children had to go home.

"Bye, guys. ♪" Maria returned the children's waves until they disappeared into the distance. She then looked back at the dome once more and smiled somewhat sorrowfully. It was as though she could see the endearing young boy from years ago standing there, and it elicited a sweet heartache.

All of a sudden, a powerful gust of wind blew, forcing Maria to hold her hair down and look away while closing her eyes. But when she looked back at the dome, the mirage of the young boy was no longer there.

"…I'll come back to see you again soon, Sah."

Maria left the park with those words, withdrawing from the memorable place with a slight frown.

(CHAPTER 11) **A Meal and a Mystery**

"Enjoying your summer break?"

"I guess. What about you, President?"

"Yeah, same. I feel like I'm using my time productively, at least."

Two guys were sitting on their beds and facing each other in the boys' room on the second floor of the vacation home. Normally, there would be so much more two guys could talk about when they were alone like this, but they weren't putting any effort into the conversation. As a result, they ended up basically talking about nothing, even though their mouths were moving. It made sense, though, since they—Touya, mainly—couldn't think about anything except for the kitchen on the first floor.

There was a spacious kitchen on the first floor of the Kenzaki vacation home, and right now, five girls were in the middle of a battle. Although this may have sounded like an exaggeration, they were, in fact, having a cook-off. It all started because of an idea that Yuki came up with on the train there. Yuki suggested that the girls in the group should all prepare one dish for dinner, but since that alone wouldn't be fun, she proposed that they have the two boys taste each dish and pick which one they liked the best. The only catch was that the girls wouldn't tell the boys who made what dish. Although Chisaki seemed to be the most enthusiastic about it, they all ended up agreeing to go along with the idea in the end.

As a result, the two boys in the group were forced to wait in their room to keep things fair while the five girls were cooking. Unfortunately, the spacious kitchen still wasn't big enough for five people to cook separate dishes at once, so they had to take turns cooking, with one group of two and one group of three. However…

"Uh… Yep."

"……"

Touya continued to stare at the door, meaninglessly grunting words and obviously feeling uneasy. It was understandable, though. Unlike Masachika, who would be able to rate the food with ease, Touya was only concerned about which dish was cooked by the girl he loved most. What was important to him was not the taste. All he cared about was figuring out which dish Chisaki made.

"So, uh… By the way…"

"Hmm?"

"Have you ever eaten Chisaki's cooking before?"

"…Never."

"Cool…"

Of course, only one dish could be the most delicious, but it was possible that they'd be asked what dish was their second favorite, especially if Touya accidentally didn't pick Chisaki's dish on his first try. And if he picked the wrong dish again—… The thought alone was terrifying. Even Masachika didn't want to see their relationship sour. After all, who would want to see such a beautiful blue sea stained dark red?

"Uh… I don't mean this in any kind of rude way…but is Chisaki not good at cooking? Or does she just not like to cook?"

"Good question. She has never really talked about it…so I guess, maybe?"

"And yet she's seemed really fired up about the cook-off ever since Yuki brought it up…"

"…Chisaki has developed a Pavlovian response to accepting competitions. That's all."

"Oh…"

Masachika thought back to how riled up Alisa got whenever there was a competition, and it started to make sense to him. After collecting himself, he spoke up in a more encouraging manner and claimed:

"This might actually be a good thing, though! All you have to do is choose the dish that looks like it was obviously made by someone who doesn't cook!"

"Hmm… I have mixed feelings when you put it that way, but maybe you're right."

Masachika firmly nodded back at the student council president, who had his head tilted back so he was looking up at the ceiling.

"First off, Ayano can cook. And according to Alya, Masha is good at cooking, too. Alya isn't a bad cook, either, and Yuki…doesn't make bad food, despite messing up from time to time. Honestly, I'll probably be able to figure out which dishes Yuki and Ayano cooked. And… Alya has a habit of cutting vegetables and whatnot absolutely perfectly, so you should be able to tell just by looking at it what dish she cooked."

"O-oh, interesting… Wait. You've eaten their cooking before? All three of them?"

"W-well, I mean, Yuki and Ayano are childhood friends of mine, and I tried a little of Alya's cooking the other day…," Masachika mumbled somewhat ambiguously before clearing his throat and adding, "Anyway, I'll give you a sign if I figure out who cooked what dish. If you know what the other three cooked, then you'll have a fifty-fifty chance of picking the right dish. Even if you mess up at first and choose Masha's dish, you can still fix things pretty easily, right?"

"W-wow, I really appreciate it, Kuze."

"…The only thing we need to worry about is Yuki or Ayano trying to be original and deliberately cooking something they wouldn't usually."

Masachika lowered his tone and expressed this concern right as Touya was beginning to see a ray of hope in the darkness. After all, it was Yuki who'd proposed this cook-off. It was very possible that she was going to make something she had never cooked before, since she knew that Masachika would be able to pick out her dish if she cooked what she usually made. It was also possible that she ordered Ayano to make something new and unique as well.

"…Are you sure you're not overthinking things? Would she really go out of her way to cook something new when she was the one who proposed the cook-off? It's too risky."

"I really hope I'm overthinking things…"

Touya made a very valid point, but Masachika knew his sister. He knew that she was more interested in making the cook-off "fun" than winning.

"By the way…I heard on TV that Russians love mayonnaise," Touya commented, looking up to the side as if he was trying to remember something.

"You what?"

Masachika tilted his head in a puzzled manner.

"A show said that Russians put mayonnaise in basically anything they make, so I was thinking that maybe this could help us figure out which dishes the Kujou sisters made."

"Russians using mayonnaise in most of their cuisine? Not sour cream? I've never heard that before, and my grandfather, who has been to Russia before, never mentioned anything about mayonnaise, either…"

"Maybe they don't use it in cuisine they serve to tourists, but they use it at home when cooking for family?"

"Hmm… I don't know if we should be putting so much faith in some random TV show… Besides, Russia's a big country. Even Japan has vastly different food culture when you compare Kanto with Kansai, so I imagine a country as massive as Russia would be far more varied, right?"

"Hmm… I guess you're right. If someone told me that Japanese people loved soy sauce, I'd agree, but that doesn't mean it's used in every Japanese dish…"

"Right? So I don't know if we should put too much faith in what you heard on that show…but if there is a dish completely covered in mayonnaise, then maybe we should consider the possibility."

"That just sounds awful," said Touya grimly, then laughed, which was followed by a few chuckles from Masachika as well. After that,

Masachika stared at the door to the room in silence for a few moments before glancing at Touya once more.

"…Want to go see how things are going?"

"What? But they told us not to step foot in the kitchen or—"

"We're just going to the bathroom. Hearing them talking might be able to give us some clues, right?"

"I see. Interesting."

After exchanging firm nods, they decided to crouch for some reason or another and left the room. Cautiously descending the stairs, they tried to listen for any voices coming from the kitchen or living room behind the closed doors, until they could somewhat hear the faint sounds of people cooking coming from the kitchen.

The steady rhythm of something thumping against a hard surface must have been a kitchen knife. The sizzling hinted that something was cooking in a frying pan. But it was Maria's sudden voice that made both of them freeze and strain their ears.

"It smells so good. ♪ The longer you cook vegetables, the better they taste, don't they? Maybe I should add some pepper and give it a little kick?"

"I know what you mean," replied Ayano.

"Add some pepper…and give it a little *kick*? Interesting…," muttered Chisaki. A few heavy thuds and smacks followed their conversation for some reason. Both Masachika and Touya began to wonder what was causing those mystifying sounds…when all of a sudden, there was silence. Another brief moment went by…

Clang…

The gratifying sound of something hitting metal echoed from the kitchen, followed by silence. After a few seconds went by, the sound of cooking resumed, like background music slowly fading in.

"…Did Chisaki cut something?" whispered Touya.

"…With what? A katana?" Masachika whispered back.

They stared off into the distance while standing in the middle of the staircase together until Ayano's voice finally snapped them out of their daze.

"It's usually better if you roast them a little."

"Really? …You're pathetic. I've never seen weaker vegetables in my life. You didn't even put up a fight when I cut you."

"Chisaki…? Why are you insulting the vegetables?"

…For some reason, chaos could be heard coming from the kitchen, especially when it came to whatever Chisaki was doing. When Masachika looked back, Touya was staring into the distance in a daze… which was incredibly understandable.

…*Don't let it bother you. It'll be okay.*

When Masachika sympathetically placed his hand on the student council president's shoulder, Touya looked back up the staircase with a philosophical gaze, then crouched as low as he could for his massive size and returned to their room. Meanwhile, Masachika decided to head over to the bathroom to make their potential excuse more credible, so he stood…and found Alisa glaring at him with a chilling gaze from the side of the staircase.

"……"

"……"

They exchanged glances for a few seconds until Masachika slowly descended the stairs, briskly walked straight over to Alisa, and crossed his arms.

"Let's remain calm," he whispered in a consoling voice as he guided Alisa away from the living room. "It's not what you think," he claimed with a pointlessly smug expression.

"What do you mean? It's exactly how it looks. And who gave you permission to touch me?"

Wearing a look of disgust, Alisa smacked the wrist holding her bare upper arm.

"Oops. My bad."

Didn't she tell me in Russian the other day that she didn't mind if I touched her? he thought in the back of his mind, promptly letting go of her. Alisa then rubbed her upper arm and grouchily muttered:

"<You need to be gentler.>"

"I'm really sorry."

All Masachika could do was genuinely apologize after that, but at the same time, he couldn't help but wonder if that meant he could touch her as long as he was gentle. He bowed, lowering his head…and found himself accidentally staring at a beautiful mountain range.

Yep. I mean, this is awesome, but when compared with the sensation of actually touching her…

The thought naturally crossed his mind. *Oh, she's actually wearing a bra this time*, he simultaneously noted as well.

"You creep…"

Alisa's lips twisted with pure revulsion while she glared at him with a reproachful gaze as if she could read his mind. She immediately took a step back, covering her chest.

"Not only were you eavesdropping, but you're a degenerate as well. There's seriously no hope for you," she hissed, her voice brimming with disgust.

"Hey, come on. I'm not a degenerate or a creep."

"Hmph! You didn't deny eavesdropping."

"Oh, uh… That's…"

After stammering out a few words, Masachika briefly sighed and decided to tell her the truth.

"I might not have anything to worry about, but Touya has to say the best-tasting dish is whatever Chisaki makes, right? So I thought I could do a little scouting. That's all."

"Oh?"

Alisa stopped covering her chest and raised an eyebrow as if she was somewhat satisfied with his reasoning.

"Anyway, I get it. But I don't think Chisaki would be happy if she figured out one of the judges was simply trying to guess which dish is hers. She's serious about winning."

"Y-yeah, that's… Yeah…"

"Besides, even if she loses, all she has to do is practice and win next time, right? Having a judge guess and choose which one is hers without considering how good the actual dish is robs her of that chance to grow and improve."

"Er... You have a point." Masachika groaned because she was absolutely right. With that being said, nobody wanted to be depressed at the beach, and a mistake like this could certainly ruin the mood... but Masachika didn't mutter a single word of this, and he grinned.

"Anyway, you don't have to worry about me. I'm going to honestly pick whichever one I like best. Even if I can guess which dish you made, I'm not going to let it influence my decision."

Alisa smirked provocatively back at him.

"Oh, wow. You honestly believe you can figure out which dish I prepared? Though you've only eaten my cooking twice?"

"Yeah, probably. I've already picked up on some of your habits."

"Oh? Have you?"

She smirked while raising an eyebrow as if to say, "I'd like to see you try." Nevertheless, Masachika doubled down and smugly smirked back at her. Before he realized it, he had challenged Alisa to a game where he would have to guess which dish she made. Regardless, he was already on a mission to figure out which dish Chisaki made, so adding Alisa to the mix was no big deal to him.

This is getting kind of exciting, though. This is my chance to correctly guess whose dish is whose and look like a badass.

Although this new challenge may have deviated from the whole purpose of the cook-off, Masachika was fired up, and Alisa could see that.

"Whatever. If you do figure out which dish is mine, you don't need to worry about hurting my feelings, okay?"

"You got it. I'm looking forward to it."

Masachika then turned his back to Alisa and began walking up the stairs to the second floor...

"<Because I'm going to make you choose me.>"

Hnnng?! She's talking about her dish, right...?

...He was struck from behind by her provocative Russian whispers, causing him to stumble the entire way.

An hour had passed, and Masachika and Touya were now sitting in front of a table.

"President Touya, Masachika, please enjoy your meal," requested Yuki on behalf of all the cooks. Her words, however, were followed by complete silence. It seemed like the girls were not going to comment or react to anything so as to not give any hints to the two boys while they ate.

""Thank you all for cooking this wonderful meal.""

Masachika and Touya clasped their hands together to express their appreciation, then shifted their gazes to the dishes lined up on the table as five girls across from them stared eerily at them in silence.

Well, there don't seem to be any dishes covered in mayonnaise.

There wasn't a single dish that looked like a complete failure, contrary to what the boys were led to believe when they overheard all those chaotic noises.

Thank goodness none of the food is so grotesque that it has to be censored like they do in comic books...

But on the other hand, it wasn't obvious who made what. From left to right, it looked like the dishes were fried rice, fried chicken, boiled pot stickers, hamburg steak, and...a mystery soup.

I wonder what that is?

Not only Masachika, but Touya was also mesmerized by the dish on the far-right end, where a large bowl was filled to the brim with some sort of dark-red soup. Seeing as there was sliced French bread lined up by its side, the bread was probably supposed to be dipped in the soup and eaten. There seemed to be diced tomatoes in the soup as well, which might be why it was so red...but it was still a mystery. There were even lemon slices floating on the top...

Is this a cold soup? I mean, there are lemon slices in there… Wait. Is that steam? More important, how is it not going to be sour with both tomatoes and lemons in it? …Yeah, I don't have the courage to dig into that one just yet.

The instant Masachika came to that conclusion, he and Touya exchanged glances and briefly communicated with their eyes. As if there was some sort of mutual understanding, Touya pulled the large plate of fried chicken toward himself and placed a few bite-size pieces on smaller plates for them to share.

They look normal… Looks like…they're garnished with lettuce and tomato. Yeah… Traditional Japanese fried chicken like this doesn't really have anything that makes it stand out visually.

The fried chicken looked good, but the lack of unique characteristics was going to make it hard for Masachika to accomplish his goal, which was discerning which dishes Chisaki and Alisa made.

Well, I guess I'll just have to try it first…

He decided to take a bite of the fried chicken alone. Rich flavors of soy sauce and garlic graced his tongue when he bit into the crispy skin, and the savory chicken itself almost melted in his mouth.

"Mm-hmm… This is good."

"Yeah, it really is."

Their impressions naturally rolled off their tongues…while they immediately glanced at the five girls across from them to see how they'd react. But unfortunately, not one of them even blinked.

I should have known they wouldn't give themselves away that easily… Anyway, this chicken is legitimately good.

Next up was to try it with the onions and lettuce, which also ended up tasting outstanding together, since the fried chicken was especially rich.

Like, I'm sure the taste is thanks to some store-bought fried chicken mix, but it isn't easy deep-frying chicken and getting it to be this perfectly crispy, so whoever made this has to be pretty good at cooking.

Masachika's chopsticks naturally reached for a second and third piece of fried chicken, but he caught himself before things got out of hand and decided to move on to the next dish. The next large plate that Touya reached for ended up being the fried rice on the left.

It looks like there's egg, scallion, cabbage, fish cake... There isn't any meat? It's pretty simple as far as fried rice goes.

On the other hand, whoever made this probably had to be pretty confident to go with something so basic for a cook-off.

I'm actually looking forward to this one.

With a dash of excitement, Masachika scooped some of the fried rice off his small plate and into his mouth.

It's pretty good...but it's kinda bland...

It was honestly a little bit disappointing. Maybe it tasted so bland because he ate such rich fried chicken first. You could say it had a very refined taste if you wanted to look at it positively, but for someone like Masachika, who usually stuffed his mouth with garlic fried rice when he cooked at home, it was slightly underwhelming.

Well, I guess it's good that I can keep eating it without getting sick of it...but I'd kill for some yellow pickled radish on the side.

Although he personally wasn't a huge fan, that didn't mean the fried rice tasted bad, so he simply reported that it was good and left it at that. Regardless, none of the girls reacted.

Touya grabbed the plate of boiled pot stickers following the fried rice. These weren't particularly garnished. In fact, it was basically nothing more than pot stickers being around 70 percent submerged in soup. What stood out was the fact that there weren't any creases in the edges.

It sounded like Chisaki was using vegetables in her dish when we were eavesdropping, so this most likely is not hers.

With that in mind, he brought a single pot sticker to his mouth—

"Mn...?!"

The ingredients inside the pot sticker took him completely by surprise.

Th-this isn't ground beef... It's mashed potatoes!

The soup tasting like consommé caught him off guard, but even then, the flavor of the pot stickers absolutely blew his mind. The sweetness of the soup-flavored mashed potatoes tickled his meat-expecting taste buds.

What the...? But...this is actually pretty good.

After exchanging stunned glances with Touya, Masachika simply uttered, "This is good," which he truly believed, and that was why he also started to doubt that Chisaki was this dish's chef. On the other hand, if Chisaki was cutting and mashing potatoes, it would explain all those mystifying sounds, thuds, and smashing they heard earlier.

This is bad... This is a lot harder than I thought. If only Alya and Masha went with something easy to pick out, like Russian cuisine...

That was when Masachika was hit with an epiphany from the heavens.

W-wait...! Is this...? Now it makes sense!

He didn't pick up on it at first because they genuinely looked like pot stickers, but he was almost sure of it now. These weren't pot stickers.

These are pelmeni! These are Russian dumplings!

Pelmeni was a popular Russian dish even in Japan. Although Masachika had heard of it, he had never eaten it before, but he was able to figure out what it was due to the thought of Russian cuisine crossing his mind.

I vaguely remember Grandpa mentioning that pelmeni can have various different ingredients for the filling... So...this...

This meant that there was a high chance of this dish being either Alisa's or Maria's. The taste was nothing like anything Masachika had ever experienced before, so it would be hard to believe that Yuki or Ayano had anything to do with it.

These are...surprisingly really good.

He only grew more excited with the taste of something new on his tongue as he felt like he was one step closer to finding out which dish Alisa cooked. However, the instant he saw Touya reaching for the next dish, his burning excitement was doused with a cold glass of disappointment.

Oh... He's going for it.

The dish Touya grabbed next…was the mysterious soup on the right. Inside the soup was tomato, bacon, and finely cut vegetables here and there…

The green powder floating on the top… Is that basil? …I seriously can't imagine what this is going to taste like.

After staring hard at the soup in his bowl for a few moments, he decided to come back to the French bread later and take a sip of the soup first.

"…?!"

Immediately, a chill ran down his spine; Touya's eyes opened wide in astonishment as well. That was just how dumbfounded they were. If they could describe the unexpected taste in one word…

"It's pizza…"

"Yeah…"

Masachika took another sip…and the rich flavors of pizza…margherita filled his mouth.

A pizza-flavored soup? …This is seriously puzzling.

But it was good. It was actually good. Masachika took a piece of bread, dipped it into the soup, and tossed it into his mouth.

"This is good, too…"

Every bite was packed full of soup thanks to how spongy the French bread was. Although the soup itself was somewhat on the sour side, the sweetness of the bread really helped bring synergy to the dish.

This is incredible… Hold on. Is this also…?

Another tidbit of knowledge popped into Masachika's mind. Russians often had soup and bread for lunch. In fact, he had also heard that there was a lot of soup in Russian cuisine, so it wouldn't be a complete surprise if this was one of their traditional dishes.

But we're having dinner now, and I think traditionally Russians mainly eat black bread…

Even if this was Russian cuisine, would Alisa or Maria serve this for dinner? If anything, it was probably more likely that someone who had little knowledge of Russian culture simply looked up the recipe and made this dish in order to throw the judges off…

Hmm… I guess I should reserve my judgment until after finishing the last dish, though.

After reaching that conclusion, Masachika decided to hold off on a decision for now and moved on to the next plate. The final dish was a Japanese-style hamburg steak with grated radish on top, doused in a thick sauce that was garnished with mushrooms, broccoli, and a variety of colorful bell peppers. A single hamburg steak was a little too much for one person, so he and Touya ended up cutting one in half and sharing it.

This is like the fried chicken. There aren't really any visual characteristics or clues that make it stand out…

There wasn't even any cheese inside. It appeared to be an ordinary hamburg steak, which proved to be just as tasty as it looked.

"I usually have mine with tomatoes and demi-glace, but this is great, too."

The grated radish, which had absorbed a lot of the thick sauce, was perfectly sweet and went surprisingly well with the hamburg steak. The steak itself was decent, as one would expect by how it looked, but Masachika's tongue was really enjoying the new combination of flavors.

But if you asked me who made this…

He wasn't confident, since he had never had something like this before. His curious mind continued to consider all the possibilities until he finished eating and placed his chopsticks down.

"I think it's time to hear what our judges thought," Yuki suggested gleefully as soon as Touya finished eating. The moment of fate was upon them…but Masachika still hadn't identified which dish was Chisaki's.

The only one that was obviously not hers was the pelmeni. That had to be Masha's or Alya's. That mystery soup could have been their creation as well…but I can't deny the possibility that Yuki made that to throw me off…

Regardless, Chisaki most likely didn't cook either of those, which Masachika let Touya know under the table by using the hand signals they had come up with. Nevertheless, they still had to worry about the fried chicken, hamburg steak, and fried rice, which were all dishes that countless young men from all over the world enjoyed. In addition, there wasn't really much of a gap in the level of perfection among the three dishes, even though Masachika personally wasn't a huge fan of the fried rice.

Was the fried rice made bland on purpose, or did it just end up bland due to a lack of skill in the kitchen? Because that would change a lot...

If it was the latter, then it was highly possible that Chisaki made it. However, if it was the former...

"...All right, I've made up my mind," muttered Touya, catching his fellow judge off guard. Although Masachika still hadn't narrowed down his choices, Touya's eyes were brimming with confidence and determination as he faced forward and clearly stated:

"I liked the fried chicken the best."

A moment of silence swallowed the room. The air was so tense that it felt like an eternity had gone by, until eventually...

"Yesss!!" cheered Chisaki with an elated note in her voice, jumping out of her chair while throwing her fist in the air. Despite the other female members' furrowed brows due to her eliminating one of Masachika's choices, they still congratulated her from the bottom of their hearts.

"I'm so happy for you, Chisaki. ♪"

"Congratulations! You two really are meant for each other."

"Congratulations."

"I'm happy for you. Congratulations."

But amid the applause, Masachika found himself smiling wryly for a different reason.

Heh. You didn't need my help, after all. Ha-ha... Unbelievable.

He felt his fellow judge was full of something for being so nervous, and it wasn't food.

"Touyaaa, come on. Was it really that good?"

"Yes, it...really...was...delicious."

"Really? I'm so glad I've only been focusing on practicing how to cook fried chicken."

"Hmm? 'Only'?"

"*Giggle!* If you really liked it that much, then I guess I could make it for you every so often."

"O-oh, really? That'd be awesome."

Chisaki wasn't even trying to hide how joyful she was as she repeatedly slapped Touya's back. On the other hand, Touya seemed to be struggling to talk as he desperately tried to swallow something back down that he coughed up due to said slapping. Meanwhile, Masachika bitterly narrowed his eyes at the happy couple.

Incidentally, Touya's dietary habits were going to change permanently in the not-so-distant future, for he was going to be blessed with fried chicken for lunch almost every day. And in a way, it would be the ultimate fried chicken lunch box of...only white rice, vegetables, and chicken. But that was another tale for another time.

"That only leaves you now, Masachika. The floor is yours."

"Hmm? Oh..."

After Yuki urged him to go on, Masachika faced forward, where he saw Yuki's amused, ladylike smile; Ayano's blank stare; Maria's bubbly grin; and Alisa's serious, smug expression, as if she was trying to make it seem like she wasn't interested in what he had to say.

"I liked the soup," he honestly admitted amid the stares.

"Oh my. ♪ Really? Hooray! ♪" shouted Maria with delight, clasping her hands together after a moment of disbelief. Immediately, Masachika noticed a crease appear between Alisa's eyes...but he didn't have a choice. Alisa said this was a serious match, so he treated it as such.

"That was your dish, Masha? It was really good. I've never tasted anything like it. By the way, was it some kind of Russian cuisine?"

"Yep. ♪ It's called solyanka."

"Solyanka? I've never heard of that."

"Hmm..."

Maria placed an index finger on her chin as though she was deep in thought for a few moments before nodding firmly.

"If borscht is the Russian equivalent of miso soup, then solyanka would be kind of like the Russian equivalent of pork miso soup, I guess?"

"Seriously? *This* is equivalent to pork miso soup?"

"Come on. It really is similar." She pouted, shaking her fists up and down in frustration.

Yuki suddenly asked, "By the way, do you have any idea who made the remaining three dishes?"

In spite of her ill intent, Masachika's expression was filled with confidence. He was always planning on identifying who cooked what, so he became convinced he had it all figured out after learning who the chefs were behind two of the dishes.

"Let's start with the fried rice. You made this, Ayano, didn't you?"

When he pointed at the fried rice while looking at Ayano, she lowered her gaze and nodded.

"Yes."

"I figured. You purposely made sure it was only lightly seasoned because everyone else was making something very rich, right?"

"Yes... I figured it would complement the other food better this way."

"Ha-ha-ha. Even during a cook-off, you prioritized the judges' enjoyment of the overall meal. That's so like you," said Masachika with a gentle smile, making Ayano jump slightly in embarrassment. Masachika then pointed at the next dish. "And Yuki made this hamburg steak."

"...Yes, you got me. I am impressed."

"I figured you were serious about winning this time. That much was obvious when I tasted it. I did notice you used a little camouflage, though."

The fact that it was a proper, traditional dish made the fact that she seasoned it differently than she usually would stand out all the more. But even then, Yuki continued to feign innocence and merely replied:

"I decided to give it a more refreshing taste when I seasoned it. It is summer, after all."

As if he had been waiting for this moment his whole life, Masachika put on the biggest, smuggest grin he could and pointed at the pot stickers.

"And this…was yours, Alya."

"…Yes," Alisa replied with a grumble, and yet she seemed somewhat happy when she nodded. It was a difficult expression to describe, but she was most likely thrilled that he picked out her dish correctly and, at the same time, annoyed that he saw right through her.

But, well…it was all thanks to that mystery soup. Solyanka, was it? I was only able to figure out what Alya made because I realized that was Masha's dish…

"Incredible. You really have a wonderful talent and exceptional taste buds," complimented Ayano genuinely, unaware of how he'd really done it.

"Hmm? Oh, I guess. Alya's dish was really obvious, though."

As if Ayano's sparkling eyes had given him a confidence boost, Masachika looked smug as he shifted his gaze to Alisa once more.

"I thought they were pot stickers at first, but when I tried one… Pelmeni, right?"

He said this while trying to look like the coolest, smartest guy in the room…but Alisa knit her brow and replied:

"No, it's varenyky."

"The hell is that?"

An astonishingly awkward silence followed.

CHAPTER 12

My Love, My Lord

"Shall we begin?!" asked Yuki playfully, on the edge of her bed in pajamas. It was the first night of the student council social gathering at the Kenzaki family vacation home. Across from Yuki in the girls' room for first-year students was Alisa, who hesitantly replied:

"Are you sure we should really do this? On the bed...?"

She tilted her head as if she was feeling a little guilty, her eyes focused on the bedside table with drinks and snacks on it. There wasn't enough space on the floor for them to sit in a circle, so they decided to sit on the two beds with the table in the middle to share the goodies...but Alisa was so straitlaced, she was reluctant to eat on the bed.

"It will be fine. All we have to do is make sure we don't get any crumbs on the bed or spill anything," assured Yuki, who was on the other side of the bedside table, before she took a bite of a chocolate chip cookie. Ayano, who was sitting by her side, grabbed one of the individually wrapped miniature doughnuts and took a small bite as well, making sure not to get any crumbs anywhere. How she didn't make a sound when she opened the wrapper was a mystery. Incidentally, unlike Yuki and Alisa, Ayano was wearing a negligee. Why? The reason was simple: Because if anything were to happen, she wouldn't be able to swiftly unsheathe her weapons in anything other than a skirt. It was unclear when or why such an emergency would arise, though.

"Hmm... Well, I suppose it'll be okay if we clean up afterward, right?"

Seeing her two schoolmates start snacking seemed to be too much for Alisa, so she negotiated with herself. After leaning forward a little, she threw a piece of chocolate into her mouth and broke into a blissful smile, and seeing Alisa indulge in the sweets made Yuki smile devilishly.

"*Giggle.* Yes, Alya. Just like that. Half the fun of pajama parties is being able to consume all the snacks and drinks you want before bed without worrying about the calories!"

Alisa froze when she heard the word *calories*, but when she saw Ayano quietly take another bite of her doughnut without a care in the world, her eyes naturally drifted toward Ayano's stomach. After a few seconds of contemplation, she naturally reached for the chocolate once more.

…If she thought about it rationally, Ayano's stomach didn't give her enough information to form a decision. Furthermore, the calories she was eating now wouldn't immediately turn into fat in the blink of an eye, but Alisa refused to face reality.

"…I guess if I considered this dessert after dinner, then it would be okay… Besides, I swam a lot today."

She continued to make excuses for herself as she took another bite of chocolate. Meanwhile, Yuki's smile only curled more maliciously, like a demon enjoying watching a human's life spiral out of control into destruction. However, that smile immediately vanished the instant Alisa looked up at her.

"Yes, I agree. Unfortunately, we got so into that cook-off that the idea of making a dessert never even crossed anyone's mind."

"*Giggle.* Maybe we should have a baking contest next, then?"

"That would be so much fun… Oh, I almost forgot."

Yuki appeared to remember something as she grabbed a cup and lifted it somewhat high in the air.

"We may have lost to our upperclassmen in the end, but at least we have our snacks. Let us make a toast to celebrate this moment."

"Ha-ha. Sure, why not?"

Although she smiled wryly at Yuki's suggestion, Alisa grabbed a cup as well. After seeing Ayano quietly pick up a cup, Yuki took the lead and said:

"We may have lost…but at least we are not an idiot like Masa-chika! Cheers!"

"…?! Pfft! Yeah, what an idiot!"

"…?! Ch-cheers?"

After a moment of disbelief, Alisa suddenly burst into gleeful laughter. Ayano hesitantly raised her cup in the air, blinking in surprise. Although it was an awfully rude thing to say, it really helped Yuki and Alisa relax.

"*Sigh*… He really is a jerk, isn't he? Of course, Masha's dish was delicious, but would it have killed him to be a little more specific about what he liked about our dishes?"

"Yeah, and he looked so smug thinking my dish was pelmeni."

"Yes, that was really embarrassing, wasn't it?"

They looked at each other and giggled. But though they were all joking, Ayano was fidgeting uncomfortably, since they were talking poorly about her master.

"Surely, you have something you wish to say about Masachika, too, right, Ayano?" asked Yuki as if she was trying to drag her into the mud with them.

"Huh?! N-no… He is a very kind, wonderful person…," she replied, hunched over.

"…Kind? Wonderful?"

Alisa knit her brow as if she couldn't comprehend the words she was hearing, then thought back to how Masachika treated her. Almost every interaction she could remember was her being teased by him, him poking fun at her, and him messing around.

"…He's kind of a jerk," muttered Alisa, feeling somewhat irritated thinking about him, but Ayano simply blinked and tilted her head curiously as if she had no idea what Alisa could mean.

"A jerk? Really?"

"Y-yeah, he's always teasing me…," complained Alisa, recoiling slightly due to Ayano's innocent, quizzical gaze. But even then, Ayano continued to stare in wonder at Alisa, so Yuki promptly chimed in to clear the air.

"*Giggle.* You could insult Ayano directly, and she would look back at you with a straight face and not even know she was being made fun of. You, though, Alya—you take things so seriously, and your reactions are always so perfect that he must have so much fun teasing you."

"Wait. Really?" Ayano wondered aloud.

"Oh, wow. I'm *so* happy," Alisa responded sarcastically.

"You know how people our age are. The more they like someone, the more they want to tease them."

"Oh? Hmph."

Alisa's eyes widened for a brief moment before she immediately put on a cool, composed expression.

"Yes… I suppose you're right. Maybe—," she said, playing with the ends of her hair… She imagined herself teasing Masachika.

"No. Absolutely not."

She immediately took back what she said and stopped messing with her hair as all emotion vanished from her expression.

"Huh? Is everything okay?"

"Of course? That's not what this is at all. This is an eye for an eye. Nothing more, nothing less."

"…??"

Alisa lightly cleared her throat in the midst of Yuki's bewilderment.

"Wanting to tease someone you like doesn't make any sense to me."

"They want the attention. You know how boys are. They try to flirt with girls they like and mess with them so that the girl pays attention to them. Surely, this has happened to you before?"

"Oh… Yeah. I usually ignore them, though. Do they honestly think girls will like them if they annoy them enough?" Alisa snorted, which made Yuki smirk.

"There are some things that guys never grow out of. They are so immature."

"They really are. You'd think they'd start calming down in high school, but they're always doing something stupid."

"*Giggle.* But do you never see them messing around together and think, 'Wow, that looks like a lot of fun'?"

"Not really. I'm fine with people doing whatever they want as long as they're not bothering others, but I don't think the classroom is the right place to be reading comic books."

"Yes, violating school rules is a problem. I feel that comic books are not that big of a deal, though."

"If they were normal comic books, then maybe. But these guys are looking at the ones with models in skimpy bikinis and drooling all over themselves. I really wish they'd do that at home…"

"Th-that does sound awkward. Speaking of awkward, I never know how to react when I hear them gossiping about girls. When they are whispering, I can easily hear them talking about who they think is cute and who has the biggest chest."

"I know what you mean… And then you realize they're talking about 2D girls. It's exhausting."

"…? Yes… I often hear them talking about the latest anime and arguing about which girl is the best…sometimes."

"Right? But they're arguing about people who don't exist. How can you get so obsessed with a girl who isn't real? You see them playing those gacha games, and they're either the happiest person in the world or their day is ruined depending on who they pull…"

"Hmm…? …Maybe it's easier to become obsessed because these are unrealistic, ideal partners who are too perfect to actually exist?"

Yuki continued to reply like this as a single suspicion began to grow in the back of her mind.

Uh… We're talking about guys in general, right? Is it just my imagination, or is Alya just talking about my brother?

So she decided to put her hypothesis to the test.

"And you know how some boys never help out when it's time to clean up?"

"Yeah, they'll clean only the areas they were assigned, but they won't lift a single finger to help anyone else after that."

This is starting to sound even more like my brother…

"And they always sleep in class right after PE."

"Exactly. They always look sleepy, though."

This is definitely my brother, isn't it?

"Oh, and they're always playing on their phone at school."

"I know, right? But they use some twisted logic to argue that it isn't against school rules to play before class starts."

Yep, that's my brother.

Despite the conversation being about boys in general, Alisa was obviously only talking about Masachika, and that terrifying realization made Yuki grimace.

Uh…? That's strange… Is my brother the only guy who exists in Alya's world? Is she some kind of princess locked in a tower and cut off from the outside world?

If she was doing this consciously, then hurry up and get married to Masachika already, and if she was doing this unconsciously, then you would have to wonder how little of an interest Alisa had in other boys. Whatever the case, it felt like something Yuki shouldn't even attempt to address, so she swiftly shifted her eyes to her side toward her maid.

"By the way, Ayano, is it just me, or have you been quietly eating doughnuts this entire time?"

"Huh? Oh… Yes, I guess I have."

Without the others realizing it, Ayano had already opened a fresh bag of miniature doughnuts and had been transferring each one to a new home in her stomach. Perhaps the real reason they bought two bags this morning was because she was planning on consuming a single bag all by herself.

"You really love fried sweets, don't you? I remember you eating a lot of churros at the amusement park the other day."

"Y-yes…," Ayano replied apologetically with an iron grip locked on the bag of doughnuts.

"Oh, Ayano? I'm not scolding you for enjoying something," Yuki said, smiling awkwardly, before she directed her gaze back to Alisa.

"What kind of sweets do you like, Alya?"

"Me? Hmm… Well, I like chocolate. I'll eat almost any kind of sweet, though."

"Oh, wow. I never knew you had a sweet tooth."

"I guess…? I like…spicy food, too, though…," she added hesitantly and shifted her gaze meaningfully to Ayano, who blinked back in her own meaningful way. Although Yuki had no idea what their stares meant, she could feel some sort of bond between them, which definitely made her curious.

Is this…friendship? No, if anything, it's rivalry… Wait. No. Just what is this?

Yuki decided to bring up something that was bothering her.

"Now that I think about it, you two don't talk that much to each other."

"Huh? Oh, I guess…"

"Are you listening, Ayano? You and Alya should talk more."

"That's… Yes, of course…"

Yuki watched Alisa and Ayano exchange uncertain gazes and felt like she was watching two socially awkward people in a stagnant relationship.

These two… Ugh… They can be a real pain in the ass.

But despite thinking that, Yuki slapped her hands together with an innocent smile.

"We are going to be staying in the same room tonight, so I think we should stop being so distant and really open up to one another."

"Huh…? Yeah, of course. I'm fine with that."

"Yes, I would be fine with that as well, as long as Alisa doesn't mind…"

Seriously, what an irritating pair.

Alisa and Ayano exchanged glances once more as if to make sure it was really okay while Yuki glared at them reproachfully.

"Uh… I'm looking forward to getting to know you, Ayano," uttered Alisa hesitantly.

"Oh. Yes, me too, Alisa…"

Their exchange is too innocent. Which one of them is going to blush first?

Yuki's nerdy mind went straight to the gutter after seeing their unexpectedly homoerotic exchange. It was like something out of a girls' love comic.

Hmm… Alya × Ayano? Or maybe Ayano × Alya? I could see both working… In fact, could I join them? Of course, a guy would be killed if he tried to put himself in the middle of a yuri *relationship, but adding another girl to the mix shouldn't be a problem, right? I wonder if I could get Masha in on this, too, since I know how much she loves Alya.*

"…? Yuki?"

"Oh! Uh…"

Alisa's quizzical gaze instantly dragged Yuki back to reality from her girl-on-girl fantasy, and she asked the first question that came to mind.

"By the way, Alya, why were you so against sleeping in the same room as Masha?"

It was a random question and an act of desperation in an attempt to change the subject, but Alisa didn't seem to find it odd.

"…Because she'd use me as a body pillow." She frowned.

"Huh?"

"Masha always sleeps with a very big body pillow—well, I guess it's closer to a giant stuffed animal? Anyway, sometimes when we go on trips without it, she'll be half asleep and grab whatever's closest to her to use as a body pillow. Whenever we go on family trips—especially when we stay at traditional inns—she'll even sometimes slip into my bed…"

"Oh my. In other words, you're saying Chisaki could be wrapped in her arms as we speak," joked Yuki, but after imagining it for a second, Alisa faintly smirked with a snort.

"It's definitely possible. Chisaki should be strong enough to break free, though."

"*Giggle.* Yes, she might even kick Masha out of the bed if she has to."

"That'd be great. She really needs to learn her lesson and stop using people as body pillows once and for all."

I wish Masha would use me as a body pillow, thought Yuki, despite laughing about it with Alisa. She was already too deep in her fantasy for girl-on-girl action, and it was going to be a while before she could escape. It didn't help that Ayano and Alisa seemed to be a little closer now and were actually conversing between themselves. They were slowly but surely becoming more comfortable having girl talk together.

It's time...

Once they finished discussing the current topic they were on, Yuki placed her hands together as if she was waiting for this moment.

"Ahem. Shall we begin?"

"Begin what?"

"...?"

"Is it not obvious? This would not be a pajama party if we did not discuss our love lives!"

"...Seriously?"

Perhaps unexpectedly, Alisa's reaction was less than stellar despite Yuki's enthusiasm. But after noticing Alisa's lack of interest, Yuki cheerfully exclaimed:

"I have always dreamed of having a pajama party with my friends and talking about love!"

"...!"

Alisa startled the moment she heard the word *friends*, and her uninterested expression vanished. She promptly averted her joyful gaze, then slowly brushed her hair back over her shoulder.

"O-oh, really? Then I guess...we could talk about love or whatever."

Yuki suddenly flashed a sinister grin. You could almost hear her inner voice say, "Heh. She's so easy to manipulate," but the smirk disappeared almost immediately while Alisa was still looking away, so there was no way for her to have known.

"So... How would you two describe your ideal man? My ideal man is someone who is understanding and sweet. What about you, Ayano?"

"I… Hmm… I want someone who takes the lead in the relationship, I guess?"

"I understand that. You are not the most assertive or decisive person, after all. What about you, Alya?"

"Someone serious who is always working hard to improve himself. Someone I can respect."

"Interesting…"

Although Yuki was more than a little shocked that Alisa answered so quickly, there was something about Alisa's answer that was bugging her.

"…In other words, you want someone like you?"

"I suppose. Having a similar sense of values is important, is it not?"

"It is. However, even if you found someone like that, I feel like you would see him more as a rival rather than someone you could fall in love with…"

"What?"

"I simply feel like while you may recognize someone's talent and hard work as a rival, you would never want to work as a team or as a couple…"

Alisa's eyes opened wide as if she was genuinely taken aback by Yuki's observation. She slowly placed a hand on her chin, ruminated on the possibility with a serious expression, then deeply nodded.

"That is probably what would happen, now that you mention it. I suppose I still want someone I can respect but also someone easy to talk with. Hmm… Maybe someone a little careless from time to time so that I don't get competitive would be good—"

That was when Alisa's eyes went wide again, and she lifted her head up in utter astonishment…before immediately flicking back her hair and wearing a smug expression as if to hide her surprise.

"…It doesn't matter, though. More important, I wanted to ask you something about your ideal partner, Yuki…"

"Yes?"

"Is there someone…specific you had in mind?"

Alisa was fidgeting with her hair as she glanced at Yuki every few moments, making it obvious to Yuki what she was getting at.

Ah, she's curious if I'm going to end up being her "love rival."

There was no longer any doubt in Yuki's mind that Alisa had feelings for her brother, so she understood that Alisa really just wanted to know if she liked Masachika. After all, Yuki had already admitted to Alisa once that she loved Masachika, so it would be no surprise if Alisa was using this as an opportunity to see how Yuki really felt.

It would be easy for me to tell her that I love Masachika like a brother...because he is my brother, but...

Hearing that would surely put Alisa's mind at ease, and Yuki would also, in a way, enjoy seeing the look of relief on Alisa's face, but...

But that wouldn't be fun, would it?

She was grinning evilly on the inside while showing Alisa a gentler smile, as if she was hinting at some deeper meaning.

"Good question."

"...Are you not going to answer? I thought that was the point of this girl talk?"

"Oh, come on. ♪ This is so embarrassing. ♪"

She squirmed around, putting both hands on her cheeks and wiggling her body, and yet she didn't let the serious glow in Alisa's eyes go unnoticed.

Mwa-ha-ha. She totally thinks I'm madly in love with my brother. But, well, I guess anyone would think that if they saw how good I was at pretending to be hesitant to tell her.

Yuki was thrilled that she managed to create such a misunderstanding, and she did it all to toy with Alisa—er, to help her dear brother find the love of his life. After all, having a rival always caused relationships to move faster, and Yuki didn't hesitate for a single moment to play the role of the rival if it meant helping Masachika and Alisa be together in the end.

Heh-heh-heh! I can't wait to see the look on her face after she starts dating Masachika and I tell her that I'm actually his sister...

Then again, maybe she really was doing this all for her own amusement. Her inward sinister smile was beyond devilish, but she still maintained her innocent expression as she tried to fish more information out of Alisa.

"Okay, if you tell me who you like, then I will tell you who I like. Deal?"

"Huh?"

"I want to hear more about your love life, Alya."

"But...I've never fallen in love before."

"Wait. Are you serious?"

That's a load of bull, thought Yuki, feigning shock. Alisa, however, pouted in a somewhat discontented manner at the performance.

"What's the big deal? There's nothing wrong with never falling in love before..."

"Of course. But, Alya, you are really popular, so I figured you had at least a little experience with boys."

"None... Besides, having a ton of experience isn't exactly a good thing, right? And yet you still get made fun of if you don't have any experience. It doesn't make any sense to me."

"Y-yes... Hmm... I suppose having a lot of experience does make you seem attractive as a woman... But I get the sense that a lot of people simply want to feel superior to others and brag."

"It sounds like they're just bragging about having loose morals, if you ask me." Alisa snorted, a disappointed expression on her face, as if someone had bragged to her like this before. Yuki, however, was delighted to hear such a comment, even though it did feel almost out of place, since they were supposed to be talking above love.

"Wait... Alya, am I right to assume...that you believe you should save yourself for marriage?"

"A-are we really going to talk about that, too?"

"Of course. It is part of love, is it not?"

Alisa's eyes began to tremble as she blushed, taken aback by the unexpected, sexual topic. Meanwhile, Yuki was smiling innocently and nodding as if it was a perfectly reasonable question. Although hesitant, Alisa seemed to be considering answering.

"W-well, I don't know about waiting all the way until marriage, but…like…it would have to be someone I'm hoping to spend the rest of my life with…"

The crimson in her cheeks darkened as if uttering the words made her feel all the more embarrassed. Nevertheless, her eyes sharpened, and she emphasized:

"Isn't that what all girls dream of? To fall in love for the first time, start dating, get married, then spend the rest of your lives together…!"

"Uh…"

Yuki hesitated before replying to Alisa's excited ramblings, although she knew how her schoolmate felt. You begin dating the love of your life, nobody ever cheats, and after years of falling even more in love, you get married and live happily ever after. It was a common theme in comics for girls for a reason. It was a reflection of what girls all over the world believed to be the ideal relationship, and Yuki understood that. She got it, but…

There are some girls who want to be popular and pampered by every good-looking guy they meet because they love the attention. There are some girls who believe that money, not love, is the most important thing when it comes to marriage. If anything, it feels like girls who idealize love are the minority lately.

At least, it felt that way to Yuki, since those were the kind of people she was surrounded by, so she couldn't help but look at Alisa differently now. Her eyes were gentle and loving.

"…What are you looking at me like that for?"

"Oh, uh… You really are a romantic and so pure, Alya."

"……"

Is she making fun of me? wondered Alisa, frowning at what sounded kind of like sarcasm to her, but Alisa still wasn't comfortable enough around Yuki to ask. Of course, if this was Masachika, she would have immediately snapped at him. Regardless, Yuki seemed to have picked up on something from Alisa's silence, so she immediately turned to Ayano to try to make things better.

"*Giggle.* That is such a wonderful dream. Wouldn't you agree, Ayano?"

"...!"

Ayano's eyes opened wide as if she was caught off guard. She immediately tried to respond to her master, but she had just filled her mouth with a doughnut, so speaking now would be terrible manners. Obviously, she could try to swallow the treat whole, but it would only get stuck in her throat. She didn't have enough moisture. She needed something to drink.

In pursuit of liquid, Ayano reached for a cup on the bedside table, but when she realized it was orange juice, she froze...because mixing sweet doughnuts with orange juice was a grave sin when it came to her taste buds. And yet her master was waiting for her, so if you asked her to choose, then she'd have to...!

"...! Mmm...! Bffaaah. Yes, I agree."

"Ahem. I apologize for that, Ayano."

Yuki wore a troubled expression with her head tilted, as if she felt bad after seeing Ayano wash down the food in her mouth in a panic.

"No, there's nothing for you to apologize for. I completely agree with what Alisa is saying. Being able to devote every last bit of yourself to the person you care about most is ideal."

"...Hmm?"

Yuki lifted her tilted head back up, feeling as if Ayano was talking about something other than romantic love...but before she could ask her maid to clarify, Alisa immediately lit up in excitement and replied:

"Right?! Saving yourself for just one person and remaining faithful to them is ideal. It is something that all proper ladies should strive for!"

"Y—"

Ayano opened her mouth to reply...and froze. Her dark-brown eyes looked up and to the side, tracing a semicircle in the air, before she eventually tilted her head.

"…? Ayano?"

"Oh… There's no reason to worry yourself about what I think…"

"…!"

Alisa froze as well, as if her expression was screaming, "You traitor!" But it was what Ayano said next that almost made Alisa's eyes roll back in her head.

"I don't see anything wrong with saving yourself for two people…"

"T-two people?"

"Although I may be only one person, I know I could do it if I work hard enough."

"At the same time?!"

Alisa imagined Ayano graciously smiling with a man on each side serving her. Furthermore, she naturally imagined her handling them at the same time…and her fair complexion turned scarlet. Her eyes swiftly narrowed as she impulsively yelled:

"Y-you can't! I—I mean, I guess it's okay if the two people are okay with it, b-but you mustn't engage in such immoral acts when you're still just a student!"

"…? Is it…immoral?"

"It's two people at the same time…! It's…!"

Alisa couldn't even get another word out because of all the lewd thoughts clogging her train of thought. Incidentally, the reason all the adult images in her mind were blurred was not because she purposely censored them but because she simply lacked knowledge on what stuff like that looked like. After all, the filthiest thing she had ever seen were two people embracing in a comic book where only their upper bodies were depicted.

I bet that's what she's imagining right now.

Meanwhile, Yuki had been watching Alisa as she imagined Ayano getting into all different kinds of sticky situations, and she was able to imagine every last detail clearly. If anything, she probably needed to self-censor some of the smut her imagination was creating. Of course, she realized this wasn't what Ayano was imagining when she spoke up, but…

I'm gonna let this play out some more and see where it goes. This is too fun.

Yuki maliciously chose silence while she watched Alisa and Ayano go back and forth without them even realizing they weren't talking about the same thing.

"…? It doesn't have to be a man, does it?"

"Huh?! Y-you're fine with it being a girl, then?! D-does that mean—?"

"Of course, that includes you, Alisa."

"Wh-what?!"

Alisa's voice cracked into a falsetto as she wrapped both arms around her body and scooted furiously backward on the bed. Ayano, on the other hand, simply stared at her in wonder.

…Yeah, she probably means that she's fine with serving Alya as well if Alya ends up marrying Masachika. The lack of clarity physically hurts me…

Yuki shook her head at Ayano, but Ayano didn't notice her master's stares and suddenly blinked as if she had remembered something.

"Now that I think about it…I might be serving four people eventually."

"F-four people?! H-how?!"

It appeared Ayano's comment went far past what Alisa could comprehend—to the point that she was genuinely curious as to how she could do that. Despite being completely red in the face, Alisa furrowed her brow and leaned forward on the bed. Meanwhile, Ayano wore her usual blank expression, though her eyes wandered.

"…Well, I suppose I would have to limit it to two people per day."

"Y-you're going to alternate between them?!"

"Of course. If we all live together, then I will make sure all four get what they need."

"L-living together…with four others… So, like…a giant love nest?"

"Even if it comes to that, I will not cut corners. They will have my wholehearted devotion, and I will personally make sure they're satisfied."

"You're going to satisfy them…all by yourself…"

"Yes, and I will bend over backward if I have to."

"W-would that really make it easier to—? Bfffppp!"

Alisa mumbled some gibberish before collapsing onto the bed as if her soul had left her body. The brain overload had heated her entire body, turning it red as if she had just been boiled in a pot of hot water.

"…! Alisa! Are you okay? What happened?"

"Pfft! Ha-ha-ha!"

Seeing Alisa lying on the bed with her eyes swirling and Ayano looking down at her with a blank expression was too much for Yuki, and she burst into laughter.

"Ha-ha-ha…! It looks like Alya's a little tired, Ayano. I think your potential future master needs your help." Yuki wiped her tears as she laughed at Ayano's troubled, wavering gaze.

"How should I help…?"

"Well, you could start by—"

Around ten minutes went by before Alisa regained consciousness, but when she woke up, she was lying in Ayano's lap in the bed while being fanned…so she screamed like a banshee. If only Alisa knew it was all nothing more than an unfortunate misunderstanding…

CHAPTER 13 | **Masachika and Alya**

The train was running through the countryside, and along the tracks, abundant nature spread as far as the eye could see. They were on the way back from their beach trip, and the first train car was peacefully quiet. Other than the members of the student council, there was no one there, perhaps because it was a little past three o'clock in a rural area. Not a word was spoken among them. Only the clickety-clack of the moving train filled the silence. Eventually, the soothing rocking of the train put Yuki to sleep, her head tilted to the left so that it was resting on Masachika's shoulder. Soon afterward, Ayano, who was sitting across from them, slowly began rocking back and forth before finally dozing off as well.

Everyone must be exhausted...

Even Masachika was sitting heavily back in his seat. They had stayed up rather late the night before due to the festival, and since this was the last day, they'd gone for an extremely long swim in the ocean that morning. After having lunch, they cleaned up the vacation house before getting on the train home, so it was only natural they would be fatigued to the point of dozing off. It was no surprise... It was no surprise, but...

I know you're awake, Yuki.

He glared down at his sister's head and lightly pushed her away with his elbow, but...

"Mmm..."

...the instant he extended his elbow to the side, Yuki swiftly looped her left arm around his right and held on tightly. She then carefully readjusted her head's position while getting comfortable to fall asleep once more.

You little…

Masachika frowned at his shameless sister, who was pretending to be asleep. She seemed to at least be trying to fall asleep, but her intentions were clearly mischievous.

Only couples would ever even attempt to sleep like this! She's obviously doing this to annoy Alya!

As he inwardly screamed his complaints, he glanced to his left, where…

"Masha, come on."

"Mmm."

…he saw Maria clinging to Alisa's arm with her head resting on her shoulder. It was like looking in a mirror. Masachika was surprised that someone would be doing the same thing as Yuki.

"Sigh…"

But Alisa eventually exhaled a resigned sigh and stopped trying to resist. When her eyes wandered over to Masachika, her eyebrows went up, but she just smiled wryly.

"She can be such a pain." Alisa gestured to Maria with her eyes.

"Ha-ha…ha-ha…"

Masachika awkwardly laughed, because seeing Maria nuzzle her head on Alisa's shoulder started giving him flashbacks to the previous morning.

Y-yeah, Masha can be…really unpredictable when she's half asleep…

A hint of guilt buried itself in his mind as he thought back to how Maria had gracefully fallen back asleep on him for the fourth time in a row, and he faced forward. Ultimately, there was no way he wouldn't feel a little bit of guilt after realizing the previous day that Alisa liked him, even if he didn't mean to "sleep" with Maria.

I mean, I didn't do anything wrong, but still…

He continued making excuses to nobody but himself when he suddenly realized that he was alone with Alisa. Of the five people sitting there, three were (supposedly) sleeping, so it wouldn't be that much of a stretch to claim that they were alone. The president and vice president of the student council? They were at the very front of the train car, sitting in a two-person seat that was facing the direction they were heading, and they were currently in their own little world… which wasn't a problem, of course.

W-wait. Should I be worried…?

A chill crawled up his spine, making him grimace. After the fireworks show last night, he and Alisa had met up with the others, and Masachika had explained that he had to steal Alisa away because of the little game they were playing. Of course, they didn't mention one word of the kiss. Masachika and Alisa never got a chance to be alone again after that, since they were constantly either being teased by Touya and Chisaki or bombarded with questions from Yuki. Plus, they had been avoiding being alone with each other all day today, perhaps worried that it would be awkward for some reason, so this was the first moment they found themselves alone since the previous day… which was why the conversation naturally drifted toward—

"The fireworks were really pretty…weren't they?"

Yep! Of course this is what we'd be talking about!

Masachika felt as if his stomach was turning, despite seeing it coming.

"Oh yeah. They really were."

But Alisa didn't say a word about Masachika's obviously half-hearted reply. Of course she didn't. That wasn't even what she wanted to really talk about anyway. Masachika knew that, and as a man, he knew that he shouldn't run away, but this place—this situation—was far too risky, and there was one glaring reason why.

There's no way Yuki's really sleeping!

There was no way he could talk about *that* when he knew his sister was eavesdropping. It was dangerous—far too dangerous. He would rather die than bring up the kiss. He knew that if there was one thing they shouldn't talk about, it was that. It was that, and yet…

"So, like…"

It's coming...! She's already going to bring it up!

Masachika inwardly screamed when he noticed Alisa waver as she searched for the right words. He only had a split second to react, so he weighed his options as quickly as he could to come up with an answer. He was going to pretend to be a guy who couldn't read the room—someone who couldn't read between the lines—someone who was insensitive and brain-dead.

"Speaking of fireworks...! Do you have fireworks during festivals in Russia, too?"

"Huh? Oh... Yeah, we do."

"Oh, cool. Is it different from the fireworks in Japan?"

"W-well, I haven't really thought about it much before...but I think they're basically the same?"

"Really? Oh, hey. Do the fireworks have funny names like they do in Japan?"

He had suddenly become unusually talkative. His conversation skills had always been far better than Alisa's, so once he got control of the conversation, it was simple for him to steer it away from topics he wanted to avoid.

"...Hey, are you trying to play dumb?"

But there was not much he could do if she decided to attack head-on, especially when her eyes were downcast as if her feelings were hurt. Masachika was at a loss for words.

"It's obvious you're trying to avoid talking about it, which is fine. We can just pretend it didn't ha—"

"Hold on. Can you give me a second?" he requested, holding up his left hand as he cut Alisa off.

"...What?"

"Sorry. Hold on."

After slowly slipping his smartphone out of his pocket, he turned up the volume and began to play a certain video.

"Hey, yooo. What's going on? I get that you want to save every moment you spend with me, but could you at least wait until I get dressed?"

"...?!"

The voice playing on the phone was from when Masachika was hypnotized into being an overconfident wannabe player. Despite Alisa's eyes widening at the sudden video, Masachika was focused on how the other three were reacting, but after noticing that nobody was moving, he immediately stopped the video.

"All right, it looks like everyone's really sleeping." He nodded in a satisfied manner.

"Wh-what kind of way...to check...was that?" asked Alisa, her cheeks twitching as she desperately tried to hold in her laughter. It was definitely an expression you wouldn't see Alisa make often.

"Because there's no way you could hear this video and not laugh a little unless you were really sleeping, right? I mean, look at you," replied Masachika with a somewhat detached-from-reality gaze.

"I-I'm surprised you would admit that...and I'm even more surprised you still haven't deleted that video, too..."

He ended up explaining to the other student council members that Yuki had hypnotized him and shared that video without his permission, so he got everyone to delete it from their phone, which was why him playing it now was completely unexpected.

"I bet you haven't deleted it, either, right?"

"Wh-what? Of course I deleted it. Rude...," replied Alisa with clear discontent, but Masachika noticed. He caught how her voice shook, albeit only for a split second.

Wow... She seriously didn't delete it...

Despite being reminded of an embarrassing moment in the past and suffering mental damage, Masachika still managed to get them back on topic.

"Anyway... Sorry about that. I wasn't sure everyone was actually asleep, so... No, I'm done making excuses."

Although he was partially worried Yuki was secretly awake, deep down inside, he didn't have the courage to face it—to face the feelings that Alisa had for him. He didn't have the heart or determination to come to grips with them, so Alisa was right. He was trying to avoid talking about it.

"Look, I'm sorry. I was trying to avoid talking about it, but I don't want to pretend like it never happened, either. I just… I still haven't processed everything that happened. I'm still trying to sort out my feelings," he replied seriously, looking Alisa straight in the eye. She seemed a little surprised.

"You don't need to make a big deal out of this…or sort out your feelings. That was… It was a kiss to congratulate you," she mumbled.

"…For what?"

"Because you did so much yesterday to make sure Masha and I had a good time. I know it didn't go exactly as you planned, and you were a little disappointed, right? So think of the kiss as a consolation prize…because what you did really made me happy. Got it?!"

Her speech gradually got faster and louder as she leaned toward Masachika.

"Huh? Oh. Okay." He nodded as if he felt pressured to do so, though he honestly didn't exactly understand what she was trying to say. After all, telling her he didn't get it would only upset her, and that was something he wanted to avoid.

"Well, what an amazing way to be rewarded. Like, that was worth more than the effort I put in yesterday," he blurted awkwardly due to the pressure. Even Masachika didn't know what he was saying, and he slightly regretted opening his mouth.

"…Hmph. Of course it was." She swiftly put her nose in the air, then lowered only her gaze and sternly added, "Oh, and so you know, I don't do that for just anyone. It ended up happening like that yesterday because of Yuki's order and because the fireworks were really romantic, too."

"Yeah, of course," agreed Masachika, thinking that this was probably the best Alisa could do. After all, telling him that she wouldn't kiss just anyone was perhaps the best way to express how much she liked him, and if anything, Masachika was relieved, since he now knew how she felt about him.

I don't know if she hasn't realized it herself, or if she has realized it and is pretending not to... She would never admit it, regardless.

He had no idea what Alisa liked about him, but there was no way someone as proud as her would ever admit that she liked such a laid-back, lazy guy.

Honestly, that works better for me, too...

Because he still wasn't ready to face how she felt about him, and if she could at least wait for him to sort out his feelings, then—

"<I wouldn't do that with anyone else but you.>"

...Yep. I really hope she keeps blurting out those inner thoughts in Russian only.

He still had no idea if she was merely teasing him or if she was revealing how she genuinely felt. So...

"What was that?" he asked, as if there was some kind of preestablished harmony.

"I said I wouldn't do that with anyone else but you."

"Oh...?"

Masachika froze, completely taken aback by her unexpected response, and Alisa immediately tried to hide her embarrassment with a scowl.

"I told you already. I don't do that for just anyone. And I don't want you thinking I'm some girl who is easily swayed by the mood or pressure, so I'm going to be direct... I felt a little kiss on the cheek as a reward was fine because it was you," she insisted almost as if she was complaining.

"O-oh... What an honor?"

"And there was absolutely nothing romantic about it, okay? I trust you to an extent as my p-partner, and I guess there are some things about you that I might possibly respect in a way? And most of all, I guess I consider you my best friend...but that's all!" claimed Alisa, her cheeks burning red while she glared at him.

"O-oh, okay. Thanks," he awkwardly replied, then softly snorted and faced forward. He couldn't help but smile wryly at her clumsy way of expressing how much he meant to her. Her tone almost made it sound as though she was trying to pick a fight with him, but this was so like Alisa. This was the kind of person she was...and that was why it really resonated with Masachika, because he knew that was how she genuinely felt. Alisa herself probably still hadn't realized that she was in love, but even then, she faced her emotions in her own way and gave him the answer she found in her heart. She was courageous and entirely sincere.

Who is this cute creature? She's absolutely adorable.

That thought naturally came to Masachika's mind as he observed her pouting with the reddest ears he had ever seen. He almost immediately regretted the ridiculous thought, though he kept it to himself.

Sigh... This is a really bad habit of mine. I always mess around and crack jokes to hide how I really feel.

That was Masachika Kuze's defense mechanism. After losing the love of his mother, the love of that girl, and the part of himself that he was proud of, he refused to let himself get close to anyone, and instead, he joked around, evaded his problems, and played the fool. If he didn't get attached to anyone, then he would never have to suffer losing anyone. If he never got close to anyone...then nobody would have to know the pathetic true nature of Masachika Kuze. And if nobody else knew, then Masachika wouldn't have to face himself—this person whom he hated—either.

But at least, right now...

He couldn't run away. At the very least, he wanted to be true to this girl in front of him who had showed him courage and sincerity.

"I..."

His voice was hoarse and trembling. All he was doing was being honest with himself and with her, and yet it was so hard. One corner of his lips was naturally trying to curl into a smirk. *Smile. Make a joke out of it and run away like you always do.* The inner voices were deafening, and he desperately tried to block them out as he continued:

"I wanted to kiss, too...because it was you, Alya."

Alisa immediately looked back at him, and her eyes opened wide in astonishment when she saw how unusually desperate he looked.

"If it were anyone else, I would have probably joked around and avoided the whole thing. But because it was you, Alya...I didn't. I wanted to kiss you back. I mean, I wouldn't have been able to kiss you on the cheek, and if you asked me why I wanted to kiss you, then I'd have trouble answering, but...maybe I'm just the kind of guy who gets caught up in the moment?"

In the end, he couldn't help but kind of joke about it, despite doing his best to seriously convey how he felt. He never had trouble talking, and yet it was times like this when he would freeze up. His gaze gradually lowered the more he spoke, until—

"...*Sigh.* What are you doing?" muttered Alisa in a fed-up tone, placing her right hand on his cheek. After gently lifting his chin so that he was facing her, she gazed right into his eyes and smiled as if she was truly happy from the bottom of her heart.

"*Giggle.* I've never seen you look this way."

"...How do I look?"

Probably pathetic, he thought, as he replied in a sulky voice, then almost immediately felt overwhelmed with embarrassment for acting so childish.

"...!"

As he averted his gaze without saying another word, Alisa's lips curled almost mischievously, and she replied:

"If I had to sum up how you look in one word, I'd say...cute."

"...!"

Being called cute right to his face while she devilishly smiled at him sent a sweet numbness down his spine, so he immediately furrowed his brow as if he was in a bad mood to hide how happy it actually made him.

"…Are you making fun of me?" he asked, trying to sound annoyed, but Alisa didn't even blink.

"Of course not. Anyway, I actually was wondering why you went with my hair, but it looks like you actually were just nervous, after all."

…Don't give me that. You noticed the moment I kissed you. You called me a coward.

"Come on. Of course I was nervous. Plus, I personally felt that it was weird to kiss your hair…but you don't want someone to kiss you on the cheek just because they were ordered to because of some game, right?" he interjected in an accusatory tone.

"I don't know," she replied, raising an eyebrow. She then took her hand off his cheek, began tapping hers, and said:

Masachika instantly stopped breathing. His heart felt as if it stopped beating for a moment.

"Wait. What was that?"

He was worried that this sounded awkward, though he had asked her to repeat herself like this countless times before.

"I just said I don't know about that. That's all."

But thankfully, Alisa didn't seem to care, and she lied with a brilliant smile like she always did...while slipping her right arm around Masachika's left and resting her head on his shoulder.

"Oh..."

She transitioned from brazenly taunting him to resting her head on his shoulder so naturally that his body went stiff. Alisa let out a brief but exaggerated yawn, perhaps not realizing that Masachika was entirely at her mercy.

"*Yawn...* I'm starting to get sleepy... Can you wake me up when we get there?"

"...So basically, I'm not allowed to sleep?"

"Oh my. Are you confident you can sleep with me leaning against you like this?"

"...Not really."

Alisa snickered, then closed her eyes, but Masachika wasn't joking when he said that. He was genuinely nervous. Only after realizing that she wasn't going to "attack" anymore was he finally able to relax his tense body.

Phew... This has to be bad for my heart.

He truly felt that because the gap between this Alisa and the version who was always curt was too big. Of course, Alisa herself probably just thought she was teasing him for the most part...but after Masachika realized she had feelings for him, it was hard to tell how much of this was really her merely teasing him.

Tsk. I wonder how much of what she does is on purpose...

He looked to his side with an exhausted smile and found Alisa already sleeping peacefully. Her usual overly serious expression was gone, and her guard was lowered. It was the expression of someone who completely trusted the person they were with. Masachika's heart was instantly filled with a warm yet intense emotion.

I want to protect her. I want to cherish her. I never want to hurt her. Perhaps these emotions were born of his desire to protect her… or perhaps even from his love for her.

But…this isn't a romantic love.

This wasn't the same feeling he used to feel with that girl…or at least, that was what he believed. But he could no longer remember exactly what romantic love itself felt like ever since she abandoned him. Ever since that day—

Hmm?

That was when he started to have doubts about his own memories.

Did that girl really abandon me…?

He frowned and tried to remember what happened, but it felt as if there were a deep mist blurring his memories. Her smile was still hidden on the other side of the fog. He couldn't remember, but what he did understand was that his love for her hadn't faded.

I still can't let her go…

No matter how hard he tried, he couldn't forget her. He would randomly remember her…because deep down inside, there was a part of him that didn't want to forget…since he had a lingering attachment and love for the girl of his memories.

"*<Masaaachika!>*"

He could still hear the weird way she pronounced his name in his head, and the innocent voice calling out to him from the other side of the mist was tearing his heart apart.

"Mn…"

But the soft voice coming from his left side dragged him back to reality. He blinked in wonder as Alisa, stirring in her sleep, tightly squeezed his arm, and the loving warmth began to soothe his aching heart.

…I have to find closure and move on.

The decision naturally formed in his mind as he looked at Alisa's sleeping face. He had to do it for the girl who fell in love with some-one like him. He had to move on from his first love and free his heart from his memories of her. Surely, once he did that...

"......"

That was when Yuki slowly lifted her head, and ignoring her brother's silent glare, she began staring at Alisa, who was tightly hold-ing Masachika's other arm, and she firmly nodded.

"Interesting. So this is what it feels like to be cuckolded."

"Wanna make your next nap permanent?"

Afterword

Hey, Sunsunsun here. I know, I know. "What? We're at the afterword already? But there's still more than ten pages left." You must have thought there was another chapter. You were probably in bed last night thinking, *I guess it's late, and I've got places to be tomorrow. I'll read the rest on the morning bus or train,* and now you're annoyed that it was just the afterword. This is you, right? Well, take a nap. If you even have a minute of free time, you should sleep. Surely, you've already realized this yourself. You "guess it's late"? Those are the words of someone who stays up far later than they should. Those are the words of someone sleep-deprived. Hey! Stop right there! I saw you trying to pull out your smartphone! Don't get on social media! Don't try to collect your log-in bonus for the day! I don't want to hear any *but*s about your favorite comic updating today, either! If you have time to stare at your phone, use that time to sleep! You don't even have to read the afterword! Because even if you do read it, it's not like it's going to benefit you in any way. Just sleep! And don't forget to turn your alarm on so you don't miss your stop! Oh, and don't do anything to bother the people sitting next to you! Be respectful when you sleep! I'd personally be looking at my phone if I had free time, though!

Yes, that was a terrible opening to a long afterword. Honestly, it's probably the worst there has ever been. Oh, and you there. Yes, you. You probably think you're sooo cool for making it to the afterword instead of going to bed when you should have. You should honestly just go to bed. I know I sound like a broken record, but there is really nothing for you to gain from this. Hurry up and sleep while you're still basking in the afterglow of the main story. You might be able to see Alya in your dreams if you're lucky. I mean, none of the characters have ever visited me in my dreams, but maybe you'll be luckier. Ah, how I wish I could be Masachika, even if only in my dreams. I'm cool with turning into Yuki, too.

Oh, hey. It's somebody thinking, *Sorry, but I only read during lunch, so none of this applies to me.* Well, sorry, but you should take a nap, too. You've got work or class after this, right? Even ten-minute power naps can really change your day. If you have enough time to read at the end of your lunch break, then you should be using that time to sleep, even if only a little. What? This isn't your lunch break? You don't have to worry about work or school? …Oh, you work night shifts. My apologies. Wait. If you work the night shift, then what are you doing awake now?!

And then there's *you*. You think you're the real winner here because you bought this on Friday, and you're using your weekend to read. Well, congratulations. Because you *are* the real winner here. Feel free to put the book down to do your own little celebratory dance. In fact, how about you show off your victory pose? If you can hold it for ten seconds, then you are, without a doubt, a true warrior.

....

....

…Oh, I need a moment to see everyone's victory pose. And I'm definitely not trying to reach a word count, so don't even bring it up. And for all the losers, put your book down, close your eyes, and take a moment to imagine the true winners. What kind of person did you imagine? Incidentally, I imagined the weatherperson I saw on the news this morning. Strange.

Unlike someone like me, whose head is constantly daydreaming about beautiful women, I'm sure you serious readers actually imagined the winners' courageous, godlike poses, and I'm sure you must be cringing at the bitter taste of despair. Aspiration is the first step to achieving your dream. If you were inspired to improve, then you're up next. You may have lost this time, but you will be a true winner next time.

There is only one thing left for you to do. You need to look up online when the next volume of *Alya Sometimes Hides Her Feelings in Russian* is coming out and buy it on the day it is released. That not only increases the initial sales, but it would also bring a smile to my face and my editor's face as well. Yes, the true winners here were actually my editor and me! ...Heh! You look like you're confused. Me too. What is this guy saying? Can you believe it? And he hasn't even been drinking. Isn't that scary?

Oh, hey. It looks like the others have returned from their victory dance. The embarrassment must have been too much, so they had no choice but to return to this book. But please let me tell you this: Thank you. Thank you for buying this volume the day it came out, and thank you for reading it as soon as possible. There is nothing that makes me happier than knowing you were looking forward to the newest volume that much.

"I didn't immediately read this volume from cover to cover as soon as it came out. Is my love not enough?" I'm sure some of you feel that way, but you're wrong. The depth of your love doesn't depend on when you read it. You are using your valuable time to read this story. That enough is proof of your love. Huh? You sped through the entire story in five minutes? Yeah, that's not cool. Please go back and read it for real this time... If you said, "Sure. I can read through it again," then you probably already actually enjoyed your time with this novel and understood what you were reading, right? So you probably don't even need to reread it. You're probably a fast reader. I wish I had the ability to speed-read. Give it to me.

To all those who read the afterword first, as you can see, it's extremely long. Furthermore, it's about nothing, as I'm sure you've already noticed. There aren't any spoilers for the main story, either, so it's a relatively safe read, but if you have time to read this garbage, then you should probably just focus on reading the novel instead. If you're still wanting to read the afterword first even after I said that, well, you deserve a pat on the back. I'm not going to stop you, but I did warn you, okay? I don't want you coming back yelling and complaining later that I wasted your time. Oh, and that goes for everyone who's reading the afterword, okay?

To the readers who skipped to the end to see how many pages this novel was and realized that the afterword was abnormally long, well, I doubt you're even reading this, since most people read the afterword after finishing the story.

My condolences to those of you who got a little too excited flipping pages and saw the last double-page spread before you finished reading the main story. You should have looked at the book from the side and checked to see where the illustration was first. Huh? You did check, so you already knew where the illustration was? Wait. It's my fault because of how long the afterword is? Oh… Sorry.

I always apologize when I am at fault. I'm an adult, after all. On the other hand, I am stubborn, and I will never apologize if it's not my fault. I'm still a child, after all. I'm an adult who can't adult. I'm sure most people who write light novels are like that. We still have the heart of a child that we refuse to throw away. With that being said, I only know two other light novel authors, so maybe you should take what I say with a grain of salt. One is far more mature than me, and the other is a saint… Wait. Am I the only one who acts like a kid? I think I owe all light novel authors in the country an apology. I almost damaged everyone's reputation just because I'm still mentally a child. I'm very sorry. If you're still in middle school or high school, please don't become someone like me when you grow up. Really, I mean it.

Now, I would like to say something to the beautiful, wonderful readers who are cheering, "Whoa! Look how long the afterword is! Sick! This is sooo awesome!!" …Wait. You don't exist? Come on, there has to be at least one person? Is there nobody excited about this?

…Oh, there is someone? You? You're happy that the afterword is even longer than the main story? Hmm… I don't even know what to say, so please return to your seat.

See? Nothing good came from reading all this (serious face). Whichever reader is complaining about how long this is and skips the afterword to see Momoco's illustration in the back, you're doing the right thing. I'd do the same thing, too. I can already guess what you'll be thinking when the next volume comes out: *Now that I think about it, I never read the afterword in the last volume. Well, I can't have that. Time to sit down and read it.*

Hey, you. The person who read about how long the afterword was on Twitter beforehand. Thank you for following me. If you're still not a follower, please follow me. You won't lose a thing. You won't gain anything, either.

Phew… All right, I think I covered every possible type of reader, so it's time to get real. I'm sure most of you are wondering why the afterword is so long this time. The reason…is simple. A few days after I finished writing the main story, the editor told me that the main story essentially filled up the agreed-upon number of pages perfectly, so there was probably no room for an afterword for Sunsunsun or anything for Momoco this time. I was then told that the number of pages could be increased for an afterword, but it would be an extra sixteen pages, and all the unused pages would be used for advertisements, which wouldn't be cool. I then asked if this book would be more expensive if they increased the number of pages, because I care about your wallets first and foremost. I'm a considerate man, after all. I knew that even the smallest price increase was a big thing, especially for my middle school and high school readers. That's why I asked about the price and— Okay, I'm lying. I was actually just worried that nobody would buy this novel if it was too expensive, especially when it's a collection of side stories. It was all about me. I know, I know. I said it was time to get serious, and barely two hundred or so words later, I'm already doing this. I'm awful. I know.

Anyway, when I asked if it would cost more if they added a few pages, it apparently didn't change the price at all. Why? I have no idea, but I figured there was no reason for me to hold back on adding more pages if I could. Honestly, it didn't really matter to me if we lost my afterword, but it would be a tremendous loss to the world if we lost Momoco's illustration on the last page! I'm sure all you readers would be disappointed as well! I'm sorry! I'm just trying to look like a good person again, but in reality, *I* wanted to see Momoco's illustration on the last page! I did it all for myself!

Phew... Getting all worked up is exhausting. I'm usually more laid-back than this. I'm not a total introvert or anything, but I guess you'd consider me unsociable. I know my pen name makes me sound like an extrovert, but I'm more of a Cloudcloudcloud kind of gloomy guy in reality.

It looks like we got off track again, but to sum everything up, we had to add sixteen pages in order to include Momoco's illustration at the end of the book. Then my editor enthusiastically told me I got to write a max of around six thousand Japanese characters to fill fourteen pages of afterword... That's about the size of two short stories you'd usually write for two different shops' preorder bonuses. But when I was in the middle of writing "Like hell I'm doing that ♡," my editor sent me another message saying, "I've actually never seen an afterword that long. It might even be a historic first (lol)." So after reading that, I felt like I had to do it.

Plus, having the last dozen or so pages filled with ads didn't sit right with me. Furthermore, if it means becoming a legend (← nobody said this), then fine. I'll write six thousand or so characters. I've already written about four thousand (in Japanese) just talking about this, so I'm more than halfway there. Anyway, let's get down to business and discuss our last topic of conversation.

Huh? Don't pretend like you don't know what I'm talking about. Is this really the time to be joking? Come on, you know what I'm talking about, right? Did you not stop and think why I was releasing short side stories while this deep into the main story? After how Volume 4 ended, the author would have to be insane to release side stories instead of continuing the main story. That's what you're thinking, right? I get it. So let me explain! I couldn't fit all the summer stories into one volume last time! There was too much I wanted to talk about! I only had basically a month to work with for each of the first three volumes, so there's no way I'd be able to fit every summer story I wanted to talk about in a single volume! My drawn-out, long-winded sentences take time! If anything, you should be congratulating me because they're finally starting the second semester next volume. What I'm trying to say is…I'm sorry. This is my fault. But I believe I'll be able to release the next volume within a reasonable time frame, so please forgive me. I always apologize when I am at fault. I'm… (The rest has been omitted for brevity). Heh! Despite having to hit a word count, I'm omitting stuff! That's how seriously I'm taking this…and yet I'm getting closer and closer to that word count as I sit here and brag about that.

The fact that I'm basically writing the first thing that comes to mind shows how not serious I am. I believe that before writing the afterword, you should clear your mind and write about things other than the story you just wrote. I know I got off topic again, so let me tell you one thing about this volume. It's important, so listen up…

You honestly won't be missing out on anything in regard to the main story if you skip these side stories and go straight to Volume 5. There's nothing in any future volumes that you'll be confused about if you don't read this volume. Reading Volume 4.5 will only deepen your understanding of Volume 4, and it will bring a grin to your face when you see characters introduced in this volume who show up again in Volume 5 and beyond. What was that? I should have told you that beforehand? You wouldn't have bought this volume if you knew that ahead of time? I'm sure there are people thinking that right now, which is why I'm hiding this comment in the middle of the afterword. Yes,

I play dirty. I have grown into an awful person. If you asked me if I was a good kid… Just don't ask.

…All right. You're getting tired of this. I get it. You're wondering if it's really okay that I submitted this to the great Kadokawa to be published. Well, I don't want you thinking that these additional pages would have been better if they were used for ads, so it's really time to get serious. I'm not messing around this time. I need to thank everyone for their help, so it's honestly time I start taking this seriously. And if I keep repeating myself, it's going to sound like I'm doing a bit again, so that's enough of this.

First, I'm sure some of you already know, but *Alya Sometimes Hides Her Feelings in Russian* is being made into a manga and will be handled by the artist Saho Tenamachi (aka Tenacitysaho). Please look forward to it. For those of you who saw the beautiful illustration of Alya on a promotional wraparound band, it was incredible, right? Looks like something done by an extremely experienced, popular illustrator, right? So I am extremely grateful that my editor introduced me to her and that she accepted the project. Furthermore, Saho isn't simply an extremely good artist. She excels in reproducing emotional expressions as well, so her ability to convey not only the romantic-comedy portions of the comics but also the serious parts of this coming-of-age story is impressive to say the least. A bitter old man and menace to society like me, who enjoys a glass of wine while watching young people suffer, is going to have to start looking for a good wine that pairs well with Masachika's pain. I'm not really a big fan of drinking to be honest, though.

Did I mention that Saho is a great person, too? When it was finalized that she would be handling the comics, she sent me a hand-written letter with an illustration of Alya to go with it, to boot. Never in my wildest dreams did I expect to receive a letter, so I was truly touched, and I am truly grateful for that. I put the letter in an acrylic frame on the wall, and I will treasure it for the rest of my life.

In other words, I am personally looking forward to her comics for *Alya Sometimes Hides Her Feelings in Russian*. I hear she has already started on the draft, and I just know it's going to be great, so please start downloading the Magapoke app. "Magapoke? Isn't that Kodansha?" You're sharp. But there are things sometimes that are better not knowing… This isn't one of those things, though. There isn't any fishy stuff going on behind the scenes. It would just take a long time to explain, and it's complicated, so I'm not going to get into that right now.

Next up, I want to thank two amazing illustrators for their contributions. The first I want to thank is Yuu Kuroto. There was a certain light novel cover he illustrated that I saw on his Twitter, and it was so incredible that I had my editor make him an offer to do an illustration for us. I almost never make such requests, so I was so happy when he accepted the offer. And the Alya that he drew for me in a swimsuit…is incredible. How can one make someone look so angelic? So pure? The water and sunlight were drawn so beautifully that it really makes it magical. It's as if she were a summer fairy. And her eyes…wow. Incredible. He really brought out her tsundere-ness while still making her eyes seem somewhat alluring as well. And to top it off…depicting her from a low-angle shot that only further emphasizes her incredible figure! What an amazing waistline! What thick thighs! Thank you so much! To those who have not seen the illustration, you can get your hands on it at a certain store as a bonus gift with the purchase of Volume 4.5, so please do so. Don't make a fuss about buying multiple copies. You can keep one as a spare or give one to a friend, even, which makes the illustration practically free… Of course, only a true nerd could understand this absurd way of thinking.

Next, I want to thank…the one and only Kina Kazuharu. Thank you very much. Really. I mean it. You made one of my dreams come true.

Kina Kazuharu is the first illustrator I fell in love with after becoming a nerd. The only other illustrator I guess I even knew of before then was Noizi, but the first illustrator's name that I looked up on my own was Kina Kazuharu's. The first art book, calendar, and auto-graphed book I bought were all his works. When a certain short story that reached first in the rankings on Shosetsuka ni Naro got made into a light novel with Kina Kazuharu doing the art for the cover, I was like, "Seriously? That's the Shosetsuka ni Naro dream!" I couldn't believe it at the time, and before I knew it, he drew an illustration to help promote this series. In other words, when it comes to short stories, I am the Shosetsuka ni Naro dream. Please feel free to ignore that comment.

You may be wondering who Kina Kazuharu drew. And my answer would be Aly—Yuki, of course, since he is known for his illustrations of heroines with long black hair. I know Alya's the protagonist, but I'm not some fool who's going to ask him to draw a silver-haired maiden. Anyway, the illustration he did for me was absolutely beau-tiful! It's unbelievably wholesome and pleasant, like something you'd see in an advertisement for a refreshing drink! Black hair blowing in the wind! It's too beautiful! The black hair Kina Kazuharu draws is unparalleled!

...It looks like I met my word count while doing all that scream-ing. In fact, I went beyond six thousand characters. I think I'm at seven? It looks like there's no reason to draw things out any longer. Besides, I'm sure my editor gave me that word count while knowing I was going to need some leeway, so exceeding the word count shouldn't be a problem. And if the afterword now doesn't fit the additional pages, I'll just remove some of the fluff... Hold on. When I put this all in the proof paper, it ended up being only thirteen pages? I've got an extra page. Should I put in an ad?

...Yessssss!! An extra inning!! I should be able to make sure there's no room for an advertisement if I write about seven hundred Japanese characters! Seven hundred doesn't sound like much, but that's about the size of your average two-page afterword without the special thanks included! I'm adding postscript during the editing phase. I should really apologize to my editor. I'm really sorry, and I thank you for your patience and kindness.

Now, for the extra inning… What should I write? Hmm… I'd feel bad if I kept talking about pointless garbage when I begged my editor to let me do this, so let's talk about something with a little substance. How about we discuss the main story?

There were three Russian dishes mentioned this time: pelmeni, varenyky, and solyanka, and I actually went to Russian restaurants to experience the taste and to see what they looked like as well. Surprisingly, solyanka genuinely tasted like pizza to me, and pelmeni unsurprisingly was just like a boiled pot sticker. The difference between varenyky and pelmeni was essentially the filling, but they didn't seem to be completely different dishes to me. Maybe it's because I tried them both at the same restaurant.

Also, I tried some sort of jellied chicken…but, well, that was… incredible. I was trembling. Not like Ayano, though. If you're curious, I think you should give it a try. It'd make a good story, at the very least. I recommend going as a group, since it's one of those things that you'll probably either love or hate. That way, if you're unable to eat it, you can force whoever likes it to eat your portion of jellied chicken as well. This is just a little bit of advice from someone who has been there before.

I know. The postscript was more afterword-y than the actual afterword. I've already gone way over the word count as well. I think this is around 8,200 Japanese characters? Lengthwise, I basically added an extra chapter to the story. No joke.

But what's done is done. Anyway, I want to apologize to my editor, Miyakawa, since the draft for this novel proceeded at a snail's pace again. Thank you for all your help. I would like to thank the illustrator, Momoco, for once again drawing numerous beautiful works of art, despite being so busy. I was blown away by the illustration of Masha on the cover, the illustration at the end of Alya in the bunny costume, and even the bonus illustration of Alya as a succubus. The illustrations of "nerdy" Sayaka and "cool-guy" Masachika made me laugh out loud as well. All the illustrations are amazing. And last but not least, I want to thank you all, the readers, for making this happen. You guys make me so happy, I could squeal. Thank you so much! I can't wait to see you all again when Volume 5 comes out. Until we meet again.

I'm looking forward to more volumes, Feelings in Russian! 🐰

momo